Mask of the

DRAGON

ASHLEIGH D.J. CUTLER

Crystal Prism Publications
Ohio, United States of America
www.ashleighdjcutler.weebly.com ~ ashwolf-forever.deviantart.com

First Edition 2016

Cutler, Ashleigh, 1985 –

Mask of the Dragon by Ashleigh D. J. Cutler – 1st ed.

Front Cover Art by FrinaArt
SelfPubBookCovers.com/FrinaArt

Publishing Logo Pawprint by Achiha-Azteca
achiha-azteca.deviantart.com

The title is set in Black Chancery and Broken Glass.
The body text is set in Times New Roman and Garamond.

Edited by Cassandra Mehlenbacher and Kirstin van Dyke

ISBN-13: 978-0692712160 (Crystal Prism Publications)
ISBN-10: 069271216X

TO SISTER MARY DOROTHY LEMON, OP

My example of a true Catholic, who gave me my cross of gold when I got my brand-new soul. She let nothing stop her from walking the path she chose and taught me women change the world. Thank you Sister Dorothy.

ACKNOWLEDGMENTS

You wouldn't be reading these words right now without the help and support of some amazing people. I couldn't have reached this point alone. A huge thank you goes out to my editors, my beta readers, and my friends who cheered me on all through November of 2015. I'd drop names if I wasn't sure I'd miss someone. You all know who you are. Thank you.

PROLOGUE

The smell of smoke lingered in the air. It permeated every item that had survived. Abigail Palmer stood in the driveway and stared at the charred remains of the trailer, arms wrapped around herself as tears spilled down her face. The six-year-old just stood watching Aunt Gladys' friends box up whatever she deemed "salvageable." There wasn't much; most of it was going in the dumpster.

"Don't cry," said Dominic. The small black dragon sat on her shoulder, licking at her tears. "Please don't cry; I don't like you sad."

"I can't." The tears came faster; her vision blurred. "I can't!" She spun around and ran straight toward the woods her parents had always told her never to enter.

"Abby, wait!" Dominic's claws pricked her skin through her shirt as he clung to her shoulder. "You're not supposed to go in there!"

"I DON'T CARE!" Abby pushed her way through the trees, flinching as thorns tore at her clothes and her skin. She had to get away; she couldn't look anymore.

The woods smelled strange, sweet yet not. Sunlight barely made it through the upper branches, but there was light enough to see. The only sound was the twigs snapping underfoot.

Abby ran until she was out of breath. She hit her knees, tears unchecked. She dug her fingers into the dirt. "Why?" she demanded. "Why are they gone? I want my mommy! I want my daddy!"

Dominic crawled down into her lap, nuzzling her arm, much like her cat would. "I wish I had more magic than just being invisible to other people. If I could bring them back for you, I would."

"It's not fair! They box everything up and put it away like they were never here! Like putting it away means they weren't real! Didn't Aunt Gladys love Mommy and Daddy? Why isn't she crying? I don't understand." She scooped him up in her arms and sat there hugging him tight, rocking back and forth. Sobs wracked her body. "You won't leave me, will you Dominic? You'll never go away, right?"

"Never," promised the dragon. He put a paw over her heart. "I'm right here. So are your parents; they'll always be with you."

"Don't lie!" she screamed. "They aren't here! They're gone and they're never coming back!"

"I'm not lying," said Dominic, nuzzling her neck. "You'll see them again, you know. One day, Abby, one day you'll be together again. It's all part of God's plan."

Her hands tightened around him. She shook once more. "Don't say that!" She couldn't see through her tears. "God wouldn't take Mommy and Daddy away! He wouldn't!"

Dominic stroked her face, careful of his claws. "I didn't say He did, but you know everything is planned. This was meant to happen. You just have to be strong and be brave."

"I don't want to be brave and strong! I want Mommy and Daddy!"

"I know, Abby, I know."

"So trusting, so innocent."

"Keep your distance! She's not yours nor is she your master's."

"She's not *yours* yet either, and unlike you, I've got the guts to do what it takes to gain leverage." Bjarte smirked, his blue eyes twinkling. "That was too easy."

Aeneas refused to look at the deceiver, his eyes locked on their young charge. "Only a coward would take a child's parents from her to shake her faith. Only a coward makes another do what he himself cannot."

"Get down off your high horse, Annie. It was just a *cat*; not like I possessed one of your boss's beloved *children*. Thing had been after the cords for days, anyway. Besides, I'm not the only one using that lizard in her head as a mouthpiece. Hello, Crow, I'm Raven – yes we're both black."

"The dragon is not a sentient being with a soul," replied the guardian. "And Troubadour is a beloved pet that the child now will look at knowing his actions took her parents away."

Bjarte shrugged and folded his arms. "Life sucks, and then you die."

Aeneas clenched his fists, fighting back the urge to summon his staff and knock the smug look off his rival's face. *A guardian doesn't resort to unnecessary violence,* he reminded himself. *No matter the provocation.* He watched Abby fall asleep on the forest floor, arms wrapped tight against her chest. He ached for the power to fix this; he had not lied when he had told her that. He was half-surprised the deceiver had not played on her sympathies with comfort of his own.

A ripple of energy brought his attention to the ground beside Abby, and Aeneas moved quickly. He took control of a passing fox and snatched the snake up, dispatching it in a single bite. The leaves muffled the struggle. He guided the fox away before letting it go, a meal clutched limply in his jaws.

Bjarte clapped sarcastically. "Well done, Annie! See, small animals are pretty useful, aren't they?"

Aeneas spun and glared at him, his dark hair falling into his dark eyes. "You –"

"Seriously, Annie, we aren't as different as you pretend. You'll see that sooner or later."

"I am *nothing* like you!" He returned his gaze to his charge, sleeping fitfully as she dreamed of her parents and the flames that had claimed them. *"Nothing."*

"Keep telling yourself that." Bjarte smoothed back his spiky blond hair. "I'm gonna love laughing when you eat those words." He looked from their charge to the guardian. "Love the family resemblance you got going on."

Aeneas's form *did* look like Abby's; same brown hair, same brown eyes, and the same heart-shaped face. Bjarte's form changed to match whatever poor soul he had most recently tricked into his master's hands. However, the guardian only ever wore one form – that of the first soul he had lost. The years since had not lessened the guilt. Before this little girl in front of him, another of the line had been his charge, and that one too he had failed.

Not this time, he thought, staring down at the innocent whose fate lay in hands. *I will not fail you, Abby.* His fists clenched. *I promise.*

CHAPTER 1

Abby sat beside her great-aunt Gladys, trying to keep her expression neutral as Preacher Davidson waxed on about women in the workforce. She fought to tune out the incorrectly referenced Bible verses and thinly veiled criticisms that on the surface were general, but had everyone looking out the corner of their eyes at the target of his sermon. Once again, she mentally recited her prayers from childhood, though every few minutes, the cries of "Amen!" and "Praise the Lord!" broke her concentration. She stole a glance at the clock. *Just ten more minutes,* she thought, her clasped hands turning white as she tightened her grasp. *You can do this, you can do this.*

A clawed paw rested on her hand, and his blue eyes stared up into her brown eyes. "It won't be much longer," Dominic reassured her. "Soon enough, you'll be able to have your own place and won't have to attend services like this. You'll be able to *go* to Mass again."

Abby had clung to the dragon, now roughly the size of a Golden Retriever, for ten years. Every time the thought that she was too old for make-believe crossed her mind, she rationalized it with the knowledge that Dominic was the one thing she could not lose. *At least I'm not crazy as Aunt Gladys thought,* she mused. *Crazy people never think they are, and I question my sanity on a regular basis.*

Aunt Gladys discreetly nudged her and gave her *the look*. Her eyes darted from Abby to the podium. The message was clear.

Digging her fingers into her palms, Abby turned her eyes to Preacher Davidson and tried to look like she was paying attention. *I can't wait to get home and watch the Mass.* She would be forever grateful to her friend Marlon for showing her how to program the VCR. Though he got a good laugh at the fact she still *had* a VCR.

Dominic sat at her feet in much the same fashion as a dog would and pressed against her side in silent support; she believed she felt the weight. Now and then he looked up at Preacher Davidson and curled his lip, stopping just short of snarling. He did not care for the sermons either.

You'd think I'd be used to it by now. Her great-aunt had tried to stomp all "heretical nonsense" out of her. Any time one of Aunt Gladys' television preachers hit the subject of Catholicism, it didn't matter what the sixteen-year-old was doing — not even homework was an excuse — Gladys would call her in to listen. Just to remind her of how "dangerous to her soul" it was. Just in case she was thinking of "going back to that Devil's den." Look at how her parents had died; if that wasn't proof they had lost their way, what was?

The collection plate was passed around once Preacher Davidson finally tired of his own voice. Gladys took new bills from her purse, same as every Sunday, and passed it on to Abby. From her own purse, Abby took out a crisp five-dollar bill. Since Aunt Gladys controlled her allowance, anything less than ten percent would result in losing it for a week. God came first.

Dominic snorted. "I'm sure *God* wanted the new carpet and paint."

Abby fought to keep her expression neutral as she passed on the plate. As usual, Dominic had a point. *I know; the carpet had just been put down a year ago. It didn't need to be replaced that soon.*

"Only way it would is if he wore it out with all that pacing he does. You'd get better results if you gave your money to the soup kitchen." He yawned, glaring at the plate as it made its rounds back to the pulpit. "At least it would actually go to people who need it."

No response was necessary; Dominic simply expressed her opinions without pulling punches. Sometimes she wasn't proud of what he said. Abby got to her feet and followed Aunt Gladys outside, bracing herself for the ride back to their apartment.

CHAPTER 2

"Cinderelly, Cinderelly, night and day it's Cinderelly," sang Dominic at her heels as Abby dragged the vacuum across her room. The dog-sized dragon leapt up onto her bed and curled up just like Troubadour once had. "I'd hate to see what would happen if the old bat actually had to clean up her own mess."

"It's nothing new, Dommy." Abby forced aside the thoughts of her cat. Once again, Aunt Gladys had left to play bridge with her friends in the complex, leaving Abby to clean the apartment. How two people could accumulate such a mess was always a mystery. "I've still got a few hours before she comes home. It could be worse. I'm almost done."

"Yeah, well, if you weren't such a neat freak yourself, you wouldn't even be close." Dominic laid his head on his fore-paws. "So much for Sunday being a day of rest. At least you don't have to get cat hair off everything anymore

"I'd rather have the cat hair and you know it." Abby next started to empty out the drawers of her desk. Old homework, sketch-covered scrap paper, and a handful of candy wrappers went into the trash bin. She replaced the items that she actually needed – still usable pencils, paper with only one side used, a couple snapshots of Troubadour she had forgotten. She spotted a photo stuck against the front and bottom of the last drawer. Half of it was hidden. She pulled at the photo but it wouldn't budge. Her eyes narrowed suspiciously. *Why do I have a feeling I just found another of Grandpa's hidey-holes?* She turned the drawer over, shook it, and heard a clunk and a thump. Turning the drawer right-side up, she found a board on the carpet. Upon it lay a floppy disk and a tattered, faded-tan book with a cloth cover that read *Journal*. "What the…?"

Dominic raised his head. He jumped off the bed and came to sit beside her. "Another one?"

"Looks that way." Abby picked up the book and flipped it open. The front page read "Property of Dominic Whelan" and listed a familiar address. "Looks like Grandpa's diary." She stared in awe at the faded handwriting. The first entry was from January 1991.

I should have done this sooner. Who knows how many mistakes I could have avoided simply by recording my progress? This project is ambitious, but not, I feel, impossible. Hopefully I'll finish it before I become a grandfather.

Taped to the page was an ultrasound picture. The date stamp signaled that it had been taken several months before her birth. Abby touched the image reverently.

Can't really see much of the kid yet, but still. Hope he or she gives Nicole all the trouble she gave me. Might even like this once I finish it, who knows? Either way, I can't wait to meet the little stinker.

She couldn't read the rest; her vision blurred with tears. She had never known her grandfather; he'd died the day she was born. Reading how happy he had been when he knew she was on the way… it made him more real than she thought possible.

The dragon leaned over and licked her cheek, following the tracks of her tears. "He loved you, before he ever knew you."

Abby closed the book and set it aside. She lifted the board up to try and make sense of it. It was simply a half-inch-thick piece of plywood, stained the same color as the inside of the drawer. Looking in the drawer itself, she found a cork spacer at each corner. The board simply lay in the bottom, and no one looking would have guessed what it hid. "Pretty simple in comparison with the trunk," she observed. "I swear Grandpa was paranoid."

Carefully, Abby replaced the false bottom and put her things back in the drawer. She tucked the journal in between her school books and then picked up the disk. "Then again it comes in handy." She went over to the trunk at the foot of her bed and pressed the hidden button to slide out *its* secret compartment. "I wonder what's on this." She pulled her laptop out of the drawer and examined its sides. Her face fell. "Dang it, doesn't look like there's a drive for this." It *did* have a disk drive – just for a much smaller disk.

"Reasonable," Dominic commented. "That's not nearly as old as that disk must be."

Curiosity nipped at her. "There's got to be a way." No sooner did she say it then a smile spread across her face. "Mr. Samson!" Abby put her laptop away and shut the drawer before heading out the door. "If anyone can figure it out, he can."

"Where did you get this again?" Wendel Samson pecked at keys, squinting at his screen. "It's encrypted almost as bad as the Pentagon."

Abby laughed. "Mr. Samson, be serious."

"He is," said Marlon from his spot on his father's desk. "Dad's got the world wired."

"Uh-huh," Abby leaned closer to see the screen, but it was nothing but random numbers. "It's my grandfather's – I found it in his desk. Figures he'd have it safe-guarded."

"No kidding." Dominic lay in a corner, shaking his head. "So far, you've found *three* secret compartments." He snorted. "I thought that book safe would be the last one."

"Safe-guarded?" Mr. Samson shook his head. "Safe-guarded is one thing; this is like putting something in a lock-box, putting *that* in a safe, then hiding the safe behind a picture on the wall." More clicking. "Ah, here we go." He blinked. "OK, seriously? All that protection for *this?*"

Marlon tilted his head. "Your grandfather made video games?" He leaned forward. "Geez, this looks like something out of an 80s arcade. 16-bit graphics and everything."

"I guess he did." Abby stared at the start screen which read "Path of the Dragon". *"Might even like this once I finish it." Well that explains a lot.* "Is there a way to get this on my laptop?" She wanted a closer look at something her grandfather had made. Wasn't as good as meeting him, but still.

Mr. Samson smiled. "What're the magic words?"

Abby clasped her hands and returned the grin. "Please and thank you."

Laughing, he placed a CD in the drive and clicked a few more keys. "If you figure out why this was so protected, you let me know, OK? That seemed a bit overkill for just a game."

"Hey, games are serious business." Marlon dropped off the desk and moved to lean over his father's chair. He brushed the bangs of his short blond hair out of his eyes. "You never know when a competitor is gonna steal your ideas."

"If you spent as much time as you do playing games on your homework," teased the elder Samson, "you'd be on the honor roll."

"I'm a gamer, Dad, not a geek." Marlon smiled, brown eyes twinkling. "That would be *you.*"

Abby sighed. "You two ever think of writing this down? It'd make one heck of a TV show."

They both laughed.

"Life's a TV show," replied Mr. Samson. "I can say that with complete confidence." He took the disks out of their drives, and then handed them to her. "Don't be a stranger; I'll get to thinking you only come around for my computer expertise."

"She's over here almost every day," said Mrs. Samson from the doorway. She smiled. "Knock, knock." It was easy to see where Marlon's looks came from; his mother's blond hair spilled around her shoulders. Her blue eyes sparkled. She crossed the threshold, setting a plate of cookies on the desk. "I swear, dear, you'd starve if someone wasn't around to feed you."

Mr. Samson just grinned and snatched up one of the cookies. "I'm not *that* helpless." He stood up and kissed her quickly. "Yeah, sugar's got nothing on you."

"DAD! EW!" Marlon gagged. "Sheesh, get a room!" He grabbed two of the cookies and headed for the door. "Come on, Abs, let's get out of here before I go blind!"

Abby slid the disks into her purse and dipped a curtsy to the love birds. "Thank you for your help. I don't know what I'd do without you. Have a good day, you two!" She turned and followed Marlon, closing the door behind her at his mother's request. "That was rude," she scolded. "They are your parents; show some respect."

"Dad would tease me just as bad if I had a girlfriend," Marlon said, holding out one of the cookies. "Here, chocolate chip, your favorite."

Abby took the cookie, shaking her head. "You're simply incorrigible."

"That's what Mom tells Dad all the time." He shot her the grin he'd inherited. "Pretty cool your granddad was a gamer. Must run in the family."

"Yeah, I guess it does." Abby followed him to the living room, one hand reaching out to pat Dominic's head at her side as she chewed her cookie.

"Fly bothering you?"

Swallowing, Abby looked at him curiously. "No, why?"

"You jerked your hand for a second there."

Abby choked on the bite she'd just taken.

"You OK?" Marlon moved to pat her back, but stopped himself.

She coughed for a few moments before managing to force it down. "I uh, I just… Hey you wanna test this game next time Aunt Gladys is out? I'm sure you could figure it out quicker than me."

Marlon's face lit up at the idea of a challenge. "You got it!" His eyes went to the clock and the joy turned to horror. "Speaking of which, you better be getting home. It's almost six."

Dominic nudged her. "He's right; you need to get moving."

"Dang it!" Abby gripped her purse strap in frustration. "Bye, Marlon. I'll see you in class tomorrow." She turned to go, but looked back at him. "You *did* do your homework, right?"

Marlon folded his arms and his face said "seriously?" louder than words. "Abs, I'm not *that* hopeless. Give me some credit. Come on, I'll walk you home."

Abby smiled. "How gentlemanly of you… considering I live next door. However could I get home without an escort?"

Dominic snorted. "You always have an escort."

You don't count, she mentally snapped, *Mr. Figment-of-my-Imagination!*

They stepped out onto the sidewalk. Sunlight reflected of the building's stark white paint job that contrasted with the bright red doors. Late-summer heat radiated off the parking lot and Abby was grateful that the walk was short.

"I know you're not helpless, Abs," said Marlon, putting his hands in his pockets. "But hey, who'd turn down a chance to spend time with a pretty girl?"

Abby rolled her eyes. "Very funny, Mars-Bars. Very funny." She drew her door key from her purse. "Thanks for company anyway. Seriously, you're a good friend."

Once more he flashed that grin. "Right back at ya, Abs. Check ya later."

Sighing, Abby went inside the apartment, going over what she would fix for dinner.

CHAPTER 3

Every nerve in her body felt like a guitar string ready to snap. Abby usually didn't use her laptop when Aunt Gladys was in the apartment. But curiosity had gotten the better of her. Had this game of her grandfather's ever gone anywhere? She searched "Path of the Dragon", but all that came up was a role-playing game from Japan and some short story.

"I doubt it would still be on that disk if it had become a 'real' game," said Dominic from his place beside her. Once more he was resting his head on his fore-paws, ears twitching at the faint pecking of the keyboard. "Why not simply play the game? See what it's about?"

My luck it'll be too complicated with the commands. Abby shut the laptop off, then got out of bed and put it back in its hiding place in her trunk. *I'll check the game out when she's gone. If I get stuck I'm sure Marlon can figure it out.* She crawled under the covers, snuggling into her pillow.

"You're going to be more careful what you do in public," Dominic said as he shifted to curl up beside her. "That kid almost caught you; course, if you could just tell a little white lie..."

I'm not a liar, Dominic! Abby narrowed her eyes at the dragon. *If I have to lie, then I shouldn't be doing it.*

The dragon just grinned. "Like how you aren't supposed to have the laptop in the first place?"

That's different! I'm responsible! Abby punched her pillow as she tried to get comfortable. *Aunt Gladys is just too old-fashioned. I don't think she even knows how the internet works.*

"Still, what would you do if she caught you, hmm? If she asked where you got it?" His grin just got wider. "Or if she asked if you still talk to me?"

Shut up, Dommy, I need to be up in time for the class.

"Sweet dreams, Abs. Sweet dreams."

"He is too real! You just can't see him because he's magic!"

"Child, he cannot be real as there is no such thing as dragons. Do you know what happens to people who see things that aren't there? They are sent away. You don't want that to happen, do you?"

"No! But he is *there so I'm not doing that!"*

"Listen, we'll talk again next week, but you need to understand that this is just make-believe. There is no such thing as dragons and you are simply making this up. Now, your aunt is waiting for you. Just think about what I said. Because if you keep talking like this..."

"No! No, no, no! I don't wanna go away!"

"Then you must stop this nonsense. Please rejoin your aunt and I'll see you next week. Be good now."

She went out into the waiting room with Dominic curled around her neck, and took Aunt Gladys' hand. She kept her eyes on the floor.

"Did you understand what the doctor told you?"

"Yes, ma'am, I did." She didn't elaborate verbally. I understand; if I talk about Dominic anymore, I'll be sent away.

"So we've heard the last of that dragon nonsense?"

"Yes, ma'am."

"Good. Now, let's go home. You can watch Children's Bible Heroes."

The ringing of her alarm clock startled Abby from her dream. She shut it off before it gave her too much of a headache, then sat up and rubbed her eyes. *That's what I get for thinking about stuff before I go to sleep.*

She got her clothes and headed for the bathroom for a shower. She adjusted the water and stepped under the soothing spray. As she lathered her hands, she took a moment to just breathe. She hadn't thought about that mess in years. While she'd never lied about Dominic being gone, she'd never told the truth, either. Not even the shrink had ever again asked, "Do you still see him?" So she'd let everyone believe she'd stopped pretending, even though she had not. After she washed her hair she stepped out of the shower to dry off and dress.

"Nice," commented Dominic, a grin on his face. "Very… nice."

Abby slapped the towel at him. "You are not supposed to be watching!"

"Oh, relax." He scratched at his chin with a fore-paw. "Not like I'm real anyway."

Abby buttoned her white blouse and shook her head. "I swear you're such a pervert."

"Just means you have a dirty mind." Dominic swished his tail then his expression became concerned. "How are you feeling? Nervous?"

"Of course I'm nervous! Driving is serious business, and everyone says the teacher is really strict." Abby pulled her hair back into a ponytail and smoothed her skirt. "I just hope he doesn't put too much pressure on us. I need my license." It was such a simple thing, that little square of plastic. But it meant freedom. If she could drive, she could go to college.

Dominic started singing. She could just remember the song; the words were familiar, but she couldn't place it. Something about a Catholic girl named Virginia.

She turned to him. "Maybe you should stay home today. I love your company, but you're a distraction."

The dragon looked hurt. "But… if I'm not with you… What if you outgrow me? I promised not to leave, but if you forget me…"

With a sigh, Abby slid on her shoes. "Fine, you can come. Stop the puppy eyes. Just keep your mouth shut for a change."

Dominic grinned and raised a paw and placed the other over his chest. "Dragon's honor!"

Shaking her head, Abby headed to the kitchen for breakfast. She smelled the cooking pancakes all through the apartment. She went to set the table, wishing Aunt Gladys good morning.

"Where is this driving class again?" Gladys carried a plate of pancakes to the table. She put two on her own plate, then two on Abby's. "I'm not sure you should walk there. This city isn't what it used to be, you know."

"It's in the parking lot at school, Aunt Gladys." Abby reached up to move a stray hair off her forehead before she smoothed the front of her shirt and brushed at each of her shoulders. Dutifully, she clasped her hands and silently joined the older woman in saying grace. "I've walked to school since I was ten; I'll be fine, don't worry."

Dominic smiled at her discreet Sign of the Cross, laying his head on his paws as he settled at her feet.

"I'd still feel better if someone went with you." Gladys picked up her knife and fork to cut her pancakes into perfectly proportioned bites. "A lady shouldn't go anywhere without an escort."

"Marlon said he –" Abby froze at the look on her aunt's face.

"How many times do I have to tell you I don't want you hanging around that Samson boy? That family has no concept of Christ. His father's got two women over there some days, and one's not even his wife! To say nothing of that younger boy; in my day, if a woman had another man's child she'd be a laughingstock! You hang around with them you'll end up just like his harlot of a mother! I will not have you alone with that boy! Boys like him only have one thing in mind."

Abby sighed. "All the more reason for me to spend time with their family. If – please let me finish – if no one's there to show them, how will they ever see another way? Marlon said he and Felice would be happy to accompany me. They're attending the class too."

At the mention of Marlon's twin sister, Gladys lost some of her fire. "I suppose you're right, but I honestly don't see how you stomach being around those people."

She poured syrup on her pancakes and took a sip of her milk. *Guess we're even, Aunt Gladys,* she thought as she cut into her pancakes. *I don't know how you handle Preacher Davidson's family, either.* "Some people have to lead by example," Abby said, frustrated with the double meanings she was forced to use just to live her life. Her honest nature warred with the knowledge that if she was blunt, she'd never see her friend again. "Or others will have nothing to follow."

"It does my heart good to see people your age taking ministry seriously." Gladys smiled and sipped her coffee. "I'm so proud of how you're turning out, Abigail. You'll make some lucky Christian man a lovely wife one day."

"Thank you," Abby replied automatically. She took another bite to give herself an excuse not to speak. Marriage was the farthest thing from her mind. She lost herself in daydreams of being a respected psychologist, one that had a good understanding of children and would never scare a child who talked about their imaginary friend. *Someday,* she thought, smiling. *Someday I'll make a real difference.* She put the last bite of pancake in her mouth.

Gladys finished her plate, too, and smiled when Abby cleared the table. "Yes, my dear, any good man would be lucky to have you."

Abby bit her cheek, nodding as she ran the sink. She rolled up her sleeves and started the dishes.

"You're certainly trained in housework," said Dominic, sitting beside her. "I guess if you look at it in that light, her insisting you tend to so much of the upkeep makes sense. Any good bitch learns to obey before she's of use to anyone."

You better mean a female dog, Scales-for-Brains! Abby scrubbed a pan a little harder than she needed to, then dried it before setting it in the strainer.

Dominic blinked up at her innocently. "What else would I refer to?"

Abby shook her head. *Sometimes I wonder why I put up with you.*

"You love me." Dominic's grin showed all of his sharp teeth. "Besides, you know you were thinking it. Not my fault I had the guts to say it."

Dishes done, she went to get her purse. *Come on, you over-grown gecko,* she thought as they headed out the door. *And try keeping your –* at his look, she corrected herself – *my opinions to yourself!*

"Yes, ma'am." He twisted around her legs like a cat before taking his place at her heels. "My lips are sealed."

CHAPTER 4

"Life's like a quiz," Abby offered. "You study for a multiple choice only to get true or false."

"Life's like a box of chocolates," Felice said, snickering as they stepped into the driver's ed classroom. This "classroom" was a small portable with dingy flooring parked outside of the main school building. "Some pieces are really sweet and the rest are nuts. Your turn, bro."

"Life's like a video game," Marlon began.

"*Everything* is like a video game to you, Mars-Bars."

"If I may continue?" Marlon waved a hand, taking on an air reminiscent of Mr. Harris. "Life's a video game stuck on hardest, no way to save, and no extra lives. Worst part? No manual either."

Out of the corner of her eye, Abby saw Felice mouth, "Three… two… one."

Abby flashed a smile. "The bible's the manual, Marlon."

"OK," he said with a grin, "a manual that was so badly translated that they had to add an addendum. Then the other guys made their own."

"I swear you two." Felice rolled her deep blue eyes. She brushed back her brown hair as they took their seats on the folding tables and chairs with the rest of the class. "How many times are you going to have this conversation?"

"How many stars are in the sky?" Abby sat her purse behind her and crossed her legs out of habit. Her hand played with the cross at her neck. "So how do you think you'll do on the written test?"

"We were up half the night with those flash cards you gave him." Felice smoothed her jeans before adopting the same pose. "I'd say we got this."

"Students, if I could have your attention?" Mr. Harris, a tall, thin man with long gray beard, stood behind a podium up front. "I regret to inform you that Mr. Roberts will not be teaching this year." At the protest, Harris simply raised his hand. "He said he wishes to spend quality time with his last nerve. Never fear; we've a qualified replacement." He looked at his watch. "Who apparently has been delayed –"

The rest of the principal's sentence was drowned by the roar of a motorcycle outside. Abby could just barely see the leather-clad figure pull into the parking lot and stop alongside the building. He shut the bike off and dismounted, kicking the kickstand into place before pulling the helmet from his head and tucking it under his arm. He pushed through the door, crossed over to Mr. Harris and held out his hand. "Sorry I'm late; traffic's a bitch around here – *oops!*" He looked out at the class and scratched the back of his head. "Sorry, sorry."

Abby glanced over at the snickering twins, then looked closely at the new teacher. He wasn't quite as tall as Mr. Harris, his black hair pulled back into a ponytail, and he wore tattered jeans with a white shirt beneath his leather jacket. From this distance she couldn't see his eye color, but he did have a neatly trimmed beard and mustache. *Why does he look familiar?*

Mr. Harris pinched the bridge of his nose and sighed. "Everyone, please meet Mr. Samson." He waved a hand at the podium of teaching materials. "I'll let you take it from here."

Abby leaned over to Marlon and hissed. *"Mr. Samson?"*

"Grandpa's great Abs, you'll love him." Marlon grinned from ear-to-ear. "Now hush."

Mr. Samson stepped behind the podium and sat his helmet by his feet. He placed his hands on either side of the platform and leaned toward them. "Hey, ya'll. Uh, so. Let's just cut to the chase. You are all here for one of two reasons. Either you got no one around with the guts to teach ya how this works, or your parents don't wanna have a heart attack. That's why I'm here; I've been through too much crap for ya to scare me, and I ain't gonna take no crap from ya neither. Respect is earned."

"That's no way for an authority figure to speak to his students," said Dominic with a slight growl. He stuck his head out from under her chair. "That buffoon has no *respect* for —"

Abby kicked him. *Hush you!*

"So long as you get that, we'll get along fine. My job's to turn you into competent drivers, so people don't have to watch out for ya while watchin' out for themselves. So people *like me* don't end up dead cause ya don't know what you're doin'." Samson looked out at the crowd, staring at them, one by one. "So take this seriously, or take a hike." He reached for a sticky note on the podium and squinted at it. "We got a bus to take you to your written tests today, then we'll come back here. Retakes can be taken again in one week. Busy as that place is, driving practice will start here tomorrow. Those of ya fine with those terms line up outside. Bus is waitin'."

As she shouldered her purse and followed the Samson twins, Abby nudged Marlon hard. "Why didn't you *tell* me about this?"

"And ruin the surprise?" Marlon blinked innocently. "Why would we do that?"

"Don't worry Abby, Grandpa's the best." Felice grinned. "You'll like him. He's a Christian, too."

Abby blinked. "Him?!?"

"Yeah, he's just not as wacko as your aunt." Marlon shook his head. "Then again, it'd take a lot to be *that* wacko. Likes the weird crap you listen to enough to sing it."

"At least I'll still have my hearing when I'm in my thirties." Abby followed the twins onto the bus. They took a seat in the back so they could sit together, as they had since they'd met. She leaned against the window as Dominic curled up tight under her feet. "Your grandfather knows how to make an entrance, I'll say that much."

"Grandpa's got class," said Marlon, folding his arms behind his head. "Just came off tour; think he opened for Stripes or whatever."

"Stryper?" Abby stared at her friend. "Wait, you mean he's a singer?"

"Yeah, Grandpa's pretty good, too." Felice smiled. "Dad used to tell us he was busy helping people and that's why he couldn't be around much."

Marlon kicked his foot in time with the song on the radio blaring over the conversations of their classmates. "He does benefit concerts, and those toy run things."

"Can't judge a book by its cover, I guess." Abby got the driver's education book out of her purse. "I knew I'd seen him somewhere before."

Marlon snorted. "Yeah, all over Dad's office. Then again, Grandma's shop isn't much better. Family photos everywhere."

"So where does he live? And why haven't I seen him around before?"

"Well…" Marlon dragged out the word, glancing at his sister. "He and his wife have an apartment downtown but they do come over for dinner. He's just usually on tour or at work."

Abby looked up from the book. "Your grandfather's a singer and this is the first I've heard of it? When you've told me about —" she lowered her voice "– all the other stuff? Are any more surprises going to come up?"

"Not really, but if you thought things were complicated before, well…"

"I had to ask." Abby smacked herself with the book. "You'd think I'd have learned by now."

"We never claimed to be normal," said Felice. She winked. "Besides, it's vastly overrated."

"Hey!" Marlon mock-pouted. "*I'm* the normal one in this family."

Abby shook her head and looked out the window, kicking her foot back and forth as she rubbed it against Dominic's side.

"Penny for your thoughts, Abs?"

"Just questioning how my life choices led me here, but," she shot them a smile, "I wouldn't change a thing."

CHAPTER 5

Abby shifted her purse strap and fell into step with Felice and Marlon as they stepped off the bus. She wasn't disappointed like the rest of the class; just passing the written test was a relief. She followed the twins over to their grandfather, who was waiting on them, leaning against his motorcycle.

"Need a ride home?" he asked and a familiar grin appeared on his face. His eyes, the same brown as Marlon and Marlon's father, shone with amusement. He looked over at Abby and pulled back. "Hey, who's this?"

Abby bit her cheek and curtsied. "Abigail Palmer," she said. "Pleased to meet you, Mr. Samson." She smiled. "That's going to get confusing."

To her surprise, the older Samson bowed, putting one arm behind his back and the other across his chest. "It's a pleasure to meet you, Miss Palmer." He straightened up and smirked. "Naw, I'm Bryan. Mr. Samson is my brother. Speakin' of relations, you look familiar." He tapped his head as he thought about it. "You kinda look like my friend's little girl did at your age. Been a long time since I heard from her. Least his old lady still sends Christmas cards. Guy's real name was Nick Whelan."

At her side, the dragon growled.

"Nick Whelan?" Abby repeated. *Hush, Dommy!* "Dominic Whelan was my grandfather."

"I'll be damned!" Bryan laughed.

"GRANDPA!" Felice put her hands on her hips. "You swore! Again!"

Bryan turned red and reached into his back pocket. From his wallet he pulled out a twenty and handed it to Felice. "Outta practice, sweetheart, sorry." He smiled. "That should cover it 'til I get back in the habit." He reached in again and pulled out an old photo then handed it to Abby. "Yeah, no doubt you're blood of the Dragon."

The photo showed her grandfather and a younger Bryan giving a one-finger salute to the camera. Abby stared, noticing a patch on the front of her grandfather's leather jacket. A dragon curled around a white cross. "The Dragon?"

Marlon laughed. "Bikers tend to have nicknames, Abs." He jerked his thumb at his grandfather. "His is 'Wasp'. Guess your grandpa's was 'Dragon'." He froze. "Wait, *Dragon?* The guy you talk about all the time?"

"*The* Dragon," corrected Bryan. "Cause of that patch. See?" He tapped the picture. "Guy never went anywhere without that jacket. He's the reason I'm teachin' these lessons in the first place. Some dumbass kid shouldn't have been behind the wheel."

Abby handed the picture back. "Grandpa died in an accident? I mean, I know he died the day I was born –"

"*You're* the kid he was going on about? Ain't that somethin'." Bryan tucked the picture back in his wallet and the wallet back in his pocket. "Your grandfather was a good man, Miss Palmer. I'll say that much. How's your parents doin'?"

She couldn't speak. Ten years or not, the rawness of the wound hurt. It was even worse when asked by what was clearly a good friend of her grandfather's. Tears made her blink.

"Grandpa!" Marlon wrapped her in a hug. "They're dead, OK? Sheesh, where you been, under a rock? You talk about the guy all the time and you don't even know –"

"How was I supposed to know? None of those cards said…" Bryan's voice came out sharp but softened along with his eyes when he looked at Abby. "I'm sorry, Miss Palmer." He started to reached out before reconsidering it. "Never could remember who Nicole married." He chuckled. "The Dragon always called him 'Cowboy'."

"Jesse Palmer," replied Abby, wiping her eyes and pulling free of Marlon. "Daddy was Jesse James Palmer. And I'm Abby, sir." She tried to smile. "Just Abby."

"Grandpa," said Felice with a sigh. "You have eighteen swears left, but you shouldn't just prepay for them."

Abby nudged Felice. "I'd say he's got a good reason." She turned back to Bryan. "It was a long time ago, sir. Just… caught me off guard. Same as it did you, I'll bet."

"Bryan," he corrected, smiling as he folded his arms. "Just Bryan. And yeah, it did. Sorry, again." He sighed. "Time moves on, I guess. So you three need a ride home?"

"If we get on that bike Mom will have your head and you know it," said Felice. "Besides, four people do not fit on that bike."

"I could make a couple trips." Bryan reached out and ruffled his granddaughter's hair. "So, I take it you… wait. Abby." He burst out laughing. "*The* Abby?"

Marlon's face went seven shades of red. "Grandpa, don't you need to get home for dinner? Grandma will be mad if you're late."

Bryan snickered. "OK, OK, I can take a hint." He winked at Abby and got on his bike. "See ya around, Abby." He looked over at the twins and grinned. "See you two this evening. Now stand back, you three." Once they did, he kicked the kickstand up, started it up and rode out of sight.

Dominic growled softly. "That bumbler doesn't have any common sense!"

Abby ignored the protective dragon. *"The* Abby?" she repeated. "Just what does that mean?"

"Just that Marlon talks about you like you hung the moon." Felice shook her head and started down the sidewalk. "And Grandpa loves to tease people."

"'Lice!" Marlon glared at her. "You're just as bad. Sheesh!"

Abby smiled as she fell in step behind the twins. She played with the cross she wore. "Hung the moon huh? Well, I did help hang Kenny's mobile."

"Damn it, Abs not you too!" Marlon's jaw dropped and he looked at his sister with a sheepish smile. "Uh… I mean…"

"MARLON!"

"Yeah, yeah." Marlon pulled out his wallet. "Here's your stupid dollar."

Abby walked into the apartment to find Aunt Gladys sitting on the couch with Mrs. Davidson, drinking tea. They both smiled at her, which sent a chill down her spine. *What are you two up to this time?* She greeted both politely out of habit, even remembering to curtsy.

"Good evening to you too, dear." Mrs. Davidson sat her teacup down and folded her hands in her lap. As always she was dressed modestly. She looked like someone on *The Waltons*. "Gladys was just telling me about your ministry work. I must say it's so noble of you to try and save those poor Samson children. Are you making any progress?"

Abby bit her tongue and fought to hide her reaction. "We spoke about the bible today." *And they blew it off same as always.*

Dominic's tail swished. He moved between her and the pair.

"That's wonderful! You must really be getting through to them."

"A lot's learned every time I see them." Abby adjusted her grip on her purse strap. "And I passed the written test. The teacher turned out to be their grandpa – he's a Christian too."

"Congratulations!" Aunt Gladys smiled then sipped her tea. "Grand*father*, dear. That's good news! Maybe now they'll have some direction in their lives."

"I really need to get dinner started." Abby shifted toward the kitchen. "I'm sorry. Are you staying for dinner, Mrs. Davidson?"

"Oh, no dear! In fact, *I* better get home or my family will starve." Mrs. Davidson stood, and curtsied. "But my dear, I'd hoped you and Gladys could join us Wednesday? I'm cooking clam chowder and it would give you and Drew time to get to know each other better."

Dominic growled at the mention of Drew Davidson. "Tell her no way in Hell!"

Abby didn't scold him this time; she did not like Drew either. She scrambled for a way out of this. "I... Mrs. Davidson I'd love to come, but I've already got plans."

"Really now dear, if it's with those Samson children surely you can reschedule." Mrs. Davidson's smile began to creep her out. "A dinner with a potential suitor surely is more pressing than your ministry work, and you did say their grandfather's a Christian. I'm sure you won't lose much ground."

Abby balked. "I'm sorry Mrs. Davidson, but I can't reschedule this."

Aunt Gladys glared at her. She folded her arms and cleared her throat. "What are these plans Abby dear and why wasn't I aware of them? You *know* where you go for lying."

"You are most certainly aware of them, Aunt Gladys." Abby forced her tone to stay respectful. "My birthday is this Wednesday and I always visit Grandma then. You used to take me yourself."

Gladys' expression became horrified. She rushed to apologize. "I'm sorry, Mrs. Davidson, truly. I cannot believe that slipped my mind!"

"It's quite all right, dear. Quite all right. Family first." Mrs. Davidson smiled at them both, then headed for the door. "I really must be off. See you girls Sunday!"

Once she left, Abby looked at her great-aunt. *"Potential suitor?!?"* She gripped her purse strap tightly. "Since when is Drew Davidson a *suitor?* I've barely said three words to him during the school year."

"All the more reason for you to get to know him in supervised conditions. While I'm sure such a good boy can be trusted, it's not proper for a lady to be alone with a man."

Abby stared at her. Times she'd spent with Marlon, just the two of them while his parents were in another room or not even home came to mind. They contrasted harshly with her memories of Drew Davidson in school. Preacher's son or not, he was a pushy flirt. "I need to start dinner, Aunt Gladys." She turned and sought sanctuary in the kitchen and its simple tasks. Her cooking was one of the few things her aunt didn't lecture her on.

"Nosy old bat," said Dominic as he curled up at her feet. "She should worry about her love life before she thinks about yours." He paused. "Still, she means well."

Even if she does, it's none of her business. Abby started cutting carrots with more strength than the job required. She forced her focus on the task. *Last thing I need is to slice off a finger. Though that might get me out of a date.*

"Just two more years." Dominic rubbed her leg with his cheek like True once had. "Then the choices will be yours alone."

CHAPTER 6

Abby swung her packed backpack over her shoulder. She went out into the living room to find Aunt Gladys knitting in front of the television. She fought not to cringe at the sermon that, even at normal volume, was too loud. "I'll be back before six, Aunt Gladys."

Gladys nodded. "Be careful dear. Do you have your pepper spray?"

Abby rolled up her sleeve and revealed the canister on its strap around her wrist. "Yes, ma'am. Are you sure you don't want to come with me?" Not that she really wanted her along, but she knew her grandmother would be happy to see her sister.

"Dear, you know I'm too old to be riding buses." She waved a hand. "You ask for so little on your special day; it's so refreshing to see a woman your age who's not spoiled."

"And you take all the credit for that, don't you?" Dominic pressed against Abby's side, snarling. "If you had any say in the matter she'd be married off within the year!"

Abby curtsied and smiled. "You raised me well, Aunt Gladys. I doubt I'd have turned out the same had Grandma been in charge."

"It's so good of you to visit Gail," said Gladys, returning to her knitting. "So many kids today don't respect their elders."

"Oh, now she's a *kid*? Where was this when you wanted her to –"

Dominic will you hush? Abby adjusted her strap. "I'll see you this evening, Aunt Gladys." She walked out the door with the dragon at her heels. *I swear, you are so… maybe it's time I grew up. You are a distraction more than anything these days.*

The black and white dragon hung his head. "But who will you talk to if you send me away?" He let out a pitiful whine. "I don't even know what will happen to me if you forget me…"

Abby sighed. "Just stop being such a jerk; yes, I know you're only saying what I'm thinking, but I really wish I wasn't thinking those things in the first place."

"Talking to yourself again, Abs?" Marlon came up alongside her, his hands in his pockets. He smiled. "Happy birthday, beautiful!"

Abby blushed and nudged him with her elbow. "Be serious, Mars-Bars."

"I am." Marlon tilted his head as he looked at her backpack. "Heading for the bus right?"

"Yeah," she replied, sighing as she unlocked her bike. "I wish I got to see Grandma more."

"Bus ride out that far's gotta suck." Marlon's expression turned nervous. "You know, Grandpa would take you…"

Abby stopped short and stared at him. "You're kidding, right? If I got on a motorcycle Aunt Gladys would hit the roof!"

"She wouldn't have to know." He fidgeted with his pockets. "I just… well there's been some stuff on the news and… well, mind if I come with you?"

Dominic snorted. "Overprotective fool. You can handle yourself just fine."

"Not at all," Abby replied, smiling both at her friend and the stunned dragon. "Be nice to have some company. Besides, Grandma would love to meet *the* Marlon."

"You're never gonna let me live that down, are you?" Marlon sighed loudly and unlocked his own bike. "I'm so gonna get Grandpa for that."

"Be glad you have him, Mars-Bars." Abby started to walk her bike to the bus stop. "Be glad you have him."

"Abby!" Gail Whelan smiled as she opened her door for them. "Girl, I swear you've shot up like a weed." She hugged her tight then noticed her companion. "And who is this handsome young man?"

"Marlon Samson, ma'am," said her friend as he bowed with one arm behind his back, the other across his chest. "A pleasure to meet you, Mrs. Whelan."

"Watch it, Mars-Bars, your grandpa's showing through." Abby smiled. "I hope you don't mind I brought him, Grandma? He's house-broken I swear."

Her grandmother's laughter was a pleasant change. It was easy to tell when Gail Whelan was happy. She waved them both inside. "I'm sure he is."

Marlon rolled his eyes, taking off his shoes at the door. "I'm not a dog, Abs."

Abby smiled and followed suit, patting his shoulder. "I know, Little Wasp."

Her grandmother froze and turned to look at them. "Wasp? Why would you…" She looked closer at Marlon and her jaw dropped. "I'll be darned. Samson. Bryan Samson!"

"That's my grandpa, yes." Marlon flashed a grin as he put his hands in his pockets. "I tried to get Grandpa to come, but," his face turned seven shades of red, "he and Grandma… kinda needed to get reacquainted. He's been on tour and –"

Gail raised her hand. "I hear you. Bryan and Vera were always like teenagers." She chuckled. "Nick swore he'd never seen a more love-sick puppy than Wasp."

Abby blinked. "This is so weird." She turned to Marlon as they followed her grandmother to the living room and sat down. "How did I manage to miss seeing your grandparents around?"

Marlon shrugged sheepishly. "Grandma kinda doesn't like the apartment much. Plus Grandpa tours a lot so when he's home he pretty much spends all his time with Grandma. I guess it just wasn't meant to be."

"Or he was too embarrassed by the bumbler to make sure you met," said Dominic as he curled up at Abby's feet. "Still, he was pleased to see he was the teacher…"

Marlon fidgeted and looked at Gail. "Ma'am, I hate to ask but… why didn't you tell Grandpa when Abby's parents died? I mean, he said you still exchange Christmas cards."

"Bryan really took it hard when Nick died." Gail poured some lemonade and handed them each a glass before picking up her own. "We lost contact with him for awhile after that; he wasn't up to talking to anyone." She frowned, staring into her glass like it was a crystal ball. "He used to send us postcards. After the fire, I just kept sending the Christmas cards. I couldn't bear to tell him Nicole and J.J. were gone seeing how he dealt with Nick's passing." She sighed. "Before I knew it, years had passed and I just… didn't know what to say."

Poor Grandma, thought Abby, *taking a drink. Though… I think this is the first time she's said Grandpa's name without crying. Maybe…* "Grandma, what… happened the night Grandpa died?"

"He was working late at the office trying to get them to support a project he had," said Gail, blinking tears aside. "Anyway, your mom went into labor and once we got to the hospital I called him." She blinked again, taking a drink and swallowing hard. She sat the glass down with shaking hands. "I wish I hadn't. Maybe he'd have waited out the rain. He left on his bike and was headed for the hospital when this teen – poor kid just got his license – came around the corner in his lane." She sighed, pulled a handkerchief from her pocket and wiped her eyes. "Bike went one way, he went the other. Died right there on the roadside."

Guess now I know what Bryan meant about a kid that shouldn't have been driving. Abby looked at her grandmother. *No wonder she doesn't talk about this.* She took a deep breath and changed the subject. "The project... was it a game? Path of the Dragon?"

"How did you know?" Gail shook her head and chuckled. "Let me guess: found another secret compartment? When I gave you our bedroom suit, I never thought it would be so useful."

"False bottom in the desk drawer." Abby reached out and laid her hand on her grandmother's. "I found a disk with it." She pulled back and nudged Marlon. "His dad got the game off it for me."

"Path of the Dragon." Gail sighed. "I swear Nick thought he was going to change the world with that game. A game with a good moral, instead of all the evil, he said. Well, how are things at home, sweetheart? Gladys still driving you crazy?"

"We were supposed to have dinner with the Davidsons today." Abby took another drink and sat the glass down. "Sounds like she's going to try and set me up with their son soon."

The sound of shattering glass rang out and both women looked over to see Marlon's horrified expression. He grabbed for the shards, wincing as the lemonade got into the cuts. "I'm so sorry, Mrs. Whelan! I'll clean it up."

"My heavens!" Gail got up and grabbed his hand. "Forget about the mess. You've cut yourself; you're bleeding. Into the kitchen, now!"

While Gail ran Marlon's hand under the cold water, Abby got the first aid kit from the drawer and set it on the counter. "You OK, Marlon?" *Looks like the bleeding stopped.*

"Yeah, I'm fine, glass just slipped." He winced as Gail bandaged his hand. "Clumsy, I guess."

"A bumbler like his grandfather," grumbled Dominic. He shook himself, his gold mane fluffing out as he did so. "At least he knows it."

Why do you have to be such a jerk? Abby grabbed an old dish towel and went into the living room. She knelt and cleaned up the glass and lemonade. *It's not like he meant to break it.*

Gail came up behind her with a dustpan. "So I'm guessing you got out of dinner because of our prior engagement?"

"Pretty much." Abby dropped the mess, towel and all, into the dustpan. "Mrs. Davidson was all 'family first'. Heaven forbid I'd have had plans with Marlon or Felice."

"Why's that?" Marlon came back in and took the dustpan. He carried it over and dumped it in the trash can before rinsing it out and putting it beside the broom.

Abby sighed. "Mostly because Aunt Gladys thinks when I'm hanging out with you and your family, I'm doing ministry work, remember?"

"She thinks *what?*" Gail burst out laughing. "Oh, Abby you didn't!"

"She did," said Marlon. He stuck his hands back in his pockets. "No offense, ma'am, but your sister's a nutjob." He pulled a hand free and scratched the back of his head. "Well, I mean my family's kinda weird but —"

"It works," cut in Abby. "Your family might not be 'Christian' but you all get along better than the Davidsons do. Drew acts like God's gift to women whenever he's out of his parents' sight. *You* are always just Marlon. You don't change your whole personality for your parents' approval."

"Like how *you* shift your words and actions around your aunt?" Dominic's smile annoyed her. "Practice what you preach sometime?"

You are so… Abby bit her tongue. *You know I hate it when you're right?*

Marlon flashed that grin. "Why change perfection?" He choked. "Dang it, I'm starting to talk like Grandpa again!"

Both women laughed, and then Gail got out a pack of cards. "You two want to play?"

"Sure, Grandma." Abby shot a smirk at her friend. "Unless you're too chicken."

"As if." Marlon sat back down and held out his hand. "Bring it on."

CHAPTER 7

"I haven't had that much fun in a long time." Gail put the cards away and smiled at Marlon. "You're quite the card shark young man."

He smiled back. "Learned early, ma'am. Grandpa, Dad and Uncle Richie play almost every time they come over." He folded his hands behind his head and stretched, looking like the cat that caught the canary. "Took 'em all for the Halloween candy last time."

"Next time we'll have to play for more than points then." Gail's eyes sparkled. "Oh, before I forget…" She pulled a box out of her pocket and held it out. "Happy Birthday, dear."

Abby took the box and carefully opened it. Inside was a black and white rosary with gold accents. She looked up at her grandmother. "I don't understand."

"That was your grandfather's." Gail reached out and stroked Abby's hair. "He made it himself; his college colors." She reached out and closed Abby's hands around the box. "It's yours."

Abby looked over at the dragon at her side out of the corner of her eye. *You're black and white with gold, too.* "Grandma… do you remember the stuffed dragon I used to have? Where did it come from?"

"Ah, Dominic." Gail laughed bitterly. "Nick made him for you – or rather for the baby that turned out to be you. He wanted you to have something from him always."

"And I lost it." Abby felt the tears prick at her eyes. "I couldn't take care of *one thing –*"

"You didn't lose it, dear, he just got misplaced." Gail looked at her with an unreadable expression. "I'm sure he'll turn up one day."

"Hey." Dominic came up alongside her and nuzzled her leg. "I'm still here. So long as you remember something, it cannot be 'lost'."

Abby nodded, both to her grandmother and the dragon. "I know. I know it's just…" She sighed. "I hope that game's as good as Grandpa believed it was." She smirked at Marlon. "Or I'll never hear the end of it."

"Oh, I'll only tease you for a week or two." Marlon looked at the clock. "Dang it, Abs, if we don't get going we'll miss the bus."

"You two are welcome to come back any time you like." Gail walked them to the door. She smiled at Marlon. "It was a pleasure to meet you, Mr. Samson."

He smiled back. "Thank you for the hospitality and next time I'll try not to break anything." He bowed. "Farewell, fair lady."

"Such a gentleman." Gail nudged her granddaughter and gestured with a thumb at Marlon. "You might want to think about going steady with this one."

"Grandma!" Abby's face turned red. "Not you too!" She hugged her grandmother tight. "I love you. I'll try to come by more often."

"I love you too, dear." Gail returned the hug. "Don't you ever forget it; I'm just a phone call away if you need me." She watched as they got on their bikes and stood waving until they were out of sight.

"Nice neighborhood," said Marlon. "Snob hill."

Abby looked at the neat yards, the white fences, the fenced-in trees. She laughed. "Got a point there, Mars-Bars." She skidded her bike to a stop as he turned a corner. "Hey, where are you going? The bus stop's that way." She pointed further down the road they were on.

"I'm starving." Marlon continued down the road. "I'm smellin' cheeseburgers and fries. So I'm heading that way." He looked back over his shoulder. "Come on, Abs. Your grandmother's great but those snacks she gave us don't cut it."

"You just said we could miss the bus." Abby turned and followed him. "And you want to hit a fast food joint?"

"If we miss the bus I'll call Dad or Grandpa. One of 'em will pick us up." Marlon smiled at her. "Where's your sense of adventure?"

"I lost it a long time ago," she replied. She pushed her legs hard to catch up and rode beside him. "Do you know how much trouble I'll be in if I don't get home on time?"

"Do you trust me?"

The question threw her off guard. Abby looked at him then swerved to avoid a pothole. "Is that a trick question?"

"Just answer it." Marlon stopped his bike, staring at her.

"Of course I do." Abby stopped hers, too, and met his unusually serious gaze. "Do you really think I'd be out here with you if I didn't? Sheesh, Marlon."

His smile would have lit up the whole city. "Then start building some memories. I'll get you home on time, promise."

"You have seen *Lady and the Tramp* one too many times, Mars-Bars." She smiled and shook her head.

"Only as many times as you've seen *Oliver and Company.*"

"OK, OK, lead on. But if I end up grounded I'm telling your mom."

At the mention of his mother his face went white. "Don't joke about that!"

"I'm not," she said, pushing off. She could smell the food, too, and it made her stomach growl. "So let's get moving."

"Yes, ma'am." He caught up before taking the lead once more. "You're not going to regret this."

"I'll hold you to that." Abby sighed in relief as they turned into the almost empty parking lot. *At least the place isn't busy.*

"This is stupid," complained Dominic as he swished his tail. "You told Gladys you would be home at a certain time. She may be …" He paused, seeming to be trying to think of the word. "Regardless, you owe her the respect of keeping your word."

If she knew I was out with Marlon, she'd send me to boarding school. Abby smiled at the dragon as she locked her bike. *You know, it's nice to be just hanging out with a friend. Feels almost normal.*

"Normal is vastly overrated." The dragon growled as he followed her into the restaurant.

Marlon walked up to the counter. "Good-day, sir. My friend and I would like a to-go order, please." He turned and smiled at her. "Ladies first."

Abby rolled her eyes as she moved to join him. *I wish Aunt Gladys, just once, would see this side of Marlon. Maybe she wouldn't be so against me spending time with him.* She looked over the menu, looking for something she could afford. She ordered a sandwich with fries and a drink off the value menu then reached for her wallet.

"Your money's no good here, Abs." Marlon put out his hand to stop her. "Add a cheeseburger, fries and a cola to that would you, please? Thanks." He pulled a twenty from his pocket and paid. "We'll be right over here." He took the glasses and headed for the soda fountain. "Diet cola right?"

"Marlon!" Abby followed him, horrified. "What… why did you…?"

He filled the glasses then put a lid on and a straw in both. He held hers out to her. "Abs, it's your birthday – you're *sixteen*. That's a big deal. That needs to be commemorated." He sipped his drink and ran a finger around the lid. "I mean, a meal at a burger joint's not much, but better than nothing."

She stared at him. She didn't know what to say. For something to do, she took a drink, only to choke on it.

"Hey, you OK?" He sat his glass down and patted her back. "I…"

"I'm fine." She managed to clear her throat, then looked at him and smiled. "Thank you. For caring, for… you know, just for being you."

Marlon grinned. "Now don't get sappy on me, Abs. I ain't nothin' special." He blinked and swore. "Great, I'm sounding more and more like Grandpa."

Abby laughed. "No, you sound like Mars-Bars."

"Yo, love-birds! Order up!" The cashier smiled at them as he sat the bags on the counter. "You two are such a cute couple."

They both started sputtering. Neither could get a word out.

Dominic laughed. "Marlon and Abby, sittin' in a tree…"

You hush! Abby felt her face heat up. She took a drink to avoid answering.

"Come on, Abs." Marlon snatched up the bags and bolted out the door. "I'll race you to the bus stop."

"No fair!" She followed, walking carefully so she wouldn't spill her drink. "You've got a head start!" She found him checking the bags when she got out the door.

He looked into both then put one in the basket of her bike. "You didn't really think I'd take off without you, did you?"

Abby laughed. "You had me going for a minute there." She got on her bike, putting her drink in the holder in the side of her basket. She waited as he did the same and they were off again. A suspicion occurred to her, which she voiced when they reached the bus stop. "You planned this, didn't you?"

Marlon flushed. He got off his bike and walked it to the beat-up bench. "What makes you say that?"

She followed suit and sat beside him. "Just an educated guess." She took out her sandwich unwrapped it. After a bite, she added, "You're a good friend, Mars-Bars. I don't tell you that enough."

"Hey, back at ya." Marlon got his burger out as well and flashed a smile. "Can't think of anyone I'd rather spend the day with."

"K-I-S-S-I-N-G," said Dominic, grinning as he lay down under her feet. He snickered when she kicked him. "The lady doth protest too much."

Oh, shut up, you overgrown handbag! Your mind is always in the gutter! Abby looked up to meet Marlon's curious gaze. She smiled sheepishly. "Same here. This was nice – now if Aunt Gladys doesn't kill me when I get home it'll be the best day I've had in awhile."

"You're so weird sometimes, Abs." Marlon proceeded to eat his burger in a couple bites. "But, I wouldn't have you any other way."

CHAPTER 8

"Will you be careful?" Abby tried to stop laughing as they rode up the sidewalk. "You're going to crack your skull open!"

Marlon just smirked and popped a third wheelie. "I know what I'm doing." He made a circle before dropping back onto two wheels. "Don't turn gray on me."

She shook her head as she fought to stop the giggling. "I'm serious. You don't even have your helmet on."

Marlon started to answer, but a wolf whistle cut him off. He turned to look and a sour expression replaced his cheeky grin.

Dominic mirrored him and snarled.

"Hey there, Miss Palmer! Mother was hoping you would make it back in time to join us for dinner." Drew Davidson turned his disgusted gaze to her friend. "Guess your 'ministry work' was more important."

Abby clenched her teeth. *Don't look at him like that!* It never failed. Every time Drew saw Marlon, he looked like he had smelled something dead on the side of the road. And every time, Abby longed to physically knock the look off his face. "Good evening, Mr. Davidson." She got off her bike and started walking it to her door. "Sorry, but I had other plans." She smiled at Marlon. "Thank you for coming with me to visit Grandma. I know you could have done something more exciting."

"No sweat," he replied, stepping off his bike and following her. He fell into step beside her. "She plays a good game of rum."

"Hey, I would have gone with you." Drew flashed the smile that made the girls at school swoon. "All you had to do was ask." He moved to walk on her other side. "You wouldn't have had to hang around trash."

Abby's grip on the handlebars tightened to the point that it hurt her hands. She fought to think of a *polite* way to correct him; a way that wouldn't get back to her aunt and result in never being allowed to see Marlon again.

Drew took her silence as agreement, apparently. He shot a smirk at Marlon. "Why don't you hang with someone more at your level, Samson? Someone more like your harlot of a mother?"

"What," said Abby, stopping short, "did you say?"

"Let it go, Abs." Marlon looked up at Drew, his eyes cold. "Ain't nothin' I ain't heard before."

"My apologies, Miss Palmer." Drew took her hand and kissed it. "Such language isn't proper before a lady."

Abby yanked her hand away and resisted the urge to rub his spit off on her shirt. "Don't. Touch. Me." She fought to keep her voice level. She clenched the hand he had slobbered on. The other still gripped the handle of her bike.

Beside her, Dominic growled, his tail lashing like a whip. "You wouldn't know proper if it bit you."

"It's a shame you aren't more familiar with manners, Miss Palmer." Drew's expression tried for concern and just ended up as pity. "That's what happens when you hang around slime all the –" He stumbled back when her fist connected with his nose. Both his hands came up to try and stop the bleeding. "What the Hell?"

Her bike clattered to the ground as Abby moved to stand toe-to-toe with him. "Marlon is *not* slime, he is *not* trash. He has more honor and compassion in his little *finger* than you do in your whole body!" She drew her fist back again. "And if you *ever* –"

"What is the meaning of this?" Gladys' voice rang out from behind them. She crossed the distance, took one look at Drew then rounded on Marlon. "How dare you strike your betters? Know your place, boy! You aren't worth half –"

"Marlon didn't hit him, Aunt Gladys," said Abby in a calm tone. She raised her fist, where a spot of blood decorated her sore knuckles. "I did. And I'll do it again."

"Abigail Dominique Palmer!" Gladys glared at her. "What has gotten *into* you, young lady?" She looked over at Marlon. "And what are you doing *alone* with *him*? I thought you were going to see Gail."

"I did," Abby replied. She took a deep breath. "You can call her if you don't believe me. Marlon *offered* to go with me, and Grandma enjoyed meeting him." She raised her chin ever so slightly. "He's my friend. Grandma called him what he is – a gentleman."

Gladys scoffed. "Gail is far from a perfect judge of character."

"She seemed all right to me." Marlon leaned his bike against the wall then reached down and picked up Abby's, too. He moved it over to the railing where she usually locked it and did so. "Plays a mean game of rum, I'll say that much." He turned to Drew. "That looks bad. Want me to get some ice for you?"

"No, *thank you*." One of Drew's hands still covered his nose, making it impossible to see the lower half of his face, though blood was smeared on the hand at his side. "If you'll excuse me, ladies, I need to get home and let Mother look at this."

As soon as Drew was gone, Gladys rounded on Marlon. "You, boy, have no respect for your elders." If looks could kill, she would have dropped him right there. "Obviously my niece's hard work is falling on deaf ears. Abby, you've wasted enough of your time on him and his disgrace of a family. I don't want to hear –"

"Aunt Gladys," said Abby clearly. "Please don't insult my friend. You don't spend time with him. You don't even allow him to come to *our* home. Grandma spent more time with him today than you have in all the time I've known him. 'Judge not, lest ye be judged'."

"Ma'am, I apologize for the poor picture of my home life you've developed." Marlon took a breath, much as Abby had earlier. "And for not reflecting how Abby's nature's rubbed off on me *and* my siblings. I'm grateful every day that she bothers to give me the time of day."

"Well, well, the boy knows the fine art of kissing ass." Dominic grinned. "A tradition that never goes out of style."

"And I cannot help but feel our friendship was dealt in the hand of fate." Marlon let a small smile show on his face. "As we recently learned our grandfathers were good friends as well."

"Oooh, Abs, you got a camera handy?" Dominic laughed. "I never wanna forget this!"

Gladys' dumbstruck expression was priceless. Her mouth moved for a minute before she could get a word out. "Your grandfather... her grandfather..."

Abby smiled. "Yes, Aunt Gladys. Marlon's grandfather is a friend of Grandpa Nick's." She tilted her head as her smile just got bigger. "And he's going to be teaching us *both* to drive." She picked her purse up from where she had dropped it when she took the swing at Drew. "Amazing, isn't it?"

Gladys apparently couldn't find a word to say.

That evening, Abby sat at her desk and wrote out an apology note to Drew, saying in essence that she should not have acted in violence regardless of the provocation, and that she regretted her actions and would make every effort not to repeat them in the future.

"Are you going to add, 'I hope you will also not jump to conclusions about individuals you spend no time getting to know'?" Dominic lay curled around her chair, half-dozing off.

"I'd love to, but Aunt Gladys wouldn't approve and that defeats the purpose of this." She sighed and signed the paper before putting it in an envelope and sealing it.

"Waste of a stamp." Dominic growled. "That boy is more of a harlot than Marlon's mother ever was." His tail lashed and he kneaded the carpet working softly. "That he actually had the balls to insult the boy's mother to his face is just –"

"I know Dommy," said Abby. She shut off the light and crawled into bed. "I know."

CHAPTER 9

"Now, keep the doors and windows locked."

"Yes, Aunt Gladys."

"And don't have those Samson children over here." Gladys busied herself with looking for her makeup in her purse. "I *will* give them the benefit of the doubt, but I still don't want them here when I'm not home." She turned to the mirror hanging by the door and put her pink lipstick on. "Gail might not be the best judge of character – honestly your grandfather…" She put the tube away and snapped her purse shut. "That's beside the point. She had nothing but good things to say about the boy. If their parents allow it, we will have them over Saturday, and you will see them at your next class. They can do without you for one day." She leaned over and kissed Abby's cheek. "Behave yourself, dear."

Once she was gone Abby let out the breath she was holding. She shook her head as she went to her room. She waited until she heard the car leave, then clicked the button on the trunk and pulled out her laptop. She leaned against the headboard and booted it up before connecting to the internet. No sooner did she turn on the messenger did a familiar user name appeared.

RandomWord: You doing OK?

Her fingers hit the keys as the smile spread across her face.

DragonflyGirl: Yeah, finally alone. You?

RandomWord: Pretty much. By the way, nice swing; you would have made Hermione proud.

DragonflyGirl: *rolls eyes* You know I have no clue what you're talking about.

RandomWord: One day I'll sneak you Harry Potter. You'll love it, lots of adventure and stuff. So how'd things go once you all went inside?

DragonflyGirl: Better than I would have guessed. She called Grandma. She's going to talk to your parents and invite you and Felice over Saturday.

RandomWord: No kidding? Whoa never thought I'd see the day. :) That rocks, Abs. Don't worry, we'll wear our flea collars.

"I swear that boy makes no sense sometimes." Dominic leaned around her shoulder to see the screen. He clicked his claws against the side. "At least he knows to behave."

"Marlon will be Marlon," she said, starting to type her response. She burst out laughing at the next message that appeared.

BuzzardBreath: He's going to need a flea bath if he doesn't clean up his room and take the trash out like his mother asked, I believe five times now.

RandomWord: Dad! We're talking here!

BuzzardBreath: Yeah and you've had hours before she got on to do a simple task.

RandomWord: After we talk, Dad, you know how often she can get online!

Abby shook her head as she watched the little dots that showed that his father was typing. She hit the keys as quickly as she could. She typed "Good-bye, Mars-Bars", hit send. Then she switched her status to offline and closed the window. About three seconds later the window popped back up and she started laughing again.

BuzzardBreath: :) Thank you, Abby.

DragonflyGirl: No problem, Mr. Samson. Least I can do.

Abby closed the window again. Without Mr. Samson, she wouldn't be online at all. She patted the laptop she had bought it at a thrift store a couple years ago. It had its fits, but Marlon's father kept it working. She opened the chess game and started to play. After her third loss, the messenger window popped open again. She smiled at the message.

RandomWord: I know you're there, Abs. I took out the dang trash, happy?

 DragonflyGirl: "Honor thy mother and father", Mars-Bars. :) Want to play chess? The computer's kicking my butt.

RandomWord: So you wanna kick mine? LOL I think you'd like this thing I found. Ever heard of online RPGs?

DragonflyGirl: I live under a rock, we've been over this. I know what a Role Playing Game is, but I don't see how you'd play Zelda online.

She could almost see Marlon rolling his eyes. She giggled then looked at the clock instinctively. *Still got a few hours.*

RandomWord: This is more like Dungeons and Dragons, Abs. You create a character and role-play as that character to interact with people. It's a lot of fun so far. Here.

The next message linked to a site called The Sanctuary. She clicked it and scanned the site, read the introduction. "I can see why he'd like this. It's all secret society-magical powers stuff."

DragonflyGirl: You sure this is a game? It looks more like a storytelling round.

RandomWord: I'm sure; it's a lot of fun, Abs. Just think about it OK? You don't have to be online all the time to play something like this.

DragonflyGirl: *sigh* OK, I'll look into it later, chess?

RandomWord: You got it. Still say you're gonna kick my ass.

Abby snickered and brought up the game. She kept her eyes on the clock and shut the laptop off with a half hour to spare. Once it was safely stashed, she headed to the kitchen to start dinner.

"Now I want to stress this," said Bryan Samson as he paced in front of the class, his hands clasped behind his back. "If you can't take this seriously, then don't get behind the wheel. Every time you do, you hold not only your own life in your hands, but the lives of the people around you." He locked eyes with them all one by one. "Do I make myself clear?"

The class nodded and then the first person stood up and went with him to the car.

Abby tried to ignore the gossip around her. She couldn't completely block the voices, though, mostly because some people weren't even trying to be quiet.

"I can't believe it, can you? She just hauled off and punched him in the nose!"

"What idiot would pick *that* over Drew Davidson? He's so *hot!*"

"Maybe she's just too dense to realize she's missing out?"

"Mom says she saw a shrink when she was younger. Maybe she's insane?"

Dominic growled from his place at her feet. His tail lashed back and forth as he glared at the gossiping girls. "Don't they have anything better to do? You'd think he was King Midas!"

"Doing OK, Abs?" asked Marlon. He had sat right beside her from the time class started. He stage-whispered, "Hope you're not too nervous. I mean, this is serious stuff. Life or death if you don't pay enough attention. Unlike petty bull–"

"Mar-lon," said Felice, pinching her nose. "Watch your mouth. If we're going to be around her aunt tomorrow, you *can't* talk like that!"

He just reached into his wallet and handed her a five dollar bill. "I know, Sis, but it's still the truth. Some things aren't worth worrying about."

"Just because it's true doesn't mean you should say it." Felice took the bill and tucked into her pocket. "And *stop* prepaying your swears!"

Abby just shook her head. She noticed the gossips looked stunned then looked away. *At least they lowered their voices.* "Thanks, Mars-Bars," she whispered. "I owe you one."

"No, it's payback." Marlon smiled and folded his hands behind his head. "And don't worry; I'll behave for Mrs. Lynde. You'll be doing the 'who are you and what have you done with my friends' bit."

"You just wearing real clothes will do that," said Felice. She fidgeted with her outfit. The pastel shirt and shorts looked like they belonged in a catalog, but Abby knew they were handmade. "Grandma flipped when she heard. Took Dad a good while to convince her we don't need new outfits."

"Grandma thinks *every* occasion needs a new outfit." Marlon crossed his feet at his ankles. "But this is just too short notice anyway." The conversation drifted to their plans once they finally had that precious piece of plastic. Felice admitted she was glad to drive, so she didn't have to ask her parents to take her places. For Marlon, it was just the start – he wanted his motorcycle license too. "How about you, Abs? You got any big plans?"

Abby worried her skirt. "I want to go to college," she said so softly she barely heard it herself. She looked up at their stunned faces. "I know it sounds crazy, but I want to go to Ohio Dominican, like Grandpa Nick. Like Mom wanted to."

"Didn't say it was crazy," said Felice. She reached out and squeezed her shoulder. "Brave, yes, crazy no."

"Sure it's crazy." Marlon smiled and held up his hand for a high five. "Doesn't mean it's not awesome! So what are you going to study?"

She met his hand with hers, grinning. "You'll laugh for sure."

"Yeah, right. Spill it, Abs."

Before she could answer, the twins' grandfather joined them. "You're up, Miss Palmer." Bryan shot her a grin. "Let's see how you do behind the wheel." He rubbed his head. "Can't possibly be any worse than the others…" He shook himself and put his hands in his pockets. "I mean, I'm sure you'll do fine. Nicole could park a car up someone's ass if she wanted to."

Felice smacked her forehead. "Grandpa, I swear! Between you, Marlon and Uncle Richie, the swear jar will be able to fund *our* college!"

"And you thought I was prepaying *my* swears." Marlon snickered. "I knew Grandpa couldn't keep from it dealing with this stuff." He lightly slapped Abby's back. "Go get 'em, Abs! Show 'em up!"

"Be easier to do if they hadn't already taken off like their pants were on fire." Bryan clicked his tongue. "Come on, Miss Palmer. Let's see what you got."

"Abby," she corrected. "My name is Abby, Mr. Samson." She got up and dusted off her skirt before falling into step beside him. She swallowed hard. *You can do this, you can do this.*

"Of course you can," said Dominic with a grin as he followed. "You're calm, you studied. You know what you're doing. So relax already. You'll be fine. Trust me."

CHAPTER 10

"Where's your brake?"

Abby tapped the pedal with her foot. She held the steering wheel so tight her knuckles were white. "And the gas is here." She let her foot just touch the pedal. "OK, now what?"

Bryan reached over and pried her hands from the wheel. "First, don't hold on so tight. You don't need the death grip. Loosen up." He waited for her to put her hands back. "Now, start the car."

She took a deep breath and turned the key. The engine roared to life. *I can do this, I can do this.* She put her foot on the brake and shifted the car into drive. Her foot stayed on the pedal.

"Now foot on the gas. Good. Now *slowly* press down."

Abby did as she was told with her heart hammering as the car moved forward. *This isn't so bad...*

"See I told you, you could do this." Dominic leaned around her shoulder from the backseat and smiled. "You're better than you think."

Dommy, get back in the seat, I can't –

"Brake!"

Her foot slammed down on the pedal and they all smacked into their seats. She looked up at Bryan nervously. "Sorry, I –"

"Just keep your mind on what you're doin', OK? You spaced out there for a second." He patted her shoulder and gestured forward. "Try again, hit the gas."

And this time, you be quiet! Abby pressed down slowly, watching ahead of them as the car moved forward. *I don't need your encouragement.* She managed the circuit around the parking lot, and was glad when she could turn the car off. She unbuckled her seat belt. "Give it to me straight, Mr. Samson, how badly did I screw up?"

"You did fine." Bryan reached out and ruffled her hair. "You're just going to need practice before you take the actual test, that's all. We just gotta set you up on a workable schedule." He smiled. "Send Felice over, will you? Once she and Marlon go, we'll set something up."

Abby nodded and got out of the car. "I'll do that, sir. Thank you." She crossed the parking lot, the dragon at her heels. "You're up, Felice!" She high-fived the other girl and sat back down beside Marlon. "Well, could have done worse I guess."

"What happened out there, Abs? You jerked the car to a stop like you'd seen a ghost."

Abby could not look at him; her eyes stayed on her fidgeting hands. "Got distracted." *By a certain annoying, overgrown lizard!* She resisted the urge to kick Dominic when he shot her a sheepish look. "I just hit the brake when your grandpa said to." She wouldn't lie, but there was no way she'd admit she'd been blinded by her made-up dragon. *Though I bet the crazy card would get Drew Davidson off my trail.* She watched as the car followed the track. "She's doing good, isn't she?"

"Been behind the wheel since we were kids, Abs." Marlon smiled and kicked his feet up on the chair in front of him. "Dad used to let us sit on his lap and steer. Mom did, too."

"That must have been fun." Abby kept her eyes on Felice and her grandfather. "Sounds like something out of a song."

"Guess it is," he replied, reaching out and patting her hand. "You'll catch up in no time Abs. Don't worry; there's bigger fish to fry – like us impressing Mrs. Lynde tomorrow."

"Just don't swear," she said, a small smile growing on her face. "And you'll be fine." *I hope.*

Surreal was the only word Abby could think of the next afternoon. Seeing Felice and Marlon sitting on her aunt's love seat, drinking lemonade and talking politely while Gladys smiled at them… She had to fight not to pinch herself. *OK, when am I going to wake up? No way is this really happening.*

"So, what do you two do with your free time?" Gladys poured more lemonade and pushed a plate of cookies discreetly into reach. "Idle hands are the devil's playground, after all."

"Nosy old bat," commented Dominic. He crossed his forelegs and rested his head on his paws. "Why don't you just come out and ask if they follow their parents' example'?"

Abby bit her tongue. She couldn't think of one thing the twins did in their spare time her aunt would approve of. She braced herself for the explosion.

"I help Mom with her flowers," said Felice, taking a delicate sip of her lemonade. "And I have archery class on the weekends. I'm not quite up to competition level yet, but I'm getting there."

"And you, young man?"

"I work at a store weekday afternoons," Marlon said, tapping his fingers on his knee. "I'm saving up to get my first ride."

"That's very responsible of you *both*," said Gladys. She sat her glass down and folded her hands in her lap. "And I must say your outfits today are simply stunning."

Marlon tugged at his shirt collar. Outside of school Abby had never seen him in dress clothes. "Thank you, ma'am."

"Our grandmother made them," added Felice with obvious pride. "She's got a real eye for fashion. Dad inherited it. He makes most of our clothes himself."

Gladys frowned for a moment then nodded. "She certainly is very talented. Does your mother sew?"

"No," said Felice with her too bright smile. "Grandpa does though." She giggled. "He's not as bad as he thinks he is. Still, Dad's better."

"I guess your grandfather learned in the service." Glady glanced at her deceased husband's medals on the wall. "Would have come in handy there."

"Mom likes dealing with plants, Mrs. Lynde." Marlon took a drink and ran a finger around his glass. "She's not happy unless she's getting her hands dirty."

Dominic covered his face with a paw. "Well *done*, boy. No way *that* will be taken wrong."

Abby fought not to follow suit. "You should see some of her flowers, Aunt Gladys. They're so beautiful." She smiled as she thought of it. "They smell really nice, too."

"I'm sure they are, dear." Gladys leaned back against the sofa. "Well, I must say I'm pleasantly surprised. I believe I owe you an apology, dears. I misjudged you."

"It's quite all right, Mrs. Lynde." Felice smiled again then reached out and patted her hand. "Everyone makes mistakes once in awhile."

Marlon just nodded and tugged at his collar again.

Abby just stared at her aunt. She glanced at Dominic out of the corner of her eye. He looked just as stunned as she felt. *OK, now I know I'm dreaming.*

"I wish we could stay longer, ma'am, but you'll have to excuse us." Felice stood up and curtsied. "Our grandparents are coming over for dinner tonight and Mom needs all the help she can get."

Marlon followed his sister's example. He stood and bowed. "Thank you for having us, ma'am."

"No trouble at all, no trouble at all. And of course you mustn't miss such an occasion." Gladys was all smiles. "Abby, please see our guest to the door."

"Yes, Aunt Gladys." Abby got to her feet and walked with the twins the short distance from the love seat to the front door. "Thank you for coming."

They both nodded. "No, thank you."

"We really must do this again sometime." Gladys waved. "You two take care now."

Abby sighed in relief when she shut the door behind them. Without being asked she collected the dishes and took them to the kitchen. She rinsed them off before setting them in the sink.

"I simply must commend you, Abby dear." Gladys came in behind her and sat the lemonade pitcher back in the refrigerator. "You've done wonders with those children. Why, I almost wouldn't have thought they had such a troublesome home life. Well *done*, dear. Well done."

"Thank you, Aunt Gladys." Abby managed to keep her voice level. *Not that their behavior has anything to do with me. You should be complementing their parents.*

"I'll leave you to start dinner. But I wholeheartedly approve of you continuing your work with them. Why, one day they might even know the Lord!" With that Aunt Gladys went back to the living room to watch her shows.

Dominic growled as he watched her go. "Heaven forbid she acknowledge their parents' hand in their upbringing. Still, at least she doesn't have a problem with you spending time with them."

That's a good thing, as I didn't care when she did. Abby got out the makings for tuna casserole. "It went better than I expected, I'll say that much."

"Did you say something dear?" called Gladys from the living room.

Abby flinched. "Just talking to myself, Aunt Gladys!" She put the pot on to boil. *I've got to watch what I say. Haven't slipped up in a long time.*

Dominic rubbed against her legs like a cat. "It'll all come right in the end. Just do your best and leave the rest."

Easy for you to say, Dommy. You're not real. Abby smiled at the dragon. *You're good company most days though.*

"Just because a thing cannot be seen by all," said Dominic as he gave her a toothy grin, "does not mean it is not real."

CHAPTER 11

One benefit to having company on Saturday was that there was less housework on Sunday. Abby swept the floor, dusted and had the dishes put away within an hour of her aunt's departure. She retreated to her room and got out her laptop. Marlon wasn't online and neither was Felice. She assumed they were still asleep after their grandparents' visit. She started to head to the chess site when the address Marlon had given her popped up. *I wonder if any Catholics play these things.* She typed in her go-to website for such answers and searched "online role playing games".

"I don't know why you bother with that site," Dominic chimed in. "It sucks the fun out of life."

Abby shook her head. "Honestly, if Aunt Gladys ever saw all the things that most Catholic sites are against, she wouldn't refer to it the way she does." She read the arguments for and against the topic. The cons were mostly that such games could desensitize you to violence and "evil" actions. Abby rolled her eyes. *Most kids know the difference between make-believe and reality.* Even she knew Dominic wasn't real. Telling the difference between actions in a game and actions in real life would be a breeze. One thing the topics warned about, though, was the huge time-drain most games were. "I'd love to have another game to share with the twins, but…"

"But you have responsibilities." Dominic curled up beside her. "And you don't have regular access regardless. I doubt the players want to wait a week for a response."

"Pretty much." She closed the window. "Even if Marlon and Felice can come over now, I doubt Aunt Gladys would let us play anything." She thought of the *Pokémon* theme deck she kept in the same drawer as the laptop. "Would be nice, though."

"Baby steps, Abby. Baby steps."

She glanced at the shortcut on her desktop. "Marlon would kill me if I played Grandpa's game without him. Still, I hope we can get together this week. I really want to see what he came up with."

"Don't get your hopes up. That game is almost as old as you are. It's not even up to snuff with the games you played with your parents."

"You don't know that." She booted up the chess game. "It could be really cool. I just hope it doesn't kick my butt like this does."

"Thank you for dinner, dear." Gladys gathered her dishes together then delicately wiped her mouth. "You are becoming an accomplished chef. I envy your future husband."

Abby collected the dishes. "You won't have to envy him any time soon." She smiled as she picked up the stack. "I've got a few more years of schooling ahead first."

"Just two, dear, and you could certainly marry and continue your high school education. You don't want to wait too long. Believe me, dealing with children in your forties is for the birds."

"I suppose I could marry before I finish school." Abby turned toward the kitchen. "I might even meet someone in college."

"College?" repeated Gladys. "*College?* My dear, what would you need with that? You're not going to be one of those God-less career women, after all."

Abby set the dishes in the sink and ran the dishwater. "Of course not, Aunt Gladys. I can't see a time when God will not be part of my life."

"Uh, Abs?" Dominic stood beside her, looking back into the dining room at Gladys. "I don't think that's what she meant…"

I know that, thank you. She carefully washed the dishes, setting then in the rack to dry. "I am looking forward to becoming a psychiatrist one day."

"You will do no such thing!" Gladys stormed into the kitchen and came up beside her, forcing Dominic to circle to the other side. "Proper ladies do not work outside the home. That is not the Lord's plan. I did not raise you to be some heathen!" She folded her arms. "You will find a suitor, marry, and fulfill your Christian duty. Besides, there's no money to pay for such things."

Abby continued with the dishes. "My mother had a college fund, Aunt Gladys. It's mine now. She didn't get to go because I was born." She sat the last plate on the rack and turned to face her aunt. "So, I will do what she didn't get to."

"Your mother gave that up as is *proper*; this foolish notion disgraces her memory."

Abby felt her fists clench. "The fund is for college –"

"Then save it for your son. It will have grown by that time anyway." Gladys smiled and put a hand on Abby's shoulder. "Come now, child, stop living in fantasyland."

Dominic placed one paw on her foot. "He who fights and runs away lives to fight another day," he said. "Let it rest. She does not decide your future."

Unable to speak, Abby nodded. She curtsied and left the kitchen, retreating to her room. She went through her closet and laid out her outfit for the next day to keep her hands busy.

"All will be well one day, Abby." Dominic jumped on the bed and sat down, watching her every move. "And in the meantime you have the driving lessons to look forward to."

I'm going to ace that test, she thought, gritting her teeth. *I'm going to college. It's just two years! Two more years and she won't have any say in my life!*

"Exactly. And in the meantime, look at all you've managed. You have your friends. You have your computer." Dominic grinned as he rested his head on his paws. "You have your games. You can even try that RPG one day, once everything else is out of the way."

Try this week, Dommy. She got her pajamas and headed for the bathroom. *I can join anyway, and explain I can only be on at certain times.* She stuck her tongue out in her aunt's direction. *It's my life, not hers.* She started the shower, got in, and turned it up as hot as she could stand it. *Mine.*

CHAPTER 12

"Dang it!" Abby jerked the car back between the lines. "It's not complicated, so why can't I —"

"You're being too hard on yourself," Bryan said. "You're doing just fine. No one said you had to master it overnight. Relax." He looked into the back seat and gave his grandson a stern glare. "And *you* stop with the worried looks. You ain't helping her confidence."

"I'm not worried about her *driving*, Grandpa." Marlon met Abby's gaze in the rearview mirror. "Something's eating you, Abs. Not just this. What's wrong?"

"I'm fine, Mars-Bars." Abby found her hands were tight on the wheel again and made an effort to loosen her grip. "Just got a lot on my mind." *Like ridiculous expectations of older women.* She took a deep breath and made the turn. So far her only issue was staying between the lines. She swerved so badly according to Bryan that she looked drunk.

Marlon sat back against the seat and folded his arms. "So what is it? It's distracting you."

"*You* are distractin' her," Bryan told him. "If she wanted ya to know she'd have told ya in the first place. Now sit back, shut up, and hold on."

"Such fuss over simple details." Dominic lay curled up in the backseat, not quite touching Marlon. "Just tell him what a fool Gladys is. He'll understand."

"I don't need your advice!" Abby flinched when she realized she had spoken aloud. She tried to recover. "I'm sorry, it's just... Aunt Gladys and I talked last night."

Marlon nodded as if that explained everything. "On her high horse again? What topic this time: the evils of Catholicism or the wonders of Preacher Davidson telling you how to live your life when he can barely run his own?"

Bryan looked from one to the other. "I'd be on ya for about talkin' about someone like that if your Dad and Mom hadn't already told me horror stories about this broad." He shot a glance at Abby. "No offense, Miss Palmer."

"Abby," she corrected. "And none taken." She sighed and took the next turn. "Apparently, if she has her way I'm not going to college." She jerked the steering wheel to get the car back between the lines a little harder than she needed to. "That would not be *God's plan for a God-fearing woman*."

Bryan reached out and steadied the wheel. "Easy on the vehicle, sweetheart, it's a loaner." He shook his head. "Met some of those in my time. Just don't let it get you down. It's your life."

"Easy to say," said Abby, forcing her grip loose. "She pretty much said if I do what my *mother* planned on doing I'd be disgracing her memory."

"No 'pretty much' to it, that's exactly what she said."

Dommy, shut up!

Bryan pinched the bridge of his nose. "Look, kid. I knew your mom, OK? She'd have laid the broad *out* for sayin' somethin' like that."

Abby kept her eyes on the road, swallowing hard against the lump in her throat. She pulled the car to a stop on the side of the road and unbuckled her seat belt. "Your turn, Marlon."

Her friend switched places and started the car again. After a few turns, he looked at her in the rearview mirror. "So you beat your grandpa's game yet?"

"I haven't even played it yet." She found herself smiling. "You gonna be around Thursday? So if I get stuck you can get me out."

Marlon turned and looked at her with that grin. "Sure thing! Still you can pro – OW!" He cupped the back of his head. "GRANDPA!"

"Eyes on the road," said Bryan sternly. "I swear, your whole argument for both of ya bein' in this car was that ya need to deal better with distractions. So far you're screwin' that up royally." He looked over his seat at Abby. "So what's the plan? You gonna go for the…" He paused and clicked his fingers as he thought. "Theology like the Dragon?" He shook his head. "Man, could *never* get into a religious debate with that guy, he'd hand you your ass on a platter."

"Grandpa took theology?" Abby blinked. *There's so much I don't know…* Asking about her grandfather hurt at times. Gladys would just say he took the wrong path and Gail would start crying if she talked for too long. "I thought he did computers."

"Oh, he did. Guy made Buzzard look like a kid with two cans and a string." Bryan smiled at the mention of his son. "But he had this thing… he wanted to know *why*, you know? Why stuff in the church is the way it is, why there's all these groups. Took his faith damn seriously."

Abby just looked at him for a couple minutes then shook her head. *Felice is right; they won't need a scholarship.* "I want to be a psychiatrist."

"A shrink, huh?" Bryan chuckled. "Give it a few years our family will be your biggest clients."

"You're weird, not crazy, Mr. Samson." She sighed and rested her chin in her hand. "I *need* to learn to drive; then Aunt Gladys can't stop me from going to college."

"If you're that worried about it, we can work out a few extra lessons a week. I'll make time." He smiled. "Bryan. If you're Abby, I'm Bryan."

"I'm telling Grandma if you keep flirting like that, Grandpa." Marlon reached out and slapped his grandfather's shoulder with the back of his hand. "Stop acting like a tramp."

"Bein' nice and flirtin' are two different things," said Bryan, rubbing his shoulder like it actually hurt. "And I am not a Tramp, I am *the* Tramp."

"Breaks a new heart every day," Abby said in a sing-song voice. She giggled. "I swear you two should do a comedy show. Or maybe a sitcom."

Marlon snorted. "Our family's the next soap opera, what are you talking about?" He pulled back into the school parking lot. "Honestly, Abs, you could write a book about all of us. It'd be the next best seller." He parked the car and unbuckled his seat belt. "Would beat the trash that's out now."

"He has a point there." Dominic stretched as they got out of the car. "No one would believe this could be reality."

Bryan hummed as he locked the car up, and then tossed the keys in the air as he walked. "Wouldn't take much to beat the stalker slash Prince Charmin' sh –" He caught sight of his granddaughter and froze. "– stuff."

"Seriously, Grandpa," said Felice, pinching her nose. "Act your age for once, please."

"No problem." He stood up straight and pocketed the keys. "So when do you want to do those extra lessons, Abby?"

"Extra lessons?" Felice looked at her and put her hands on her hips. "You're doing fine. Don't sell yourself short."

"Gladys has her worrying, Lice." Marlon rolled his eyes and went to unlock his bike. "I swear sometimes I wanna just –"

"Give it a rest, Mars-Bars." Abby sighed and joined him, retrieving her bike as well. "Thank you, sir, but let's worry if I still can't stay between the lines next week."

"Deal." Bryan bowed and headed for his motorcycle. "See you kids later."

A chorused farewell followed him. The three friends started home. They rode in silence for a few minutes before Felice broke it.

"Do I want to know what Gladys had to say?"

Abby shook her head. "Just that a *proper woman* doesn't go to college," she said, swerving to avoid a rock on the sidewalk. "A *proper woman* finds a husband."

"Dumb old-fashioned old biddy." Marlon snorted. "Sheesh, women are more than breeding vessels. She wants to go 'God' on it? When He saw Man was lonely He didn't create a bunch of friends. He made one woman."

Felice just stared at her brother for a moment then looked at Abby. "He's got a point, but seriously don't let her tell you what you can and can't do. You're one of the strongest people I know."

"No kidding," said Dominic as he ran beside her. "Anyone else would have broken by now." His eyes shone with an emotion she did not know. "You keep fighting."

"Thank you," she said. It bothered her that she was answering both of them. Clearing her throat, she added, "Don't worry, I'm not giving up just because she says so. In two years…" Abby raised her chin. "In two years it won't matter *what* she says. I just have to make it until then."

The twins shot her a smile and nodded.

"Hey if it gets too rough, you can always move in with us." Marlon jumped a pothole and popped a wheelie. "Pretty sure Mom and Dad won't mind."

Abby laughed. "Yeah, that wouldn't be awkward at *all*."

"Hey, don't act like you wouldn't fit right in." Felice's smile matched her brother's. She winked. "You're over almost all the time anyway; this would be a natural progression."

"I'll keep it in mind," she replied, her smile hurting her cheeks, "but I'm pretty sure my sanity would leave me after a full twenty-four hours."

"Ah, you'd survive," said Marlon, grinning. "We're weird not crazy, remember?"

"Not *yet* you aren't."

"You're just as likely to go crazy as we are," said Felice. "Pretty sure Gladys is a carrier."

All three burst out laughing.

"I can't argue with that," said Abby once she could breathe again. "She means well. She's stuck in the 1800's or something."

Felice nodded. "Some people don't mean to hurt anyone, but they still do. They just can't see that they are."

"And some set out to harm but hide behind kindness," added Dominic, looking up at Abby. "The road to Hell is paved with good intentions."

"Gee, when did you become a philosopher?" Abby blushed when she caught herself replying aloud to the dragon. *Dang it what's* wrong *with me? At least it looks like I'm talking to Felice. I haven't had trouble with this in years!* "Still, thanks for the advice."

"You're welcome."

She laughed when they both answered.

CHAPTER 13

"OK, let's see what this is all about." Abby brought up the site Marlon had linked her. She sat cross-legged on her bed with the laptop in front of her and the dragon once more lying beside her. She read through the introduction on the home page. "This might be more fun than I thought."

This world is not what you thought it was. It hasn't "changed" – no, it has always been this way. It is just now out in the open, out where all can see. And we who hid from mankind no longer can. We must brace ourselves for the battle ahead. You are not alone, friend.

What? You thought I couldn't tell you were not "human"? Psh. You are as human as I am. We might look the part, sound the part, but we are not, and never will be, human. And we must stand together, friend, or we will be destroyed. Humans always destroy that which they can't understand.

Please, come with me to the Sanctuary.

There were links to rules, the new player's character sheet, and instructions for where to post character applications for approval. There was also a leader board and as soon as Abby saw the top name she burst out laughing. "Figures Marlon would have aced everything." She continued to look around. It didn't seem that complicated. You wrote a few paragraphs, the other players responded until the scene ran its course. As you posted, you earned points to gain powers and items. "It's not *Zelda*, but…" She tapped her fingers against the bed. "I think I can handle this." Before she could go any farther, the messenger window popped open. She shook her head at the message.

RandomWord: What'cha doin', beautiful?

DragonflyGirl: You won't believe me.

RandomWord: Try me.

DragonflyGirl: I'm looking over the Sanctuary. Shouldn't be too hard… *smile* considering the reigning champ's my best friend.

RandomWord: *blush* Aw, it's more that I'm active. Not everyone is, really. That's why I suggested it. People disappear off the site for months and come back. So you'll be fine.

"That's reassuring." Abby typed that message and clicked the sign up button. *I can always quit, right?* She went to the character sheet. As she looked at the profile questions, she realized she had no idea what she was doing. *This might be harder than I thought.*

DragonflyGirl: OK, I made an account. Now what? I've never created a character before.

RandomWord: It's not that hard, Abs. Heck, my character's just me anyway. You know, if I could shapeshift and stuff. *smile*

"You know," said Dominic. "The only person here that knows you is him, right? This could be a chance to address some of the things you can't just talk about."

Abby looked at him. *That* was tempting. To be able to work through things she felt she never really got to. Her parents, being stuck with Gladys, even the loss of Troubadour to old age. *Maybe… I can finally face those things, put them to rest. That would be wonderful.*

RandomWord: CODE RED!

The message repeated five times and Abby swallowed hard as she shut the laptop down. The time it took felt like forever. As soon as it shut off she closed the lid and put it away. She sat down on the trunk just as Gladys came to her door.

"There you are, dear." Gladys smiled and held out an envelope. "There's mail for you."

"Thank you, Aunt Gladys." Abby took it from her, confused. No one sent her cards. She got her birthday cards from her grandmother and Marlon's family personally. She looked for a return address and sighed in exasperation. She opened it to find a standard "I'm sorry" card and a handwritten letter. She fought not to gag when she saw the words inside.

Miss Palmer,

I hope this card will say what I cannot. I accept your apology and hope you will accept my own. I also hope you and your aunt will accept an invitation to dinner this Saturday. It is the least that could be done, after all. I will await your reply.

Mr. Andrew Davidson

"What are you doing this Saturday, Aunt Gladys?" Abby knew the impossibility of getting around this. *Might as well get it over with.*

"I didn't have any plans," replied Gladys with a smile. "Did you have something in mind?"

"The Davidsons would like us to join them for dinner."

"Oh, of course. You send our RSVP back straight away." She fussed with her hair then turned away from the doorway. "I'll just get dinner started. So glad to see you have your priorities in order."

Dominic growled after her. "You didn't have to tell her."

"And have Mrs. Davidson bring it up later?" Abby sat down at her desk and got a piece of paper and a pen. "No, thanks."

Mr. Davidson,

I accept your apology and am glad you accept mine. My great-aunt and I are honored by the invitation and promise to be there Saturday. Thank you for your consideration.

Miss Abigail Palmer

"Do you watch the door or something?" Abby sat beside Marlon on her bed, waiting for her grandfather's game to load. "Gladys wasn't even gone five minutes."

"He always comes over on Thursday, so why are you surprised?" Dominic yawned from his place on her pillow then eyed the slowly loading screen, tail twitching.

Marlon snorted. "Don't ask stupid questions." He tapped his fingers against the covers. "Finally! Sheesh, I hope the gameplay isn't this slow."

Abby leaned closer to read the introduction as it filled the screen.

Once upon a time there was a boy. Times had changed and war was upon the people. Everyone had to fight, whether it went against their nature or not. Now, the boy trained day after day for battle. There was no such thing as too prepared! Or so his superiors shouted every day. Their foes were not human. No, they were dark beings that robbed their victims of free will. No one was safe. These dark creatures could not be seen... only heard. They whispered to all who would listen and took possession of their form once they bought the lies. People who had never harmed a living soul became monsters.

The only way anyone knew to deal with such transformations was to destroy the body of the trapped in hopes of freeing the soul. The boy believed this was the sole way, until one of the dark creatures took his brother. He could not bear to cruelly destroy someone he had known all his life. He would find another way; he would save his brother... though he knew not how

Years before, the brothers discussed the possibility of one of them falling prey to these dark creatures. The younger had asked the elder, "Will you hunt me down if I become one of the fallen? Will you slay your own flesh and blood?" The elder had smiled and ruffled his brother's hair. "Sooner myself than you." And so now the younger bore that promise in his heart. He would sooner end himself than his brother.

"This game is a bit more advanced than I would've thought." Marlon picked at the keys, causing the avatar to move across the screen. "The story's less preachy than I expected, though."

It honestly didn't look that great to Abby. It resembled the games her grandmother had at her house from the rare weekends when she'd slept over growing up. Still, it could have been poorer quality. She sat beside Marlon and watched the text fill the screen.

So the boy set out on his own, armed with only a staff, and followed after his brother, traveling in the path of destruction the monster left behind. Along the way, he faced those harmed by his brother's actions. They questioned his choices. He fought off the doubt taking root in his heart. Each time he simply helped them as best he could and continued on. He followed the dragon, bracing himself for that final battle.

The rest of the backstory was standard fare for the time period. For the first level, players learned to use the controls and how to kill various minor enemies that ranged from dark shapes to stray animals. The second brought the first real challenge to the game.

"Sheesh, not like you're on your own quest here," Marlon noted as between them they looked for various people missing in the debris. "Not like these people could help instead of just pacing or anything." He sighed as they finally reached the end of the level.

"Ha, ha, ha!"

They both jumped as laughter echoed from the speakers. A blond man appeared before the avatar, bent over in mirth.

"I thought you had the speakers off on this thing, Abs." Marlon shook his head and went for the settings and muted the system.

"So did I." She rubbed her arms and glanced at Dominic, who stared at the being on the screen, his tail lashing. "That's weird. No sound in a game until *that?*"

"Maybe it's supposed to freak you out." Marlon blinked. "Abs, what was your gramps on?"

"Well done, well done!" The man clapped. *"So good to see youngsters like yourself willing to aid others. Your parents must be so proud!"* The man grinned wide. *"Who am I? I, my boy, am the one who will help you reunite with your brother! I have the power to set all to right. Will you let me help you?"* The game paused again and a yes or no select came up.

Marlon looked at her. "On three?"

"1… 2… 3," said Abby. She said "No" at the same time Marlon did.

After the "no" option was clicked the man put his hands on his hips. *"No? Why not?"*

"Because you're creepy enough for a horror film?" Marlon suggested, rolling his eyes.

"You realize you're talking to someone who's not real, right?" Abby looked at her friend then shook her head. *Like me on a daily basis.*

"So?" Marlon hit the key for the rest of the text. "It works sometimes."

"You don't trust me? Boy, what is there not to trust?" The man straightened up and the screen went black. *"Maybe you'll change your mind next time."*

"Save it here, please." Abby glanced at the clock and sighed. "Well, it could be worse, but I don't see how Grandpa thought this game would change the world."

He did as she asked, shutting down the computer and handing it to her. "It's not bad; reminds me of a few other games, but still not bad. The story's decent too. For something he did on his own it's pretty impressive." He got up and straightened the blankets. "So we pick this up Saturday?"

"Love to, but can't." Abby put the laptop back in its drawer. "Aunt Gladys and I have dinner with the Davidsons." She sighed.

"Hopefully we can get this out of the way and *both* sides will quit trying to play matchmaker."

"And if they don't?" Marlon snapped. He put his hands in his pockets. "What if they don't give up, Abs?" He scuffed his foot on the floor. "I… I don't want you forced into something you don't want."

"We'll cross that bridge when we come to it." Abby smiled and walked him out. "Don't worry, Mars-Bars. If Aunt Gladys gets too pushy I'll just move in with you, remember?"

"Yeah," he smiled, though he looked thoughtful for a moment. "You can have my room. I'll take the couch. See ya tomorrow, Abs."

"See ya."

CHAPTER 14

"So how are your driving lessons going, Miss Palmer?"

Abby looked up from her plate to meet Mrs. Davidson's eyes. "It's not going as well as I'd like." She buttered a roll to keep her hands busy. "I still can't stay between the lines." She tried to laugh. "Mr. Samson says I look like I'm drunk."

"He would know, wouldn't he?" Preacher Davidson cut his steak a little harder than necessary. "I still can't believe they let that buffoon teach impressionable young people." He scoffed. "A biker playing the devil's music masquerading as a Christian."

"You would know wouldn't you, you pretentious know-it-all?" Dominic growled from his place at Abby's feet. "After all, you do the masquerade quite well yourself!"

"Mr. Samson does a great deal of charity work," said Abby as she sat the roll on her plate. "And he is a *Christian* biker. He's very polite." She smiled. "Just don't get him started on his wife. He'll talk your ear off."

"Be that as it may, Miss Palmer, but he is still a wolf in sheep's clothing."

"He's honest about his past, sir." Abby took a bite to give herself time to find the words. To find *polite* words. "He makes no secret about who he was. That's not who he is now and that's what counts."

"You'll have to excuse her, Mr. Davidson," Gladys chimed in. "Apparently, Bryan Samson was a good friend of my brother-in-law. Abigail naturally has some affection for someone that knew him."

79

"Naturally," replied Preacher Davidson. He took a bite of his steak. "Still, we must not forget where our true loyalty lies – with the Lord."

"Exactly, Father." Drew took a drink of his milk and smiled at Abby. "One must always put the Lord first. He died for us, thus we must live for Him."

Dominic's snarl was so loud for a second Abby had to remind herself only she could hear him. "You self-centered brat! Remind me: what's the slogan of Bryan's group again?"

I know, Dommy, I know. It's only a few words off. Please calm down!

Mrs. Davidson obviously saw her distress. "You can't save them all, Miss Palmer. It's a sad fact of life that some are just too far gone to free from the Devil's grasp."

"And some are so clenched by his hand they don't know it." Dominic reared and put his paws on the table. "You self-righteous fools sitting here, believing yourselves so superior! You wouldn't know your Master if he stood before you!"

DOMINIC! Abby took a deep breath. *Enough! Either lay down or –*

"I know it's sad, Miss Palmer." Drew's voice was sickly sweet. "I don't blame you for trying. It's noble of you." He reached out lay his hand on hers, forcing the dragon back to the floor. "Your conviction is so inspiring; I don't know how you can spend so much time with people like that and yet remain as pristine as the new fallen snow."

"DON'T TOUCH HER!"

"DON'T TOUCH ME!" Abby jerked her hand away so fast her elbow hit the back of her chair. She looked up at the shocked faces as she felt her hands clench on the table on either side of her dinner plate. For a second she considered chucking it at the preacher. "You know what? Last I checked, *Jesus* spent time with the sinners because *they* were the ones who needed Him," she pointed out. "He gave a chance to those no one else would. He turned sow's ears into silk purses so many times, yet everyone *forgets* that!"

"Abigail Dominique Palmer!" Gladys' sharp voice cracked like a whip. "You apologize this second and compose yourself! I did not raise a heathen!"

"You raised a puppet to dance to your tune!" Dominic snarled. "No, you raised a good little bitch to obey your commands! The only problem is she's not a dog, she's a wolf!"

Dommy, stop. I've got this. Abby took a deep breath. "I am sorry for my outburst. But, I was taught to be honest. If you could please refrain from speaking so poorly of my friends, I'd appreciate it." She smoothed her napkin on her lap then looked at Drew. "Please don't touch me. It makes me uncomfortable."

Dominic still growled as he glared at the Davidsons. He began to pace behind her chair, the constant rumbling reminding her of Bryan Samson's motorcycle.

Mr. Davidson spoke up first. "Your loyalty is commendable, Miss Palmer." He raised his glass in a toast. "And it's perfectly understandable that the touch of a man to whom you are unattached would be unsettling." He looked at his son. "Wouldn't you agree, Drew?"

"Yes, Father." Drew looked at his lap with the most hangdog expression she had ever seen. "I am sorry, Miss Palmer. I will respect your personal space."

"That's all I ask." Abby glanced at Gladys before she added, "After all, a proper lady doesn't relish any man's attention except her husband's."

Gladys' smile and nod had her biting her tongue. "Quite right, dear, quite right. And you've had such a stressful week. It's understandable if you lose your composure."

"She lost her 'composure' because you keep trying to mold her into something she's not!" Dominic's growls just got louder. "Why don't you let her be herself she's —"

Dominic! Abby fought not to glare over her shoulder. *The matter is settled. Enough! What is WRONG with you? Look, maybe it's time for you to go. I don't need —*

"No!" The horror in his voice was too much. "Please! I don't know what would happen if you ever forgot me!" He crawled back under her chair like a whipped dog. "I'll behave, it's just so hard to see you treated this way and be unable to do anything about it."

I know, Dommy. I know.

"Are you pleased with yourself?" Aeneas eyed Bjarte, who was leaning against the trunk at the end of Abby's bed. "You put on quite the show this evening."

"Me?" The deceiver smiled. "I think you're the one who was chewing the scenery, Annie."

The guardian clenched his fists, reminding himself that violence solved nothing. He didn't have the power to drive Bjarte away. *It was not me alone speaking* tonight *and I know it.* "I would think you'd take credit for your part in that fiasco."

Bjarte laughed. "Wow, such denial! Seriously, I keep telling you. We are not as different as you like to think. We'd do better as a team than as rivals."

Aeneas turned his gaze on their charge. So much had changed, and yet so much remained the same. "We will always be rivals. There is nothing you or your master can do to change that."

"And when you fail again? When *your* boss casts you out? Who will you serve then?"

"This is your last chance; fail and you fall as well." The guardian did not answer. There was nothing left to say on the matter. "My loyalty is unwavering. As is hers if you bothered to look."

"We'll see about that." The deceiver's smug smile had him longing to summon his staff. "Now that she's not as sheltered as she has been, we'll see who has the upper hand."

"You are a fool if you think something as simple as a game with others can turn her from her course." Aeneas folded his arms and narrowed his eyes.

"Yeah," said the deceiver, looking him up and down before he snickered. "I'm the fool."

The guardian didn't see the amusement until he looked from the deceiver to himself. When he had crossed his arms he had unintentionally mimicked Bjarte's pose. Rather than shift position and admit the other had a point, he crossed his feet at the ankle and leaned against the wall, making the mirror image complete. *Laugh while you can,* he thought. *This is one fight you will not win.*

CHAPTER 15

"You could have picked a more original name."

"No one asked you." Abby looked over her profile one last time before submitting it. She opened the chess game to kill time. She didn't think it would be approved any time soon. She had just moved her first pawn when a knock at the door made her jump. She shut her laptop and slid it under her pillow before going to see who was there. She peaked out the curtain and groaned. "Great, just great."

Dominic sniffed at the door and growled. "Don't answer it!"

"And have his mother tell Aunt Gladys I couldn't be hospitable?" Abby sighed and unlocked the door, keeping the chain in place. "May I help you?"

"Good afternoon, Miss Palmer," said Drew Davidson, smiling. "I was hoping to find you here. May I come in?"

"I'm sorry, but no." Abby fought off the smile. *At last Aunt Gladys' rules pay off.* "I'm by myself at the moment and so can't have anyone inside without supervision."

"Yet it was perfectly fine to go out to your grandmother's alone with the Samson boy?" Drew's expression fought to stay pleasant. "You trust him more than me?"

"With good reason," said Dominic, growling beside her. His tail lashed and his claws dug into the carpet. "Don't let him in!"

"It's not a matter of trust, Mr. Davidson." Abby braced herself against the door ready to slam it if she needed to. "It's a matter of courtesy. I had no warning you would be coming over, and I wouldn't think you'd want to see me after my behavior last night."

"That is why I came over, Abigail." Again that smile. If he kept that up she'd end up hitting him again. "Your behavior is more than understandable."

If your next words are "what with the company you keep" I'm shutting the door. Abby raised her eyebrows. "You came over because my behavior is understandable?"

"Well, yes, but more because I hope we can start over." He put his hands in his pockets and tilted his head. "I was hoping you might accompany me to a movie this Thursday?" At her frown, he hurried to amend his statement. "My father will be there to chaperone, no need to worry."

"Aunt Gladys does Bingo on Thursdays," she replied. *It's the one of the few days I get time to myself.* "And I have driving lessons Friday."

"Right, right, you wouldn't want to be out late and be tired the next day." He tapped his chin with his index finger. "Lunch, perhaps?"

"Tell him no!" Dominic pressed against her legs growling.

"That sounds fine, Mr. Davidson." Abby forced herself to smile. "Please, though, you must ask Aunt Gladys first." *Like she'd say no.*

Drew's smile became sheepish as he glanced to the side. "I'll do that right now, Miss Palmer. Thank you." He turned and started off. "Mrs. Lynde! If I may have a word?"

Oh, crap! Abby closed the door and ran back to her room, jerking her laptop out from under her pillow. She winced as she popped the battery out, killing the power. She opened the drawer and stashed it away, then straightened her covers. She heard the front door open.

"Abby dear! Come in here please."

"Yes, Aunt Gladys!" She walked into the living room to find Drew and his father already seated. She curtsied. "Hello, Mr. Davidson, Mr. Davidson."

"Please get our guests some lemonade, Abby?" Gladys looked to Preacher Davidson and smiled. "I am sure you're parched after sitting in that hot car."

Abby escaped to the kitchen and took her time getting out glasses, filling a pitcher, and putting the whole set on a tray. She carried it back into the living room and sat it on the coffee table and poured each of them a glass.

"Well, it's not like my boy here would be alone with a young woman." The preacher sipped his drink and smiled. "This is quite good. Thank you, Miss Palmer."

"You're welcome, Mr. Davidson." Abby looked and saw the only place to sit was beside Drew on the loveseat. She fought not to groan as she sat as far from him as she could.

"I am pleased to see you know better than to allow anyone in when you're home alone, Miss Palmer." Mr. Davidson nodded. "It speaks well of your upbringing. Now, about lunch this Thursday…"

"Here we go," said Dominic, curling up at her feet.

"You needn't worry. I won't hover over you two. I'll just be there as a reminder that some actions are not appropriate." He smiled again. "Not that you seem to need it, but better safe than sorry, after all. We'll pick you up at noon, yes?"

Abby glanced at Gladys, who nodded and did the same. "That will be fine, Mr. Davidson." She looked at Drew. "Thank you for the invitation."

"Not a problem, Miss Palmer." Drew shot her that smile again.

"So, read any good books lately?"

"Not really." Abby's hands smoothed her dress for the thousandth time. She picked at her chicken tenders, not even sure she should have chosen something this greasy, but it had been one of the cheaper items on the menu she actually liked. "How about you?"

"Same." Drew kept sneaking glances at his father at the next table as he tried to keep the conversation going. "Are you looking forward to going back to school?"

"Yes, I am." Abby looked up from her plate to meet his gaze. "I really like my class list and I can't wait to start studying again."

"That's cool." Drew took a drink and swallowed hard. "I like woodshop myself. I've made Mother a few tables and such. What do you like to do for fun?"

"I play chess as much as I can." Abby took another bite. "Do you play any games?"

His eyes lit up and the smile, for the first time, seemed legit. "Yeah, I play –" He stopped himself and glanced at his father again then lowered his voice as he leaned forward. "I play RPGs sometimes. There's this really cool one out now." He blinked and took another drink. "Oh right, you don't know what that is, RPGs are a role-playing game." He paused. "Like uh… like if you could be Bilbo Baggins or something. You play as a character in a story."

"She knows that, idiot!"

Dominic you were SUPPOSED TO stay home! "I understand. So you play video games?" She took another bite of her chicken for something to do. "I didn't know they made Christian ones."

"Well, these aren't strictly *Christian*," he said, his voice still low. He glanced back at his father, but the elder Davidson seemed focused on his paperwork. "And it's not a video game either. It's online."

"Oh?" Abby fought to keep her face blank. She picked up a French fry and dipped it in ketchup. "That sounds … nice."

"It's a lot of fun. You should try it sometime." He suddenly blanched. "Just don't tell my parents, OK? It's nothing un-godly or anything I just well…"

Abby looked up at him. *Did he just admit to doing something behind his parents' back?*

"Sounded like it." Dominic sat up to look at Drew and tilted his head. "That's… strange."

"I'm not allowed online," said Abby. She smiled. "I'm sure your parents' gave you permission in the first place, so no worries."

"Thank you." He took a bite of his burger then took a drink. "So chess and you play rum with your grandmother right?"

Abby blinked. "Yes, I do. She's quite the card shark, though." *He remembered that?*

"Maybe next time you visit I could give you a lift." Drew took another bite. "Then you wouldn't need to take the bus."

And bring your father along? No thanks. "Grandma was looking forward to seeing Marlon again." She broke a tender apart, waiting for the scorn.

"Car's got four seats," said Drew. He smiled and leaned closer. "No reason I couldn't give you both a ride." He started to reach his hand out before pulling it back. "City's not as safe as it used to be."

"Uh, Abs?" Dominic looked at her sideways. "Did we fall into the Twilight Zone?"

I was just going to ask you that. It didn't add up. Drew Davidson, who sneered every time he saw Marlon, offering to let him ride in his car? Before she could say anything, their waitress appeared and set two takeout boxes and two carry out cups on the table. She raised an eyebrow when the waitress pocketed a five that Preacher Davidson handed to her as he stood up.

"Get your things," said Preacher Davidson. "We're leaving." His gaze went to a couple a few tables down. "The clientele is no longer suitable company."

Drew immediately emptied his plate and glass into his containers, then, when she did not move, did the same with Abby's. He pushed the box and cup into her hands.

Abby stared at the couple who had attracted the elder Davidson's attention, trying to understand just what made them so "unsuitable". When they passed the table on their way out, she understood. Sitting at the table were Marlon's grandparents.

"Are you kidding me?" Dominic glared up at Preacher Davidson. "*That* is 'unsuitable company'? Are you out of your mind?!?"

What had offended the preacher? Bryan had even been wearing a suit, for heaven's sake! Abby had never even seen him in one. She opened her mouth several times but could not get the words out. *Just what's wrong with the man having dinner with his WIFE? You pompous –* She glanced over at Drew. *And YOU just go along with it?*

Drew gave her a sheepish look and shrugged. He opened the car door for her and waited until his father got behind the wheel to shut it. Right before he did though, unless her eyes were playing tricks on her, he mouthed the words "I'm sorry."

CHAPTER 16

Ava followed the stranger through the dark streets, curiosity overwhelming her common sense. She had to find out how they had known what she tried so hard to hide. She had tried several times to get them to tell her who they were, where they were going. Every question fell on deaf ears. She could barely keep from running into walls as she fought to keep up. Of course stuff like this has to happen at night. She flinched as she kicked a rock, stubbing her toe. Secrets can never see the light of day.

"You do know how lame that sounds, right?"

Abby made a face at the dragon. "Hey, I never claimed to be Jane Austen." She proofread her first post then submitted it. "I'll get better." The writing *was* stilted, she knew that. But she was trying to have some fun, not write a bestseller. She smiled as the messenger window popped up.

RandomWord: Avalon Rose… seriously Abs? Remind me to never let you name anything.

DragonflyGirl: Yeah, Brock Dent is so much better. *claps* So now what?

RandomWord: You gotta wait for WhiteQueen to reply and follow along on your first mission to join your society. It's not hard but she's not usually on until Saturday. How'd you get roped into lunch with Drew Davidson?

Abby stared the message for a moment. She sighed and typed, "I take it your grandpa saw us, huh? Long story short he showed up Sunday with his dad. And I just figured, might as well get it over with you know?" He didn't respond for a moment. She fidgeted.

DragonflyGirl: Mars-Bars*?*

RandomWord: I take it Grandpa and Grandma cut it short, huh? Glad they helped some.

DragonflyGirl: I couldn't even figure out why Preacher Davidson wanted to leave in the first place at first. *sighs* It wasn't right for him to do that. I honestly don't get why he has such a problem with your family.

RandomWord: *snorts* Gee, I dunno. How about the fact no matter how discrete Dad is, it's kinda obvious that Mom's not his only lover? Dad's bi, Abs. Heck, so's Grandpa he's just loyal as heck.

Dominic growled. "Here we go again. I swear that boy has some screws loose."

Abby shook her head. She typed, "Mars-Bars, stop. No one has the right to judge your family. It works. I don't even know how sometimes, but it does. Better than Drew having to hide the fact he plays online RPGs from his parents."

RandomWord: Say what now?

DragonflyGirl: You can read. We talked at lunch… believe it or not he wasn't so pompous for once. He likes games. And *snickers* he remembered Grandma plays rum.

RandomWord: … Whoa. Well, unless you wanna do a quick round of chess, we better get off here. Don't need Mrs. Lynde to catch you. I'm betting you didn't tell him you were joining one?

DragonflyGirl: As if. I'm not that stupid. See ya tomorrow Marlon.

Abby smiled at his sign off and shutdown the laptop. Once it was safely stashed, she sat back on her bed and stroked Dominic's mane. "Remind me to thank Bryan. That conversation wasn't too bad, just *painful.*"

"Speaking of grandfathers," said Dominic with a growl that sounded more like a purr. "When are you going to look more into my namesake's journal? Just 'cause you won't play the game by yourself doesn't mean you can't read up on it."

"You just want me to see if there's any more creepy stuff." She got into her desk drawer and took out the old book. She sat back down on the bed to read. She wasn't sure what she expected to find. As she leafed through pages of technical notations she could not even begin to read, she found herself tracing her grandfather's handwriting. *I make my A's like he did. I write the same size too.* She stopped. This entry she *could* read.

OK, that's the last time I go out for a drink with Wasp. Seriously, what was in that stuff? The nightmares I had last night just didn't make any sense. These two guys were talking to me, like I was supposed to know them or something. One looked a bit familiar; I'm sure I've seen his face before. It's going to eat at me until I figure it out. Either way, might be time to swear off liquor. Still some good did come out of it. Creepy as those two were, they'll be a good fit for the game's hero and villain.

Dominic snorted. "He based this on a *dream*? Oh, now that's just lovely. How stupid can you be to use a *dream* for inspiration?"

"Abigail!" Gladys' voice carried from the living room. "Dear, are you home?"

"Yes, Aunt Gladys!" Abby tossed the journal in her nightstand drawer and rushed to the living room. "How was your Bingo game?"

"Oh, just a blast!" Gladys hung her hat up by the door and gestured to a couple bags on the coffee table. The smell of fried chicken filled the room. "I picked up dinner. I figured you'd be too tired to cook. Did you just get home?"

"No, I've been back a couple hours." Abby took the bags into the dining room and began to set the table. "Mr. Davidson cut the lunch short."

"You didn't lose your temper again, did you?" Gladys looked at her sternly as she sat at the table. "Really, dear, I know you're stressed but such is unbecoming of a lady."

"As a matter of fact, the conversation had just started to relax when Mr. Davidson insisted we leave." She set a plate and utensils in front of her great-aunt. "We didn't even get to finish our meal."

"So why did he insist?" Gladys helped herself to a breast and some mashed potatoes. "I'm sure he had a good reason." She broke a soda off the six-pack.

Abby fixed her plate and sat down, placing a napkin on her lap. "He found the 'clientele' unsuitable." She helped herself to a soda. "A loving husband taking his wife out apparently ruined the mood."

"Some people just don't understand that some things belong behind closed doors."

"They were perfectly chaste as far as I could see."

Gladys' confusion was palatable. She shrugged and started on her dinner. "One of those … mixed couples I gather?"

"No… The Samsons." Abby opened her mouth to explain it had been the elder couple when Gladys cut her short.

"Abby I know you don't want to hear it, but Mr. Davidson has much more experience with those people than you do. Things just haven't been the same since they moved in. You were too young to remember how things were then."

You mean boring? Back when I had no friends in the building and you dragged me to Sunday School to watch wannabe preachers act out bible stories? Abby bit her tongue. Remembering when Marlon and Felice moved in next door was not hard. She'd been elated to see other kids her age. It just got better when they were in the same class at school.

"So until the Samsons arrived, did you enjoy your time with young Mr. Davidson?"

"Why don't you just ask Abby if she's ready to set a date?" Dominic curled up under Abby's chair. "I swear you need to get laid, you old bat. Maybe then you'll stop playing matchmaker."

Abby choked and grabbed for her drink. She coughed for a good minute before she could speak. "Sorry, went down the wrong pipe. He offered to drive next time I visit Grandma."

Gladys smiled. "That would be lovely. I'm sure Gail would enjoy his company and perhaps Mr. Davidson could convince her to come back to the church."

Abby took a few bites. *Do I tell her Drew offered to take me and Marlon? I know there's no way Preacher Davidson would approve.*

"And you know she'd tell him faster than you could get the words out." Dominic nipped at her ankle. "Don't you dare. The kid showed you some respect today, return the favor."

"I'm sure it would be fine." Abby smiled at the idea of Marlon and Drew both in front of Gail Whelan. "Who knows, we all might play a few hands of rum."

Gladys laughed. "Oh that would be a picture. Gail would sweep the floor with them. I'd almost pay to see that." She sobered. "Forgive me dear, but I know my sister. I lost far too many times."

"Join the club, Aunt Gladys," said Abby, smiling.

CHAPTER 17

"Take it easy, now. See, you're getting it."

Abby kept her eyes focused on the road. Her hands weren't as tight as before and she had only gone over the line for a split-second so far. They went further out this time, Bryan was content to let her go where she liked so long as she followed the laws. The familiar streets faded and yet she did not feel lost. The surroundings seemed off, somehow. Nothing about them was quite right.

Dominic sat up in the backseat, looking around with his ears perked. When they reached an intersection, he nudged her shoulder. "Turn right."

Abby glanced at him in the rearview for a second, then at Marlon, who shot her a smile. *Why?*

"Please?" Dominic gave her a hangdog look. "Trust me."

She sighed and took the turn, wincing when Bryan reached out and steadied the car. "Sorry."

"You're doin' fine, Abby, relax." Bryan looked around. "Nice neighborhood."

It was a nice neighborhood. Not quite on par with where her grandmother lived, but it fit the definition of "ritzy". It seemed quaint, yet it unsettled her. More from curiosity than anything else, she let the dragon guide her, the uneasy feeling increasing with every turn. When they came to another intersection, she looked up at the street sign and understood. She turned onto the road, her hands once more holding the steering wheel in a death grip.

"Uh, Abby?" Bryan sat up in the seat. "Where are you –"

"It's OK, Grandpa," said Marlon, reaching out and touching his shoulder. He met her eyes in the mirror. "It's OK."

Figures he understands. It didn't look the same, yet it did. It didn't look *right.* She followed the road until she reached her destination and pulled over. She stopped the car, looking past Bryan at the house a good ways back from the road. *It's not the right color,* she thought. *Where are the trees? Where's the fence?* She turned the engine off, unbuckled her seat belt, and got out of the car.

Dominic slipped out and followed, coming to heel at her side as she walked around the car and stood on the apron of the driveway.

Why did you bring me here? She felt tears prick at her eyes. Her mind forced the view in front of her to back to the way it belonged. A trailer parked to the left of the gray house, cars in the driveway, tall trees bordering the property, a chain link fence surrounding the backyard, two tall willow trees… Then she blinked and it was gone. She was staring at a brown house much like the others around it; no trailer stood there anymore. It was wrong. No other word for it. It was *wrong.*

"You needed to see," said Dominic, pressing against her leg. "You needed to know."

Know what? I already knew it was gone! I knew that! Abby started crying in earnest, the tears falling unchecked. She started to sway and felt two strong arms wrap around her, holding her upright. She turned and cried into Marlon's chest, hugging him tight.

Marlon rubbed her back and rested his chin against the top of her head. He didn't say anything. Just let her cry until the tears stopped.

When they finally did she pulled back and wiped her eyes with the back of her hand. Then she looked up at him sheepishly. "Sorry about that."

"No biggie, Abs." Marlon smiled as he let go, resting a hand on her shoulder. "Are you OK?"

"For now," she replied, turning to find Bryan had come to stand beside them. "Mr. Samson? Are you OK?" When he didn't answer, she tried again. "Bryan?"

He reached out and laid his hand on Abby's other shoulder, but otherwise didn't take his eyes off the property. "Why'd you come out here?"

"I don't know," she replied, sneaking a look at the dragon still pressed close to her side. "I didn't mean –" She didn't know how to explain without sounding insane. "I just turned down roads that seemed familiar and… they led here."

"Let's get outta here, OK? This is just surreal. And you *lived* here, no wonder ya broke down." Bryan turned back to the car. "You all right to drive?"

"I think so." Abby took a deep breath and got back behind the wheel. She waited until Marlon and Dominic took their places in the backseat and pulled into the driveway long enough to turn around. Then she headed back for the city and away from the past.

"Do you promise to guard the society's secrets with your life?" Jade looked at the new recruit, assessing her for possible weaknesses. "To aid the cause to the best of your ability, and not betray your comrades even under threat of torture?"

Torture? OK, seriously? What the heck did I walk into? Ava met Jade Dis' stern gaze with her own. She stood up as straight as she could. "I do not betray my friends."

"Good, now…" Jade circled her before coming to a stop in front of her once more. "What powers do you possess?"

Powers? Ava tilted her head in confusion. "Uh, I can do this." She stepped back and a flame-point Ragdoll cat took the human's place. She sat and meowed.

"I see." Jade reached down and examined the cat, noting the unusual markings. "Not a perfect disguise, but a decent one nonetheless." She turned and gestured for one of the people standing in the shadows to come forward. "You'll be partnered with Jenner. His skills are similar to yours."

Harley Lawrence stepped into the light. His smile was genuine. He kept his hands in his pockets. "I'm sure we'll work fine together," he said then crouched down before becoming a large rat.

Jade smiled. "Your mission will be to infiltrate the League Headquarters and find out when they are planning their next raid. You must not get caught. Is that understood?"

Ava morphed back into her human form. Cats couldn't talk. "I get that we can't get caught but I don't know where the Headquarters is."

"Jenner does, he'll lead the way." Jade grinned. "You'll be fine."

Harley Lawrence resumed his human form and gave her a smile. "No worries, done this a few times before." He gestured for her to follow. "Let's get to planning."

Ava nodded and trailed him, questioning her judgment in following Jade in the first place.

Abby shook her head as she read the "out of character" reply that informed her they could pick this up next week. She thanked WhiteQueen and JennerTheRat and closed the window. She was about to shut her laptop down when the messenger window popped up.

RandomWord: Looking good, Abs. You'll be a pro at this in no time.

DragonflyGirl: If you say so, personally I feel like I fell down after the White Rabbit. Jade Dis? Seriously? And you were teasing me?

RandomWord: *snickers* Yeah well Harley Lawrence isn't much better. Still, he's a good guy. Just had his first mission not that long ago. He'll walk you through it.

DragonflyGirl: So, we pretend to sneak into some league and get info? Is there a map or something? I mean, this is kinda weird.

RandomWord: You get used to it. Yeah there's maps and stuff, not that most people use them anyway.

DragonflyGirl: Yeah, well I'll look at those some other time. Right now I need to go fix dinner.

RandomWord: Hey, you doing OK? I mean, you looked like someone sucker punched you yesterday.

Abby twirled her hair around her finger. Yes, seeing the place where she'd lived with her parents so changed had shocked her, and despite knowing for years that it belonged to a new family, it was seeing the differences proving the fact that it hadn't been *home* for a long time that hurt.

DragonflyGirl: I'm fine, Mars-Bars. It was just a bit of a surprise. See ya tomorrow?

RandomWord: You bet, if I can make it. Sleep well, Abs.

Abby closed the window and shut the laptop down. She put it away and headed to the kitchen. *Something quick and easy,* she thought as she set the oven.

Dominic padded into the room and lay down by the door. "The boy had a good question. Look, I'm sorry for taking you out there. I just noticed where we were and …" He hung his head. "It felt like the right thing to do. I didn't realize it would bother you that much."

"It's OK, Dommy." Abby got out a bowl and the ingredients she needed. "No blood, no foul." She found her mind wandering as she crumbled up a package of crackers. *The trailer's gone of course; it didn't survive the fire. I wonder why they cut the trees down?* She mentally kicked herself. It didn't matter why. "What's done is done, no use crying over spilled milk."

"Who are you talking to, dear?"

Abby almost dropped the crackers. "Aunt Gladys, don't do that, please." She opened the package and dumped it into the bowl on the counter. "Sorry, I was just thinking out loud."

Gladys leaned around the door frame, her head tilted curiously. "My apologies, dear. I'll be in the living room if you need me."

Sighing with relief, Abby went back to her preparations. "At least meatloaf isn't complicated."

Dominic rested his head on his paws. "I'm just glad you aren't using a knife. The way your mind's been, you'll cut your finger off."

Abby turned and glared at him. She opened her mouth to retort and caught herself. *I'm not that dense, Dommy. Sheesh.* She turned back around and opened the hamburger. *You're a real ray of sunshine lately, you know that?*

"You're growing up," he said, not bothering to raise his head or look at her. "You're going places I can't protect you. So sue me if I don't like it."

Abby looked at him over her shoulder. *You're protecting me?*

"Don't thank me."

She laughed and put the mix into a pan before sliding it into the oven. *Don't worry, I won't.*

CHAPTER 18

"This is pretty creepy."

"Don't be such a wimp." Marlon guided the avatar through the level. "The graphics aren't even close to how real games are these days." The last enemy was slashed through. "There, now the crazy man shows up again and says some psycho crap and –"

"I wonder who this guy's supposed to be," said Abby. She leaned against Marlon's shoulder so she could see the screen better. "I mean, there's some pretty dark themes going on."

"Dark? Abs, this is about as dark as *Billy and Mandy*."

"Would you not refer to things I don't know?" Abby read through the now-familiar speech. The words changed, but the gist was always the same. Just accept the guy's help, and you'd get your brother back. The offer always seemed sincere on the surface, but something about the *way* it was offered made you shiver. The graphics might have been lower quality, but that grin as he offered up his services belonged in a nightmare. And when you refused…

"Ha, ha, ha! You'll change your mind when you see how much pain and suffering has been laid at your feet. Mark my words!"

"Well, I'll give your gramps this," said Marlon as he saved and shut the laptop down. "He knew how to make use of a decent story. Might have been better as a book, though."

"He got the ideas for the characters in a dream apparently." She snickered as she put the laptop away. "After he got drunk with *your* grandfather."

"Speaking of Grandpa, he says you're really improving. You just need to lay off the death grip."

"That'd be a bit easier if I didn't think I might crash and kill us all."

Marlon just shook his head and started to speak when his phone buzzed. He flipped it open to reveal a text from his father. He blanched. "'CODE RED!' Oh, crap!" he said and jumped to his feet. "Of all the times for her to come home early!"

"Keep it down," said Dominic from his spot at the end of her bed. "Some of us are trying to sleep."

Gee, thanks for the support! "Be glad this is a ground floor apartment," said Abby as she popped the window screen out. "Go! She catches you in here and we're both dead!"

Marlon did not have to be told twice. He slipped out and dropped to the ground then took off down the alley.

Abby just managed to get the screen back in place before Gladys knocked against her door jam. "There you are, dear. You'll never believe it! I have wonderful news!"

"Ten minutes' silence says it has something to do with the Davidsons."

I don't take sucker bets. "Do tell, Aunt Gladys." Abby moved to sit beside Dominic, smiling. "I haven't seen you this happy for a while."

"Dear, it was the darnedest thing," said Gladys, coming over to sit beside her. "Dolores and I *both* got BINGO at the same time! Down to the *second*. Well, to be completely fair we decided to split the prize. Guess what it was!"

"An all-expense paid trip to the loony bin?"

Dominic, hush! "I've no idea, Aunt Gladys, but it must be big to get you this excited."

"A *week-long* trip!" Her smile threatened to crack her face. "There were only two tickets, so she and I are going together. Just to be fair." At Abby's shocked expression, she patted her shoulder. "Don't worry dear. I'm sure you'll be fine on your own. You're a responsible God-fearing young woman. And Mr. Davidson and his son will look in on you from time to time. So no worries."

A week to myself? Abby had to bite her cheek to keep from grinning. "When do you and Mrs. Davidson leave?"

"Tomorrow," replied Gladys, taking her hand. "Why do you think I'm home so early? Come on, dear, I need you to help me pack!"

"Sure, Aunt Gladys," she said, the grin breaking free. "I'll be happy to help."

"You're kidding!" said Felice after driving class was over. "A week with no one else there?" She laughed. "Dang, Abby, you lucked out!"

"Tell me about it. All I have to do is keep the apartment clean and I can do whatever I like!" Her face hurt from smiling so much. "I can listen to music without headphones for once! Watch what I want on TV… Heck, I might check out a few books at the library!"

"Whoa, slow down there, Abs!" Marlon started snickering. "Next you'll want to stay up past ten! Don't do it! Resist the temptation!"

A car door slammed. Bryan had parked the student car for the day. "OK, so what's got you three hyenas in an uproar?" Bryan asked as he joined them. "I could use a laugh. Let me in on the joke."

"Aunt Gladys is going on a trip with Mrs. Davidson for a week." Abby fought not to dance. "A *week*!" She looked up at the sky and clasped her hands. "Thank you God!"

Bryan just shook his head chuckling. "Just remember, you try throwing any parties, my boys will be playin' bouncer. Pretty sure neither of 'em will stand for it."

Marlon gave his grandfather a look. "Dad and Uncle Richie? The same two whose music taste, like yours, can best be described as…"

He made air quotes with his fingers. "Loud?" He shook his head. "Those 'boys'?"

"Grandpa, be serious," said Felice. "This is *Abby*. She's so straight you could use her for a ruler!"

"I'm trying to decide if I'm honored or insulted."

"Knowing those two clowns, I'd go with honored." Dominic pressed against her leg. "They have a point though, you're thinking pretty small."

"There you are, Miss Palmer." They all turned at Preacher Davidson's voice. Drew stood by the family car in the school parking lot. The preacher ignored the Samsons and moved to stand in front of Abby like a sergeant standing over a new recruit. "I figured with Dolores out of town we should make arrangements for you to get to the service Sunday."

Abby frowned. She had actually hoped that her usual ride being gone meant she could skip one service. *I should have known better.* "I didn't think of that, Mr. Davidson." She rubbed her head with a sigh. *Great, riding in the car with him again.*

"I'll take her." Bryan shrugged when they all looked at him. "You go to the morning one, right? That works out since Vera and I go to ours in the afternoon."

"I wasn't aware you attended *any* service."

Bryan raised his head and met Davidson's gaze. "Been a Christian for a good few years now. Owe that to the Dragon, really. Never met anyone else that could knock ya for a loop with the words in red like he could. Couldn't let that goodness die." He nodded at Abby. "Got no problem gettin' up a bit earlier to make sure his blood gets to church."

"The 'Dragon'," repeated Preacher Davidson, the scorn barely contained in his voice.

"My grandfather," Abby said, biting her cheek to keep from snapping. "And thank you, Mr. Samson, I'd really appreciate that." She smiled. "That way Mr. Davidson doesn't have to go out of his way before the service. This works out best for everyone."

You could almost see the wheels in Preacher Davidson's head turning as he fought to find a reason to protest the arrangement. "Very well, Miss Palmer," he said, clearly frustrated. He glanced at Bryan and gave a curt nod. "Thank you for your assistance. Good day."

Once Davidson turned his back, Bryan flipped him a one fingered salute, then looked at Abby. "If ya like, I can 'get lost' on the way."

Abby laughed. "Don't tempt me, sir. Still, thank you. I don't know what I'd do if I had to go through another car ride with him commenting on the news."

Felice rubbed her nose. "Grandpa, are you *ever* going to stop swearing? Gestures are just as bad."

"I wouldn't bet on it, sweetheart." Bryan smiled sheepishly. "Sorry but there's some people in this world that you'll never get along with." He made a face at the preacher's retreating figure.

Abby reached up and played with the cross she wore around her neck. "Sir? What *is* his problem, anyway?" She looked down at her shoes. "I know your family's different, but that doesn't mean –"

"That's what it *does* mean, Abby." Bryan shrugged. "When you're *different*, nobody trusts you, you're always the first to be blamed, and no matter what you do it's always, *always* your fault."

"But that's not fair!" Abby flinched at the whine in her voice. She felt like a child complaining because there weren't enough cookies to go around. "You're not bad. You're just *different*."

Bryan looked at her sideways and smiled. "You know as well as I do that life's not fair. If it was, there wouldn't be orphans like us."

Abby blinked. "Like us?"

"Grandpa's parents died when he was a kid, Abby." Felice frowned then tugged at her tank top. "It's a really long story."

"One I need a few shots in me to tell properly." Bryan patted them all on the shoulder then turned for his motorcycle. "You three get on home. Abby, I'll stop by tomorrow and you can fill me in on what time I need to get up. Sound fair?"

"You got it, sir." Abby smiled and waved. "Thanks again." She turned and unlocked her bike as her friends did the same then she followed them down the sidewalk.

"I'll say one thing for that bumbler," said Dominic as he took his place beside her. "He might be rough around the edges but at least he's honest."

You have such a way with words, Dommy. "So you two want to come with me to the library? Or is that too *boring?*"

"I ain't got a problem goin' with you, Abs." Marlon shot her a grin. "But I think you're thinkin' pretty small. How about a movie? My treat." He looked at his sister. "What ya say, Lice?"

"I say we stick with *Abby's* plan," replied Felice, grinning. "Let her make a choice for a change."

Marlon's face turned seven shades of red. "That's not what I meant and you know it!"

"It's OK, Mars-Bars." Abby smiled again, coming up alongside him. "How about this? Library tomorrow, movie sometime next week? I don't even know what's playing."

"Sounds like a plan."

CHAPTER 19

Abby smiled as they walked out of library. The bag of books hung heavy from her shoulder, but it wasn't that bad. "Now I'll finally get some of the references you make all the time, Mars-Bars."

"I still don't see how you're going to read all those in a week, Abs." Marlon tried for the fifth time to take the bag from her. "You're going to hurt your back."

"She'll be fine," said Felice as she unlocked her bike. "You worry too much, bro."

"I do not!"

"Do too!"

"Do NOT!"

"Do TOO!"

"How old are these two again?" Dominic shook his head, keeping his place at Abby's heels.

Abby pinched the bridge of her nose. "Last I checked we were all about the same age," she said. "Could you two quit acting like preschoolers?"

Marlon shot her a cheeky smile as he unlocked his bike. "Of course we *could*," he laughed.

"The real question," added Felice, "is if we *would*."

Abby put the bag in her bike's basket then unlocked it. She got on and started down the sidewalk. "Sometimes I examine my life and wonder how I ended up with you two."

"God thought you needed some excitement in your life," said Felice as she rode up alongside her, "and we needed someone to stop us from doing something *completely* insane."

"Or fate likes screwing with you," Marlon said. "Either way, you're stuck with us now."

"Clowns to the left of me," Dominic said in a sing-song, "jokers to the right."

"Here I am," Abby added, "stuck in the middle with you."

"Seriously?" Marlon shook his head. "You shoulda snagged a few CDs too. This ain't the 70's, Abs."

"I couldn't keep them." Abby sighed. "I can return the books and remember the stories. Not being able to hear a song I like?" She shuddered. "I don't even want to think about it." They rode in silence for a while and she enjoyed the simple pleasure of knowing no one was waiting at home to ask questions. *I wish I could do this more often.* She sighed. *Can't wait until I turn eighteen... Then the only one I'll answer to is myself.*

"Abby?" Felice swerved to avoid a hole in the sidewalk and pulled ahead of her. "Earth to Abigail Palmer."

Abby blinked and glanced at her friend. "Uh, what?"

"You want to stop for lunch?" Marlon asked as he pulled up beside her. "Geez, if I didn't know better I'd say you were high."

"Very funny, Little Wasp." Dominic shook his head. "Freedom suits you, though, I agree."

"Sure, we can stop." Abby ignored both her friends' comments. "What do you have in mind?"

"Up to you." Felice's smile was bright. "The world is at your feet... or at least the neighborhood. Lead the way."

Abby looked around. She thought hard, trying to remember her surroundings. The image of a dark restaurant came to mind, the name Longhorn. But she had no idea if they were connected or if the place was nearby. "Maybe you guys should pick. I'm drawing a major blank here."

The twins looked at each other then took the lead.

"No offense, but…" Felice's voice was carefully neutral. "Are you OK?"

"Of course she is," said Marlon, shooting them a smile. "It's just a side effect of finally being able to make a decision. It'll take some getting used to."

Only I'm not going to get to *get used to it.* Abby sighed. *Who am I kidding? One week of no one telling me what to do doesn't change anything.*

"Think of it as a taste of the future," said Dominic. He kept pace alongside her, now and then glancing up at her. "Just two more years, remember?"

Yeah, she thought. *Just two more years.*

"So now what?" asked Marlon, as the bus pulled away and they started home. "You gonna hit the RP then hit the sack, Abs?"

"Most likely." She smiled at her friends as they bounced along the sidewalk past the park. "I do have to get up in the morning. Thanks for coming with me."

Before either of the twins could reply a familiar voice called out, "Hey, Miss Palmer!" Drew jogged over to join them as Marlon frowned and his sister face-palmed. "Evening, Mr. Samson, Miss Samson." He put his hands in his pockets and grinned. "How are you all doing?"

Dominic said what Abby assumed they were all thinking. "Who are you and what have you done with Drew Davidson?"

"We're just fine, Mr. Davidson," replied Felice, regaining her voice first. "And yourself?"

"Just fine, just fine, thank you for asking." Drew gestured with a thumb to the basketball hoops. "You up for a game? We were just getting started."

"What's the catch?" Dominic growled softly, his wings twitching as he shifted into a crouch.

"I don't think a skirt is conducive to playing basketball, Mr. Davidson." Abby released a handlebar to tug at her own.

"You could keep score," Drew suggested then looked back at the twins. "What'd you say?"

The twins shared a look then turned back to Drew and nodded. "You're on."

They followed Drew back to the court and parked their bikes by the bench.

Abby took a seat on the bench and watched the others take position. A coin flip established who was going first and the game began. It might have helped had she actually watched sports more often. The only thing she really understood was that they scored a point if the ball went through the hoop.

"Hey, Samson." Drew tried to get the ball away from Marlon but couldn't seem to manage it. "You to play like a girl."

"Oh yeah?" Marlon tossed the ball to his sister who turned around and sent it straight into the basket.

"You were saying?" she said with smirk, twirling a lock of her hair around her finger.

Drew caught the ball on the rebound and passed it to his teammate then went around Felice. He caught his teammate's pass and sunk it. "I dunno. What were you?"

Abby found herself smiling. None of the players were that good, but they were having a good time. *I wonder why Drew decided to invite Felice and Marlon to play?*

"You've defended them several times now." Dominic rested his head on his paws and watched with thinly veiled amusement. "If he's really trying to court you, being nice to them is an easy way to get on your good side. He obviously knows he can't outright insult them."

Honestly, I think he's just teasing. Abby kicked her feet as he watched the four players dance around the court. *I wonder if you were right about that Twilight Zone comment.*

"OK, let's end it here." Drew caught the ball and tossed it back and forth in his hands. "Some of us –" he nodded at Abby "– need to be up early tomorrow."

Marlon's cough sounded suspiciously like "yeah, right". He flashed a grin at Davidson.

"Yeah, right." Felice's expression matched her brother's. "You're calling it quits 'cause we were kicking your butt."

Drew's teammate rolled his eyes. "As if." He folded his arms. "We were cleaning your clock."

"Abs?" Marlon spun around and looked at her, rocking back on his heels. "What's the score?"

Abby picked up the paper they'd handed her when the game started. She tried to add it up but couldn't make the numbers make sense. "Uh, I think you're tied."

Dominic wasn't the only one who burst out laughing.

That evening, Abby waited for JennerTheRat to come on, tapping at the keys as she wrote out as much of she could ahead of time. It was already late and she'd have to post quickly if she wanted to get the mission over before she needed to crash.

RandomWord: How ya doing?

DragonflyGirl: Just fine, just waiting on Jenner so I can move on. You?

RandomWord: Taking a break from cleaning my room. *rolls eyes* Apparently it's not up to par with Mom and Dad's standards.

DragonflyGirl: *laughs* Mars-Bars…

RandomWord: I know, I know, I'll get off here and finish. Good luck on the mission.

DragonflyGirl: Thanks.

She refreshed the page and found a reply at last. She laughed at the fact they apparently had to crawl through a vent to get into the boardroom. She posted her reply, waited a few minutes and refreshed. Someone called GreenQueen posted and gave the intel they were supposed to gather. She posted an out of character reply, asking what they were supposed to do with it, as they had no way to write or record it. Jenner finally posted, showing that there was apparently a "common speech" for animals. He told her to remember half of the information, while he would remember the other half. The rest of the "mission" bored her a little. They got back to the society hideout and gave their report, then were dismissed after Ava was named a probationary member of group.

RandomWord: Nice, you broke my record for quickest finish.

DragonflyGirl: *grin* I don't quite get the point but at least I'm one step closer to being a full member. Well, I'm gonna crash. Night, Marlon.

RandomWord: Night, Abs. Sweet dreams.

She shut the laptop down and put it away out of habit. Then she got out her CD player and put on one of the few discs she still had her parents had given her. The familiar music filled the room and she curled up in bed, smiling. *One day,* she thought. *One day this will be normal.*

"It's just two years," said Dominic, curling up beside her. "Get some rest; something tells me tomorrow's going to be a rough one."

Abby rolled over on to her stomach and hugged her pillow. *I hope you're wrong…*

CHAPTER 20

"I turn your attention to John chapter two verses thirteen to sixteen. What happens here? Why, the Lord finds the temple has become a market place. It no longer serves its intended purpose, does it?" Davidson waved his hands as he paced up and down the pulpit. "That would be like removing these pews, putting tables in their place and having a flea market and calling it a service."

Abby fidgeted with her dress as she sat beside Bryan in the pew. Everyone studied them out of the corner of their eye, sneaking glances in between looking down at their bibles and looking back up at the preacher. She wanted to say something, but wasn't sure what.

"You'd think they'd never seen a man in a suit before," commented Dominic.

Bryan Samson was almost unrecognizable. The deep blue suit he wore contrasted with his black tie. He'd pulled back his hair, and while he had not shaved, his beard was combed neatly. He tapped his fingers against his knee but otherwise appeared impassive.

"Just as you cannot turn a place of worship into a shopping mall and expect it to still be the spiritual place it once was," continued Preacher Davidson. "You cannot turn something that was the Enemy's to start with into something that serves the Lord." He flipped his bible back open. "In Mark chapter twelve verses thirteen to seventeen, our Lord reminds us to give to God that which is His and to give to the world that which belongs to it. One cannot, I repeat, cannot take something of the world and make it of the Lord. You just cannot do it."

The cries of "Amen!" began the second Davidson paused for breath. Abby felt her nails dig into her palms. *Hail Mary, full of grace, the Lord is with thee. Blessed art thou among women and –*

"This is why so-called 'Christian rock and roll' and 'Christian gangs' are the height of foolishness. These are the Enemy's greatest weapons, brothers and sisters! He hopes to convince you that you are still following the Lord while you are really trailing behind him. This rhetoric is the flute music and he is the Pied Piper, and you are but the children being led away to your deaths."

And blessed is the fruit of thy womb, Jesus. Abby gritted her teeth. *Holy Mary, mother of God, pray for us sinners, now and at the hour of our death.*

"AMEN!"

"So my brothers and sisters don't be distracted by the Devil's honeyed words. Don't fall for his lies – for he is the Master of Lies. He is the Great Deceiver. Remember that anything that draws your eyes from the Lord, no matter how small, can lead to damnation. You might think it harmless fun, but whenever something causes you to neglect your Christian duty, it opens the door for the Devil. It allows him a foothold in your soul. Stand strong, brothers and sisters, and put aside the world's temptations!"

Dominic began to growl. He pressed into the floor. His ears pulled back against the noise as his wings – usually folded tight against his body – flexed as he considered flight.

Don't move! Abby gripped the seat as she fought not to flinch. Davidson was in his element and she hated the fact an act of kindness was being repaid so poorly. *You're always happiest when you can cut someone down without calling them out, aren't you?* She struggled to keep her expression passive.

"So simple a pleasure as a game can be an invitation. You cannot set up shop within sight of Hell's gates and expect to keep people from it. You cannot allow anything to take your eyes from Heaven's grace." Davidson smacked his bible against his palm. "When something does, no matter how small, you have lost the battle. Do not lose the war."

At last the collection plate was passed around. Abby got into her purse for the weekly five dollar bill. She glanced up when the plate reached Bryan. The woman who extended the plate to him looked terrified. Abby bit her cheek. *It's not like he's a leper and he asked you to shake hands.*

Bryan simply laid the plate on his lap and took his wallet from his jacket pocket. To Abby's shock he dropped a hundred in the plate and passed it over to her.

She placed her offering in and passed it on, following his example and not reacting to the disgust of the person beside her. She smiled.

"I ask those of you here today, who have allowed yourselves to be led astray, to ask the Lord's forgiveness. Say: Lord, I have sinned. I have let myself be drawn from Your side for my own sake. But from this day forward I give myself to You and put away the temptations of the world. From this day on I will put You first in all things and in all ways. Amen." Davidson set his bible on the podium and looked out at his flock. "Those of you who have not accepted the Lord as your Savior I beg you to do so today. It is not simply a matter of your own soul, but that you put those around you at risk. Every step you take in shadow can lead others from the light." He nodded. "I hope to see you all here next week. God bless."

Thank you God. Abby had never been so happy to see a service end. She got to her feet and led the way outside. She tried not to roll her eyes as people went out their way to keep their distance. She leaned closer as they passed the doors. "Thank you, sir."

Bryan winked and smiled, putting his hands in his pockets. He unlocked what she assumed was his wife's car and went around to hold the door open for her as he had that morning. Once she was inside he closed the door and got in the driver's seat. "Geez, what a wuss." Bryan checked the mirrors and backed out of the space and pulled onto the road. "Whining 'cause his wife left him on his own for a week. He might have to cook for himself. Oh, the horror!"

"Say what now?" Abby tilted her head. "When did he say anything about Mrs. Davidson?"

"Ya missed that? All that griping about games and pleasures that distract from 'your Christian duty'?" Bryan snorted. "I can read between the lines."

"I guess I did." Abby fidgeted in the seat. "I honestly thought he was taking shots at *you*." She curled her hair around her finger. "He does that to everyone. Someone does something 'un-Christian' and you can guess what he'll talk about next service."

Bryan laughed. "Now don't you wonder what the preacher's gonna preach about Sunday mornin'," he sang then shook his head. "Hakuna Matata, Abby. If he's talkin' about me, he's leavin' someone else alone."

"Did a grown man just use a Disney movie catchphrase?" Dominic lay in the backseat shaking his head. "Well, that's one way to turn the other cheek."

"I don't know what to say, sir." Abby just shook her head. "That's mature of you."

"Shh!" Bryan shot her the grin she saw so often on his grandson's face. "Don't ruin my bad reputation. It's a sellin' point for *Bonfire and Brimstone*." He popped a CD in and a song she'd never heard began. "Thinkin' we should use this one in the next show."

She listened to the words, nodding along at the wholesome lyrics. "Who was that?" she asked when the song ended.

"Jars of Clay," he answered. "But they aren't the only band on there." He skipped a couple songs then ruffled her hair. "If Marlon's got his facts straight you should know this one."

Her jaw dropped and her smile hurt her face. "Speak of the Devil; he's no friend of mine." They sang along until Bryan pulled to a stop in front of her apartment. Abby unbuckled her seatbelt as he did the same and walked over to open her door. "You don't have to do that, you know," she said as she got out of the car. "But thank you, sir, for everything today."

"No big deal, ma'am." He took off his jacket and slung it over his shoulder. "I've been through worse. Besides, gave my lady a break."

"That she needed," said Dominic, padding alongside them. "Considering he's a love-sick puppy at her heels."

Abby shifted her purse strap then got out the key and unlocked the door. She turned and looked up at him. "I'd invite you in, but my luck some busybody would tell Aunt Gladys when she gets back."

"I need to get home anyway. See ya around, Abby."

"Good-bye, Mr. Samson." Abby turned and went inside, Dominic right behind her.

CHAPTER 21

The game is progressing at a decent pace. I wish I could say the same for my sleep. Maybe putting those two clowns in was a mistake. I don't know how much more of these nightly discussions I can take. I swear I can almost hear them when I'm working too. It's frustrating but I'm sure it's just stress. That or I've lost too much blood making this blasted dragon toy. I don't know how Wasp stays sane being a tailor. Still, the thing doesn't look too bad. Less scary than the version in the game at least.

Abby traced the words. "Looks like your original form was made by hand. Poor Grandpa Nick, sewing is a pain with something that size."

"Should have just bought a teddy bear or something," said Dominic. "Would have been easier and you would've loved it just as much."

"The way Mom was into dragons?" Abby sighed as she recalled dim memories of the films she had watched with her parents. Hadn't one had a dragon that lived in a train tunnel? Some of the voices in those films had been familiar, too. "That's probably why he did it. He knew she'd make me a dragon freak." She reached out and pretended to run her hand through his mane. She could almost feel the fur. "A dragon freak and a Jesus freak."

"You're a freak no matter which way you look at it." Dominic nudged the book in her hand. "What are you hoping to find in there?"

She paused, looking at the open pages. "I don't know. It's just like… well, I can see why Grandpa and Bryan got along."

"Yeah, two complete nuts."

She swatted him with the book. "Be serious." A tap at her window made her jump. She turned to find Marlon smiling. She got up and opened the window. "What are you doing?"

"Mom wants to know if you want to come over for dinner."

Abby sighed and pinched her nose. "And that somehow warranted knocking on my window? Instead of, you know, using the phone like a normal person?"

"Figured it'd be easier just to walk over. Window is 'cause most people don't look this way so nobody runs their mouth to Mrs. Lynde. How'd the service go?"

She reached up and popped out the screen. "I'm not having this conversation through a screen. Besides you're letting the cold air in. Get in here."

Marlon heaved himself over the windowsill. "That bad huh?"

"Same old, same old really." Abby set the screen against the wall and shut the window. "He took shots at your grandpa *and* Mrs. Davidson, which I missed until your grandpa pointed it out."

"Sounds like *fun*." Marlon smiled as he got her desk chair and sat down backwards on it, resting his arms on the back. "So how'd Grandpa handle it?"

"Put a hundred in the collection plate and said 'so long as he's talking about him, he's leaving someone else alone.'" Abby got out her laptop. "Up for more of Grandpa Nick's game?"

Marlon nodded then put the chair away and joined her on the bed. "It's a good game," he said as they waited for it to load. "I bit repetitive but good."

"And you are so qualified to judge its merits."

Considering he plays games almost as much as he breathes, I think he is. "I wonder if… sometimes I wonder if I can get this out there, you know? Like Grandpa wanted."

"This day and age, anything's possible." Marlon gestured for her to go first. "I wonder how many levels this thing has?"

"Nine," she replied, tapping the journal. "Well, ten if you count the first 'learn how the controls work' level."

"That explains a lot." He tilted his head she finally dispatched the wolf that popped up. "I wonder if he just ran out of ideas on the levels?"

"It's supposed to teach patience and they *do* get harder as they go on." Abby passed the game back. "I think we're on the last level anyway."

"Does that book say how this ends?"

"If it does I haven't got that far."

The level's background was – for the time – a detailed illustration of a cave. The enemies were more annoying than dangerous aside from the fact engaging them meant "spilling" oil from your lantern and if the oil ran out, game over. They finally reached a spot with no way to go any further. They walked right into the wall a couple times but nothing happened. They looked at each other.

"OK," said Marlon, "where's Mr. Creepy?"

"Good question." Abby reached out and touched a few keys, turning the lantern up and brightening the cave. "Shouldn't he have popped up by – WHOA!"

The cave started shaking and then the dragon – which had so far only been seen in what Marlon called "cutscenes" – landed beside the avatar and roared. A text box appeared.

"Why have you come? Will you slay your own flesh and blood?"

Marlon snorted. "Uh, *no*. Seriously, we've been asked *how* many times to accompany the idiots gearing up to kill him?"

"He doesn't know that though, I mean since we've never seen him, he most likely just assumes we're out to get him, too."

Before they could hit anything, another text box popped up. *"Choose your answer carefully."* The rest was a blank where you could type a response.

"Oh-kay." Marlon looked at her. "Now what?"

"*You're* the game master," said Abby, "you tell me. I mean, I love games, Mars-Bars, but how often do I play? *You* play all the time."

"This would make more sense if it was multiple-choice." Marlon tapped his fingers against the bed. "I don't even know what to type."

"Uh, 'No, I'm here to save you'?"

"I don't think that was it, Abs," he said as another text box appeared – *"LIES!"* – and the dragon attacked. They were given no chance to talk again. The player quickly fell. Game over.

"Well," said Marlon. "That was anti-climatic."

They were about to try again when the messenger window popped up.

BuzzardBreath: You two coming to dinner or what?

DragonflyGirl: Be right there, Mr. Samson.

Abby shut the computer down and put it away, then opened the window. "Meet you over there, Mars-Bars." Once he'd climbed out she replaced the screen and locked the window. "Come on, Dommy. Let's spend some time with sane people."

Dominic laughed. "Sane and the Samsons only belongs in the same sentence with 'are not' in between."

"Still more sane than Mr. Davidson."

"I'll give you that one."

"DAMMIT!" Marlon's words were followed by the rattling sound of something hitting the floor. "What is *with* this game? Did we miss a clue somewhere?"

Abby looked up from the pages of the fifth *Harry Potter* book. "Watch the walls, please. And don't forget you owe Felice a dollar."

"How can you take this so calmly? This thing is kicking our butts!"

"I'm used to disappointment," she replied. She understood Marlon's frustration. They'd been trying for three days now, but no matter what they "said" to the dragon it attacked. Once, they'd managed to kill it but had *still* gotten the "game over" message. "Give it a rest. You're stressing yourself out."

"I've never seen a game I couldn't beat eventually."

"Maybe Grandpa Nick's a smarter programmer than the others were." Abby turned the page. "You know, you're right. These *are* good books."

"I still can't believe you're reading them this fast." Marlon shut the laptop off and shut it, then went and picked up the tumbler of pens he'd knocked over. He picked them up, each pen rattling against the plastic. "It took me a month just to read *one*."

"I don't have a job." She put a bookmark in the book and sat up on the side of the bed. "This is gonna sound *really* dumb... Drew Davidson offered to give us a ride out to Grandma's."

Marlon almost dropped the tumbler. "*Us*. You and me. *Us*." He put the tumbler back on the desk and turned to look at her. "You're kidding right?"

"Nope, he said no reason he couldn't take both of us." She kicked her feet. "I'm… thinking about taking him up on it."

"*Why?*"

"I'm with the little wasp." Dominic yawned and stretched. "Why would you want to subject yourself to his company?"

Abby reached up and played with her locket. "Mostly, I'm hoping to open some eyes."

Marlon sighed. "Abby, look. There is nothing you can do about people like Drew's dad, OK? The only thing getting him to spend more time with me and Felice will do is get his father in an uproar and get him in trouble, which will then spill over onto *you* once your aunt hears about it."

"It's more... when he's not around his dad so much, Drew doesn't seem like such a... What's the word?"

"Total prick?"

"Three dollars." Abby folded her arms. "Seriously, Mars-Bars."

"Hey, if the shoe fits." Marlon turned the chair around and sat facing her. "Maybe I'm wrong, but the guy's been a jerk for as long as I can remember. One basketball game's not gonna change that."

"Still say he's a two-faced little creep." Dominic kneaded the bed with his claws. "He only started being halfway nice to those kids after you put your foot down. Don't forget, if Gladys has her way, you'll be walking down the aisle with him."

"I know," she said, shrugging because she was, again, answering both. "But just because his father doesn't give others a chance is no reason not to give him one. It's one visit. How bad can it be?"

"I hate questions like that." Marlon shook his head. "Fine, set it up. Just don't hit me when it comes time to say 'I told you so'."

"Thank you so much for the vote of confidence." The phone rang and she jumped up, running into the kitchen to answer it. "Lynde residence, Miss Palmer speaking, may I ask who's calling?"

"I see you still remember your phone manners." Aunt Gladys' voice came through clearly. "I'm just checking in on you dear. Are you getting along all right?"

"Just fine, Aunt Gladys." Abby pressed a finger to her lips as Marlon followed her. "I was just reading for a bit."

"Good, good. Like I've always told you, read and you will stay out of trouble."

Abby smiled. She had heard the same advice from her grandmother as well. "So how is your trip going, Aunt Gladys?"

"Just wonderful dear! I've taken so many pictures! It's beautiful!" Gladys paused and Abby could hear ice rattling. "I was glad to hear you attended the service. I am so sorry I didn't make arrangements for you. I just was so excited."

"It all worked out in the end. Marlon's grandfather took me."

"Yes, I heard about that. Dolores spoke with her husband just this evening. I must admit I'm impressed he showed proper respect. Mr. Davidson said he was silent all through the service."

Abby bit her lip. "The sermon was on the evils of the world's pleasures. How anything that draws you away from your Christian duty is wrong and should be avoided at all costs – even something so simple as a game."

"That's very true, dear. I'm glad the elder Mr. Samson got to hear that. It just might save him."

"He doesn't need to be *saved,* you bitter old bat!"

Dominic hush!

"He got more out of it than I did. We discussed it on the way home."

"Wonderful! Now if that only trickles down. Do you have any plans this week, dear?"

"I might go see Grandma," Abby admitted.

"That will be good for Gail. We'll I'm going to get off here, mustn't run up the bill. Good-bye, dear. I love you."

"I love you, too, Aunt Gladys," Abby said. "Take care." She hung up the phone and looked at Marlon. "Well, Mr. Davidson was sharing and caring."

"I'm not surprised." A knock sounded at the front door. "Sheesh! What'd this place turn into? Grand Central Station?"

"Bedroom, now!" Abby headed for the door.

CHAPTER 22

Speak of the Devil, thought Abby, *and he's bound to appear.* She opened the door, leaving the chain in place. "Hello, Mr. Davidson. What brings you by?" *And is your father out in the car this time?*

"Just in the neighborhood," said Drew, running his hand through his hair. "I wanted to see if you had any plans this week, what with your aunt out of town."

"Actually," said Abby, smiling, "I was just thinking of calling you. Is that offer to take Marlon and I to visit my grandmother still good?"

Drew looked surprised. "Of course it is, why wouldn't it be? Are you wanting to go this week?"

"If it's not too much trouble. I think it would give everyone a chance to get to know each other on neutral ground." She arched her neck and tried to look past him. "Would you and your father like to come in?"

"My father's at home. Like I said I was in the neighborhood – had to pick up dinner since casserole is getting old. I better be getting home." Drew put his hands in his pockets. "How about tomorrow? Say three?"

"That sounds fine, we'll see you then. Thank you." Abby shut the door, glancing down at the disapproving dragon. "That went well. Now, if he doesn't tell his dad we'll be good."

"Something tells me that boy keeps more from his parents than just his gaming habit." Dominic followed her back to her room.

"All clear?" asked Marlon. He bounced slightly on the bed. "Whew, that was close. So who was it?"

"Drew. He agreed to take us to see Grandma tomorrow at three. Can you make it?"

Marlon rolled his eyes. "Yes, Abs, I can make it. I just think this is ridiculous. You're not going to change anything anymore that *Path of the Dragon* did."

"It never got a chance to," she replied, picking the *Harry Potter* book back up. "If something never gets a chance, you never know if it works or not."

Drew arrived on the dot the next day. He got out and opened the car door. "Beautiful day, isn't it?" He gestured to the backseat. "Hop in, Samson. How have you two been?"

Marlon slid into the seat. "Been better, been worse."

"Just getting some reading done," said Abby as she sat down in the passenger seat. "How have you and your father been, with your mother gone?"

"Bet you two are enjoying the guy time," Marlon added. "Not having to worry about making a mess for a few days has to be fun."

Drew shook his head. "Father wouldn't stand for it if the house was out of order. 'Cleanliness is next to Godliness'." He sighed. "Mother left frozen dinners she made, but the lack of home cooking is driving him nuts."

"What, he can't cook?" Marlon tilted his head. "Heck, even Grandpa can cook, admittedly instant stuff, but it's still food."

"My father wouldn't know a saucepan from a frying pan," said Drew then flinched. "I mean, he hasn't had to cook in so long he just doesn't remember how."

"Mom taught me to cook when I was ten," Marlon said, leaning back in the seat. "She said that way I could take care of myself. I'd only 'have a woman because you want one, not because you need one'." He folded his arms behind his head. "Then again, my parents aren't normal."

"Normal is *vastly* over-rated." Drew turned on the radio then quickly moved to change the channel when *Amazing Grace* came on.

"You can play that stuff, it doesn't bother me." Marlon sat up and jerked his thumb at Abby. "She's as bad as my grandfather with the Christian music."

Drew looked interested. "Really? What bands?"

"Something with stripes," Marlon answered then looked at Abby. "And DC something..."

"Stryper and DC Talk," corrected Abby, rolling her eyes. "Seriously Mars-Bars, we've known each other since *grade school* and you can't get my favorite bands right."

"I wouldn't say either of those names too loud around my father." Drew shook his head. "I swear I missed a lesson in Sunday School because I just don't... get it."

Dominic raised his head from his forepaws. "Where was this confusion at his parents' dinner?"

"You didn't talk like this when Aunt Gladys and I were at your house for dinner."

"You've never talked like this *at all* that I've ever heard." Marlon crossed his arms in front of him and leaned back again. "Who are you and what have you done with Drew Davidson?"

Drew kept his eyes on the road. Well..." He glanced over at Abby. "When I told you I played RPGs, you didn't judge me for it."

"Wait," said Marlon boisterously, "you do RPGs? Seriously? That's cool!"

Abby fought not to roll her eyes.

"You'd think that," Drew said with a smirk. "I forgot you're the guy with his nose in his Game Boy all the time."

"Better than buried in a b –" Marlon caught himself. "I mean, uh, um..."

"Yeah," said Abby, crossing her arms. "I'd rethink that statement if I were you."

"Anyway," said Drew, taking back control of the conversation, "being honest about it felt good, so I'm going to try and be more upfront with you guys."

"You 'guys'." Marlon stared at him then facepalmed. "OK, look – what is *with* you lately?" He ignored Abby's gesture to stop. "You don't like me. You've *never* liked me or my sister, yet all of a sudden you're all buddy-buddy and it's *creepy*. Excuse me if I'm not buying it."

Drew twisted his lips into a frown. He came to a turn, took it, then reached down and set the cruise control. "I don't know you. I just know what my father *says* about your family, and how much Mrs. Lynde complains about her niece's friendship with you – when she's not bragging about what a good missionary she is."

Um, I'm sitting right here? Abby looked between the two boys. She wondered how many people had seen this side of Drew – or if this side of him was real at all. But what motivation did Drew have to be their friend? Was there anything to gain, or was he truly trying to make amends? Abby wanted to give him a chance, but she knew Marlon wasn't easily persuaded by the 'new' Drew. "That's my aunt for you."

Drew didn't look at her, but he made a face like he'd remembered that he was talking about her. "Really, I do my darndest not to get on my parents' bad side. Everything I do, and I do mean *everything*, they take as a reflection on them. I cannot screw up because that makes them look bad."

"Which is why you flirt with every girl at school," said Abby, folding her arms. *Might as well get this out in the open.* "That's *really* Christian."

Drew's face fell. "Yeah, that's kind of going to stop. I mean the 'boys will be boys' line worked for a while but I, um, well..."

"Am dealing with my parents thinking it's time I settled down," finished Dominic, growling slightly. He looked up at her. "Why did you think this was a good idea again?"

I'm beginning to ask myself that. You could cut the tension with a knife. Abby scrambled to come up with something to say before Marlon beat her to it.

"Deep subject." Marlon smirked. "So a change of heart, huh?"

"Yes, Samson." Drew said, his tone cool. "So what is your grandmother like, Miss Palmer? I've heard some from Mrs. Lynde, but I'd like your perspective."

Abby fought the urge to shake her head. *"Well." "Deep subject."* She sighed. *Maybe but we won't be getting anything else out of Drew for awhile.* She unfolded her arms and made herself relax. "Grandma is a wonderful person, if a bit eccentric." Abby smiled. "She hasn't really slowed down much, she just isn't up to the house work and likes being around the friends she's made among her neighbors. It's a very nice community."

"She's Catholic?"

"Yes," she bit out. "She is. She attends mass every Sunday when her health permits. She is very secure in her faith." *And if you rub that in her face or try and convince her she's "wrong" I will punch you all over again.*

'Mrs. Lynde made it sound like you ministered to her as well as the Samsons." Drew shifted gears literally. "I'm guessing she just assumes as much."

Abby glanced in the mirror at Marlon as she told Drew about her grandmother and saw that he was gripping his arms so hard he was likely going to have bruises. "Aunt Gladys knows how committed Grandma is to her faith," she said, neither denying nor confirming his suspicions. "You're going to need to turn at that next intersection."

"Thank you."

Marlon shifted in his seat. "So you RP? What type?"

"I'm not into the pagan nonsense of D&D," Drew replied then drew a deep breath. "Dang it, I'm too used to talking like that... I'm just not big on playing a wizard or whatever. I don't know what kind you'd call the one I'm on. It's mission-based mostly."

"Mission-based is cool." Marlon sat up, resting his arms on his knees. "And yeah, in a world where there's magic, people tend to god-mod too much. There's nothing worse than an OP character."

The rest of the drive was a back-and-forth on the pros and cons of the differing types of online roleplay. Most of it went over Abby's head, and she ignored what she did understand, fearing Drew could realize she had more than theoretical knowledge and rat her out. She breathed a sigh of relief when they pulled up in front of her grandmother's. She unbuckled her seatbelt and got out of the car before either of the boys opened her door for her. She walked to the door and rang the bell, one ear on the boys' conversation.

Gail opened the door, smiling. "Well, isn't this a pleasant turn of events? Come in, dears, come in." She looked over the pair behind Abby. "Hello there, Mr. Samson. And who might you be, young man?"

"Drew Davidson, ma'am," he replied, taking her hand and kissing it. "Thank you for your hospitality."

"My, what did I do to have *two* gentleman's company?" Gail lead the way to the living room. "May I offer you three something to drink?"

"Ice water will be fine, ma'am."

"Pish, water when I have lemonade? I think not. Abby dear will you come help me in the kitchen?"

"Of course, Grandma."

Once they were out of sight, Gail lowered her voice. "Why is the boy Gladys is trying to pair you off with *here*?"

Abby rubbed the side of her head then got out the pitcher and tray. She'd been asking herself that. "I'm hoping to change people's opinions of each other and decrease hostility, especially with school starting. That would be nice, right?"

"I see," said Gail as she got out four glasses. "I hope your plan succeeds then." When they arrived back in the living room the boys were seated and animatedly continuing the conversation they had begun in the car. "It's nice to see young people getting along." Gail set the glasses on the table and sat down. She picked her card deck up off the table and began to shuffle. "Can I interest you young'uns in a game?"

Abby set the tray and pitcher down, poured them all a glass, then sat down beside her grandmother.

The boys agreed and Gail dealt out the cards for a game of Five Hundred Rum. They sat there a moment, taking in their hands. Abby's was going to be an uphill battle. "I hope my cards are good enough, ma'am," Drew said. "I hear you're quite the player."

"You remembered that after Abby socked you?" Marlon remarked.

"Abby did what now?" Gail froze, looking at her granddaughter in confusion. "You did what?"

"Went Hermione on his butt," said Marlon, gesturing with a thumb at Drew. He drew a candy bar out of his pocket and dropped it in the center of the table. "It ain't much, but it's more than points."

"Good memory, Little Wasp." Gail shook her head. "I swear, people claim each generation is a change from the last, but I just don't see it."

Abby gaped at her friend. *Traitor! Did he really just* —

"He did," said Dominic, lashed his tail. "I still say the boy deserved it."

"In her defense, ma'am, I did deserve it just as much as Malfoy." Drew's face was seven shades of red. He reached into a pocket. "I really shouldn't gamble, but then I don't think gum counts anyway." He dropped a pack of mint gum on top of Marlon's candy bar.

Gail shuffled her cards. "Well boys, I'm afraid I'm worse off than either of you." She pulled a peppermint out of her pocket and added it to the pile.

Abby lay her cards face down on the table and rummaged in her pockets. She came up with a box of tic-tacs. "This is the most pathetic pile to play over."

"Could be worse," said Marlon as he rearranged his cards. "We could be playing for drugs."

"MARS-BARS!"

CHAPTER 23

The card game got interesting when Drew finally broached the subject of religion. "So, about this praying to statues thing," he said and lay down a pair of aces. "How does that work?"

Gail shifted her hand and shook her head. "Catholics don't pray to statues, dear, sorry to burst your bubble." She laid four kings on the table. "Your move."

Abby fought not to smile. *Drew's in for a surprise if he thinks he's gonna knock Grandma out of with those default objections.*

"The second commandment says no idols." Drew waved his hand at the crucifix on the wall. "What do you call that?"

"If you bothered to read the ten commandments," said Gail, gesturing for Marlon to take his turn. "You would know that what the Lord forbid was the adoration of images, not their creation."

"How you figure?" Drew looked genuinely curious.

"He commanded Moses to make the brass serpent, did He not?" Gail kept her eyes on her cards. "He commanded the Ark of the Covenant to be built, with images upon it, did He not?"

Drew blinked. Clearly neither of these things had ever occurred to him. "OK, maybe that's right. But you can sin as much as you want and then when you go to confession, *boom*, forgiven! And you can go out and do it all over again and just go back."

Marlon rolled his eyes. "Your move, Abs."

Abby drew a card and tossed one into the discard pile. "You might as well save your breath," she warned. "Grandma can destroy every objection to the Catholic faith you can come up with."

Marlon rolled his eyes. "Way to ruin the show, Abs."

"When your husband studies the faith day and night, you can't help but pick some of it up." Gail reached out and lightly slapped Marlon's hand. "And don't you roll your eyes young man. Wasp made some of the same objections during his arguments with Nick."

"Sorry, ma'am." Marlon rubbed his hand then looked at Drew. "And Wasp is my grandfather before you ask. He usually credits the Dragon – Nick Whelan – with his conversion."

"Anyway, as to your assumption, Mr. Davidson, a Catholic who acts in such a way clearly has no understanding of the sacrament. When you confess your sins, you are *supposed to* repent and make every effort not to make those mistakes again. You're allowed mistakes because to err is human."

"Right. Well," said Drew, clearly grasping at straws. "Catholics changed the bible!"

Gail slapped her cards face down and walked over to a bookshelf. She took down a book and handed it to Drew. "Did we really? Sonny, without *our* bible you wouldn't have yours."

Abby recognized the book, a collection containing the four most popular versions of the bible. She had one herself; Gladys allowed her to keep it when Gail had said Abby could see for herself which version was the truth. "Or do you doubt how you've raised her so much that you think a little exposure with turn her away?" was how she had challenged Gladys. She smiled. *Game, set, and match.*

Drew kept turning pages, staring. "What do you mean we wouldn't have ours?"

"King James would have had nothing to translate *from* had the Church not kept the scrolls." Gail sat back down. "You can keep that if you like."

"What?" Drew almost dropped it. "But – but ma'am I couldn't –"

"Boy," said Gail, giving him a look. "I keep parallel bibles just for situations like this. It's yours. Maybe next time you visit you'll have a more open mind." She laid the last of her cards on the table. "And I'm out. Add it up."

Dominic snickered. "Anyone who dares come against that lady simply gets their asses handed to them."

Will you watch the language? Abby laid her cards down and added up her score. She passed the pad to Marlon. *If you weren't just in my head I'd start a swear jar for you.*

"Since I *am* in your head, maybe you should set the jar up for yourself?"

Funny, scales-for-brains, funny.

Drew stared at the bible until he sat it beside him and started adding up his cards. "Thank you, ma'am."

"You're quite welcome, Mr. Davidson." She took their scores. "And I win." She smiled. "Round Two?"

"You weren't kidding when you said she was a card shark." Drew buckled his seatbelt and started the car. He glanced at the bible on the console beside him. "I don't know what my father's going to make of this."

"Hey, Davidson?" Marlon leaned back in his seat again. "Quick question: when did you read *Prisoner of Azkaban?*"

Drew jolted and smacked his head on his seat. "Say what now?"

"Last I checked, your dad was dead-against *Harry Potter.*"

"Wondered who would point that out," said Dominic. He curled up beside Marlon in the backseat.

"I've never read the book," said Drew, pulling out onto the main road. "I did see the movie and I gotta admit that kid's a creep. Who laughs when you get someone's pet killed?"

"That does sound like a pathetic thing to do," said Abby. She kept her eyes on her hands. "And I am sorry for hitting you, but –"

"You got nothing to be sorry for," said Drew. He glanced into the rear view mirror. "I on the other hand, do. It doesn't mean much, Samson, but I am sorry."

Abby looked in the mirror to see Marlon's eyes narrow. *Oh, no, please don't –*

"I reserve judgment," said Marlon through his teeth. "I don't trust you, Davidson, and don't think playing nice is gonna change that overnight. In my family, actions count more than words. So if you're sorry, prove it." He folded his arms across his chest. "I appreciate the fact you're not shuttin' me and my sister out lately, but I keep waitin' on the other shoe to drop."

"And I've never given you any reason not to." Drew turned on the radio. "So I think that's fair. I'll keep that in mind from now on."

Abby shook her head. "Does this mean we can call ceasefire?"

Marlon shot her that grin. "Works for me."

"Agreed," Drew chimed in. "Ceasefire."

CHAPTER 24

"You have any books on shape-shifters?"

Ava looked up from restocking the shelves to find a tall man speaking with Mr. Burton. She returned to her task but kept an eye on her boss out of the corner of her eye.

"Of course we don't," replied Mr. Burton. "I don't carry any propaganda for those monsters!"

"Well, you are going to start." The man set a box on the counter. "The mayor believes educating the people on the enemy will be beneficial." The man flashed an ID card at Burton. "Is that clear?"

"Ava!" called Burton, waving her over. "Please get these stocked and make sure they're on display!"

She got down off the ladder and came over to the counter. She took the heavy box to the front window first and moved the books around before placing it front and center. Then she carried the box back to the reference section. Safely out of sight, she looked at the title.

The Wolf Among the Dogs: How to Identify and Defend Yourself from Shape-shifters.

She gulped and stocked them. I better tell the Society...

Abby clicked submit on her latest post. The forum stagnated during the week, making her grateful she normally only had weekends to play the game. She would have to wait for a reply from one of the Queens before her post would be "canon", but it felt like a good start. *I can't believe this week flew by so fast.* She sighed. *Just two more days of freedom*. She glanced at the chatbox on the bottom of the page and shook her head. *Looks like Marlon's on a Harry Potter kick.*

RandomWord: Oh, come on! Malfoy is a total pansy!

JennerTheRat: He's just trying to make his father happy, it's not like that's a bad thing.

RandomWord: It is when your dad's idea of fun is genocide.

JennerTheRat: The way Draco was raised he didn't know that! He clearly wanted out from the moment he joined! Kids always want to believe the best of their parents.

RandomWord: I'll give you that one. So you believe people can change? Not be what they were raised to be?

JennerTheRat: Some people change. You see it every day. Not everyone can or wants to, but that doesn't mean they can't.

GreenQueen: OK, Plato and Socrates, knock off the debate. This is a chat not a discussion forum.

DragonflyGirl: Isn't this kind of thing going to come up in the RP? How good and evil isn't black and white and such?

GreenQueen: Look, new kid, knock it off OK? Don't go trying to mini-mod I've got it under control and if I don't WhiteQueen does.

Abby started to reply when her messenger window popped open.

RandomWord: Don't try and defend yourself. GreenQueen doesn't take being corrected well.

DragonflyGirl: Seriously, Mars-Bars?

RandomWord: Turn the other cheek, Abs. It's not worth it.

With a sigh, Abby typed, "Glad to hear it. I've got to go to bed. See you all when I get a chance" in the forum chat and logged out. She typed, "There, happy?" to Marlon in their usual chat.

RandomWord: Discretion is the better part of valor.

DragonflyGirl: You are so weird.

RandomWord: You have no idea!

Rolling her eyes, Abby bid Marlon good-bye and then did a double take at the laptop's clock. *When did it get so late?* She closed the laptop. *Third time this week. It's too easy to get caught up chatting with everyone.* She yawned. *I really do need some sleep.*

"What do you want?" In a cold sweat Abby stared up at the dragon as she shouted the words. "I just don't know!"

"You know," said the dragon, it's fiery breath lighting the chamber, "you've always known. SAY IT!"

"I don't know! I swear I don't KNOW!" She screamed as fire filled the cavern. She felt the heat against her skin, fought to get away when a ringing sounded from somewhere. Wait, ringing?

Abby bolted upright in her bed, the sound of the phone cutting her nightmare short. She looked at the clock and stared. *It's four pm already? Crap, there goes my day!* She got out of bed and ran to the kitchen, barely making to the phone before it disconnected. "Lynde residence," she said with a yawn. "Abby Palmer speaking."

"Good evening, Miss Palmer." Drew sounded panicked despite his dictation. "I... I was wondering if you could do me a favor?"

"What kind of favor could *he* want?" Dominic demanded. He leaned into her side, growling. "Should have known that ride would have to be repaid."

"Maybe, depends on what it is, Mr. Davidson." Abby glared at the dragon. "I just woke up."

"Are you um, are you feeling well?"

"I'm fine," said Abby, shrugging even though he couldn't see. "Must have needed it. Are you going to tell me why you called?"

"Sorry, sorry, it's just uh, well..." Drew was scrambling. "Oh, this is a mess. We're out of the stuff Mom fixed and Dad's going to be home soon and if there's nothing on the table he'll flip."

"Did you just call your parents 'Mom and Dad'?" Abby rubbed her eyes, trying to fully wake up. She ran what he had said back over in her head. "Are you asking me to fix dinner?"

"Uh, yeah." Drew sounded embarrassed. "I don't know what to fix – never mind how, and I don't want any, I mean I don't –"

"I get it. I get it," said Abby, wracking her brain for some way to help. She could have just told him to look something up, but then she'd never hear the end of it when Gladys found out. "What have you got in the fridge?" She started pacing. "There's some simple things I can walk you through." Silence came from the other end of the line. "Hello?"

"You can't come over, maybe?"

Abby pinched her nose. *Should have seen that coming.* "One, being alone with anyone is against your parents' rules *and* my aunt's. Two, you're alone obviously, or your dad would be on the phone by now. Thus I can't come over because there's no one else there."

"Right," said Drew. "OK, let's see." She heard him put the phone down and mutter something before he finally came back on the line. "Uh, some onions, green peppers, a bag of potatoes –"

"Do you have *any* meat in the house, at all?" Abby fought not to sigh. "There's a couple things I can tell you how to fix otherwise..." She went to her own fridge. *OK, we still have hamburger.* "I can fix something here and you can come get it."

There was more noise on Drew's end of the line. "Uh, there's some chicken breasts in the freezer. That count?"

"Does that 'count'?" Dominic repeated. He covered his face with a paw. "That boy is hopeless."

"Yes, that counts," said Abby, closing the fridge. "OK, here's what you do. Put two of those in the sink, fill it with hot water." It took the better part of an hour to explain how to bake chicken and sliced potatoes with onions and green peppers. "You can read the directions on the biscuits right?"

"Yeah, I can handle that... Thanks, Miss Palmer. I owe you one!"

"You're welcome, Mr. Davidson." She debated correcting him. Her name *was* Abby. *But that would give him the wrong idea anyway.* "I need to start my own dinner, take care." After he said good-bye she hung up the phone.

Abby tapped her fingers on the counter. *I really don't want to cook.* She opened a can of chicken noodle soup and got out a package of crackers. "I wonder why I slept so long. It's not like I've been doing a lot lately." She put a bowl of the soup in the microwave.

"You've been reading non-stop and trying to beat that game." Dominic curled up at her feet. "That takes a toll on your brain, if not your body."

"There is that," she said, taking her bowl to the table. "It can't be that hard. Grandpa wouldn't have made the game impossible to beat."

"You would think that," said the dragon. "Who knows? Maybe it's just his last joke."

"I hope not." She thought back over her dream. "That dragon kind of looks like you."

"What dragon?" Dominic asked innocently. "Oh, the one in the game? Yeah it does look like the stuffed one." Dominic's tail swished as he lay under her feet. "He just couldn't think of more than one design."

"I guess." She blew on the spoonful and ate in silence. She stared unseeingly at the *Footprints* plaque on the wall. "I wonder what the dang password *is*. It can't be more than one sentence there's not enough room."

"Maybe you'll find it in the journal."

"That would be cheating." Still, after she finished her soup and put the bowl away, Abby went back to her room and got out the journal. *It can't hurt to look, right?* She flipped past several passages of coding and computer language she didn't understand. *Can Marlon or Mr. Samson read this?* Finally she reached plain English.

These dreams... I need some real sleep. Either that or I've read the Screwtape Letters *too many times. Those two, always arguing. I hear this stuff even when I'm awake. It's like my conscience has taken on their voices. Still... the game is ready to present. I can't wait to watch them try and solve the last puzzle. It's so simple yet I doubt they'll get it on their own. That's going to be a laugh. This game is different from what's out now. I believe it will make a difference. And at least I got that stubborn plush done in time. Baby should be here any day now. God willing, by the end of the week things will be looking up.*

"Yeah, a real laugh, Grandpa." Abby flipped the pages, hoping for at least a clue or something, but the rest of the journal was blank. She looked back at the entry. She saw the date and realized the significance of what she'd just read. "July Twenty-Fourth, Nineteen-Ninety-One..." The day before she was born. The day before her grandfather died. *This is the last entry.*

Dominic reached out and knocked the journal from her hands. It fell to the floor with a thump. "Stop looking at it like you've seen a ghost. It's just some old ink on dead trees."

Abby glared at him then reached down and picked the journal back up. "How did you do that?" She turned the book over in her hands. "You... you touched it." A chill came over her as her heart skipped.

The dragon rolled his eyes. "Seriously? You just dropped it. You don't want to admit it so you're pretending I did it." He shook his head. "You know I'm not real."

Abby resisted the urge to roll her eyes as well. She returned the journal to the drawer. *You state the obvious way too much.* "I think I need more sleep." She quickly shut off her lamp and curled up under the covers, silently saying her prayers.

"I still can't believe you read all seven of those in one week."

"Don't be so surprised, Mars-Bars." She smiled as they rode their bikes back to their apartment complex from the library the next afternoon. "I read fast that's all. At least now I'll know what you're talking about."

Marlon shook his head. "Reading fast is one thing, Abs. You binge read like some people watch TV shows." He smiled at her then swerved to avoid a pothole. "It's impressive."

Abby bounced along the sidewalk, crunching leaves beneath her wheels. Summer was definitely over. "Not really. I just like reading. It's quiet and I get to picture things my way."

"Whatever works for you." He zigzagged along, popping a wheelie now and then. "You've been doing really good in the RP."

"I just hope no one minds when I go back to only being active on the weekends."

"You'll be fine, Abs. Like I told you, people bail all the time."

Abby started to reply when her cell phone rang. Her heart raced as she scrambled to answer it. "Hello, Aunt Gladys." She fought to keep her voice level.

"Abigail, where *are* you, dear? I just got home and you're nowhere to be found!"

"If she bothered to check the note on the fridge, this wouldn't be a problem." Dominic shook his head. He jogged along with the bikes. "What is she? Blind?"

Dominic will you hush? "I'm on my way home from the library, Aunt Gladys," said Abby, fighting to keep the bitterness out of her voice. "I left a note for you just in case. I'm sorry traffic was bad and the bus was late."

Rustling came from the other end. "Oh, I see it here. I'm sorry, dear. Be careful all right?"

"I will. I love you. See you soon." Abby listened to Gladys return the endearment and end the call. She put the phone away, shaking her head. "Sometimes I wish I didn't have a phone."

"That thing is more of a leash," said Marlon. "You're *sixteen* and she still makes you use a phone that only calls home and nine-one-one."

"I'm honestly surprised she went that far." Abby sighed. "Well, at least school starts next week."

"You are the *only* person I know that actually *wants* to go back to school, Abs." Marlon shook his head. "Not that I blame you."

Abby sighed. *You have no idea.*

"So how was your trip, Aunt Gladys?" Abby hung her purse on the kitchen chair and got out the makings of tuna casserole.

"Wonderful, dear. I took so many pictures. Dolores and I had such fun!" Gladys leaned against the doorway. "And what about you? What did you do while I was away?"

That didn't take long. Abby had been hoping that her aunt would go on about her vacation through dinner. "Cleaned, checked out a few books at the library, went to see Grandma with Marlon and Drew Davidson – that was fun, he and Grandma got into a religious debate."

Gladys laughed and sipped her lemonade. "That had to be something. I'll bet Drew showed her a thing or two. Who won?"

"More like she showed him," said Dominic, chuckling. He curled up in the corner out of the way.

"I think it was more of a draw." Abby put the pasta on to boil. "I'm glad you enjoyed yourself, Aunt Gladys. Really, it was a good week."

"Yes, yes it was." The phone rang and Gladys answered. "Lynde residence, Mrs. Lynde speaking. Oh, hello, Dolores. How is everything at home? I see... Yes..." Gladys looked up at Abby with a calculating expression. "Yes, as a matter of fact she's at the stove now. Yes, I'll tell her. Thank you for calling and for a lovely week. See you in church." She hung up the phone. "Mrs. Davidson said to thank you for helping Drew fix dinner the other night. Apparently he bragged about how you walked him through it. Over the phone."

"And you're going to get out of shape because she didn't rush over there and show off what a good little housewife she would be." Dominic growled.

Abby placed the tuna can she'd opened on the counter and turned to face Gladys. "I couldn't go over there. No one else was home. If he hadn't had anything to fix I would have made something here and invited him to pick it up or them to come over."

"I'm very proud of you for handling that so responsibly," said Gladys, surprising her. "Admittedly, it would have been better to simply invite them over, but you did think it through instead of rushing over there unchaperoned."

"Thank you, Aunt Gladys." Abby turned back around and went back to opening the can. "I'm just glad I was able to help." She drained the tuna and started on the next can. "It's a shame neither Mr. Davidson knows how to cook, though. Drew sounded so worried."

"He knew who to call though, didn't he, dear?" Gladys smiled then turned toward the living room. "He's starting to depend on you! And why not when you're the definition of dependable? It's so sweet."

Dominic's low rumble would have shaken the floor as he watched her leave. "You … I wonder if that lack of food was a test you somehow *passed?*"

If it was, it was. Abby stirred the pot of pasta, her hand shaking a little. *Just be glad they haven't set a date yet. I'll be so glad when school starts.*

"Yeah, that will stop the match-making attempts." Dominic rolled his eyes.

I wonder why Drew started to open up to Marlon and I and then suddenly… just stopped? She got out the plates and scooped the casserole onto them. Something big must have happened. *He's changed so much in so short a time.*

"You're guess is as good as mine," said Dominic as he followed her into the dining room.

No kidding, scales-for-brains, since it is *the same as yours.*

CHAPTER 25

"Hey, Miss Palmer."

"Hello, Mr. Davidson." Abby hugged her books closer to her chest. She tried to ignore the cold looks sent her way from the other girls in the hall. The last thing she wanted was his attention. *How can he act like he doesn't completely agree with his parents, yet insist on this courtship?* After two weeks of his hovering, she wanted to scream.

"Mind if I walk you to class?"

Abby bit her cheek. She couldn't refuse without being offensive. "Don't make yourself late on my account." She glanced down at the dragon at her side. *Behave, you!*

"I am behaving," said Dominic, growling slightly at Drew. "It's the boy that had better mind his manners. If he crosses the line I'll –"

Growl at him? Dommy, you're not real remember? You can't do anything to him.

"No, but Bryan, his son, and grandson can."

You seem to be under the impression they would. Abby shifted her grip on the books. She could see her fourth period classroom door ahead.

"You're a fool if you think they wouldn't take care of this rat for you."

They reached the door and Abby dropped a half-curtsy to Drew. "Thanks for the company." Then she spun and escaped into the classroom. She took her seat in the back corner, getting out her homework. *Study hall is a Godsend.*

"Yes," said Dominic, curling up at her feet. "Considering you have *so much* to do at home."

Abby ignored him. Yes, doing her homework at school meant she had almost nothing to distract herself with in the evenings, but she had her last couple of driving lessons this week. Doing the work ahead of time meant she did not have to rush it when she got home. She spread her papers on the desk, wincing when her pencil hit the floor. She reached for it but someone else beat her to it.

"Here," said Melissa Hilary, holding it out to her.

"Thanks." Abby took it then watched out of the corner of her eye as Melissa took the desk beside her. "Can I help you with something?"

Once upon a time, she would have considered Melissa a friend. That was before she'd reached out to the Samson twins. Before people started to look at her like she had lost her mind for keeping company with such a "deviant" family. Melissa had not come within two feet of her willingly for at least two years.

Melissa did not respond a first. She got out her homework and set up her desk. Once everything was in place, she whispered, "What do you have that I don't?"

"What do you mean?" Abby busied her hands with her math homework.

"What does Drew see in you that he doesn't see in me?"

Crap! Abby looked up, but Melissa's eyes were still on her papers. She followed the other girl's example and returned her gaze to her own work. Abby's cheeks burned. "I don't think *he* sees anything in me."

"Don't play dumb. He's walked you to almost every class, sat with you and those twins at lunch..." Melissa blinked rapidly. "He's got it bad. Why you and not me?"

"It's not him," she said, frustrated. "It's his parents." Her grip on her pencil tightened as she stared at her homework. "Them and Aunt Gladys."

"You're kidding, right?"

"No, I'm not!"

"Miss Palmer!" called Mr. Cooper from the front of the class. "Please keep your conversations low enough so as not to disturb those working."

"Yes sir," replied Abby. She felt her face heat up. *I haven't been called out by a teacher since...* She could not remember when.

"She's just helping me with my math homework, Mr. Cooper." Melissa smiled in a way that was everything men seemed to like. "We'll keep it down."

"Thank you, Miss Hilary."

"Thanks," Abby whispered, squirming in her chair.

"Don't mention it." Melissa tapped her pencil against her desk.

"And I'm serious. This mess has more to do with what *they* want than anything else. It's like something out of a Jane Austen novel."

Melissa frowned. "That does explain why he said we couldn't see each other anymore."

"Say what?" Abby looked up again, catching herself before her jaw fell open.

"You heard me. I wondered why the sudden change of heart."

If he was dating Mel... She'd never really paid attention to who Drew hung around. He had always been such a flirt, so how could she tell which girl he was actually with? *"That's going to change."* Could this be the big thing Drew had avoided discussing?

Melissa shook her head. "I never thought I'd hear the 'it's not you it's me' speech." She looked up at Abby. "Which brings me back to my first question: what do you have that I don't?"

Now that she knew what Melissa meant, Abby tried to think it through. What *was* the reason for Drew's parents preferring her? She was a brown-eyed brunette who was too short and stocky. Melissa was blond, blue eyed and looked like every boy's dream. Both were polite to authority figures, neither swore... The only differences she could come up with between them were rather petty, so much so that Abby hesitated to say them out loud.

"Which means they *are* the reasons." Dominic yawned and placed his head on his paws.

Abby twirled her pencil in her fingers. "I don't know how to put this politely."

"So be blunt; I can take it."

"I go to church. I don't flirt. I dress modestly regardless of where I am," she said, tugging at the skirt of her school dress. "I don't wear jewelry aside from –" here she drew her locket and cross out from under her shirt before tucking them back in, "– these. I cook and keep house at home – and Heaven *knows* Aunt Gladys brags on that." She looked up at Melissa sadly. "It sounds petty as heck, but honestly those are the only differences between us I can come up with." She sighed. "I could be an extra on one of those *TV Land* shows."

Melissa did not reply, tapping her fingers on her desk as she stared down at its surface. Her gaze went distant in thought and her brow furrowed. She pursed her mouth. Finally, she said, "Can you teach me?"

"Teach you?" Abby blinked. "What?"

"Teach me how to act..." Melissa paused, clearing trying to think of the word. "Presentable? Proper? Whatever. Teach me how to get his parents' approval."

Abby looked up at Melissa. "Why should I help you? This is the most we've spoken in years."

Melissa met her gaze. "Do you like Drew?"

Abby rolled her eyes. "I think we could be good friends if our guardians would quit playing matchmaker. He's not as much of a stuck up jerk as I used to think. Please don't change the subject; why do you want them to approve of you? The truth, holding nothing back."

"We were dating for almost all of last year." Melissa started tapping her desk again. "He's a flirt – or he *was* – but you could tell he wasn't serious."

"I'll take your word for it."

"When we were dating, I really thought we had a chance at making it work, you know? Then out of the blue he says we can't see each other anymore. Then I get back to school to find he's chasing *you*. So." Her eyes hardened. "If this is all because his *parents* made him break it off, then I want to fix it. You don't want him anyway."

"That could work," Dominic noted. "If you can make her seem like a better candidate than you, they might get off your back."

Yeah, but...I don't want to set Drew up with someone he doesn't want to be with. It doesn't matter if it's me or Mel. He should choose who he spends his life with. She had to admit to the possibility. If Mr. Davidson had seen Drew with Melissa outside of school... it would have depended on what they were doing, but with his narrow world view, she could see Mel being labeled as a Jezebel.

"I can't promise that you'll get back with him. I *can* teach you how to behave so you're more 'proper,' but that doesn't mean it'll work." She looked Mel in the eye. "To be honest, you can't fake it – you'll have to *really* change."

"It's worth it," Melissa said. "My wardrobe's nothing to write home about anyway. I don't need the bling. I gotta admit, he made living 'Christian' sound pretty good."

"It is," she agreed. "Even with the weirdos in it." Abby held out her hand. "OK, I'll teach you what I can. I hope it *does* work out, but even if it doesn't you'll be attracting the right kind of attention for the future."

"Fair enough." Melissa shook her hand. She looked up as the bell rang. "Dang it, I didn't get a dang thing done!"

"Me neither," said Abby, gathering her homework. She thought as she put her papers in their folders. "You want to come over after school? We can get started."

Melissa smiled. "Works for me. Mind if I sit with you at lunch?"

"Seriously?" Abby stared at her. "Not at all." She narrowed her eyes. "Just not one *word* about the Samsons or deal's off."

"Scout's honor."

They walked out of the classroom together and found Drew leaning against the wall. His eyes popped before he nodded to both of them. "Miss Palmer. Miss Hilary."

"Hello, Mr. Davidson," said Melissa, nodding back. "We're off to lunch, care to join us?"

"Of course," he replied, averting his eyes. "So... hot dogs, huh? I wonder what's in those things?"

Abby watched how he reacted to Mel out of the corner of her eyes. Now that she knew to look, she could see it. *He acts like a kid caught with his hand in the cookie jar.*

"Because if his dad saw him, that's most likely what he *would* be."

Well, it shouldn't be too hard to change that. Mel's not a bad person.

"The Samsons aren't either; doesn't mean he likes them."

Sadly, Dominic had a point. Still... *It's worth a try.* She looked over at Melissa. *It'll be nice to see friends happy.*

"You consider him a *friend* now, do you?"

As a matter of fact, yes. He's been a lot nicer lately and everyone deserves a chance to change. She subtly kicked Dominic as they walked down the hall. *You be nice!*

The dragon rolled his eyes. "Yes, ma'am. Just watch you don't get burned again."

I don't think I will.

CHAPTER 26

"I'm sure Daddy could help with your wardrobe," said Felice. She was all smiles. "After all, he helped Mom when she decided she needed a change."

"I'd appreciate that." Melissa smiled back. "I just... I really want to think about the message I'm sending, you know?"

"Oh, yes!" Felice nodded. "Appearances shouldn't be the first thing people judge on, but they often are. Making a good impression is *crucial!*"

"Are you kidding?" Marlon leaned across the table toward Drew. "Raiden *rules*, man! The guy's unstoppable!"

"Johnny's the best, and you can't change my mind."

"A movie star versus a *god?* Come on!"

"I think calling a guy who can do magic tricks a *god* is a bit of stretch."

"*Magic tricks?* Summoning lightning is a *magic trick?*"

Abby looked around the table, pleasantly surprised. *No fireworks... yet. Everyone's getting along a lot better than I thought.* Granted, Drew had been sitting with her and the Samsons pretty much since school had started, but seeing Felice and Melissa bonding over clothes was something she hadn't expected. *Though I should have. Anyone that actually gets to know her loves Felice.*

"You really think my old clothes can become presentable?" Melissa played with her hair then took a bite of her hot dog. Once she had swallowed, she added, "I was just going to donate them."

"Mom used to wear some..." Felice paused. "How did she put that?"

"Slutty," said Marlon bluntly, wincing as his sister smacked him. "Ow! OK, trashy! That better? OUCH! Lice!"

Abby laughed. "You know he's right, Felice. That's exactly what Mrs. Samson would call it."

"*Both* of them." Marlon rubbed his head. "Grandma and Mom used to – OW! SIS!"

"Stop airing dirty laundry, then." Felice dusted off her hands. "Anyway, Mom had some really revealing dresses, and Daddy managed to make some really nice ones out of them. I'm sure he could show you how to do the same with yours."

"I'd like that," said Melissa, smiling again. "So what do you like to do?" She looked over at the boys. "I gather hot-shot here's a gamer."

"Who doesn't know that?" Drew laughed. "He's usually got his nose stuck to a screen."

"Better than spending all my time on a basketball court!"

"Yeah, actually moving around is so stupid."

"I take archery," said Felice, cutting off the debate. "And help Mom with her garden. She's really good with coaching seeds."

"In more ways than one. Ow!" Dominic growled softly. "Hey, don't blame me, you were thinking it!"

Mind out of the gutter. Abby smiled. "You should see her flowers, Mel. They're so pretty and some are *huge*. The vegetables are really good, too."

"Wow, a garden in the city?" Melissa sounded honestly surprised. "That is impressive."

"You can come over this evening if you'd like."

"I was supposed to go over to Abby's." Melissa looked nervous. "She's helping me with some things."

"Really?" said Drew. "What things?"

"She's just got some skills she let get rusty," said Abby. *That's true, technically.*

"It's nice of you to help out." Drew nodded. "Seriously, you're a real humanitarian."

"She'd do the same if the situations were reversed." Abby shot Melissa a smile. "Right?"

"Of course," she replied. "What are friends for?" She took a drink of her water. "Still, Felice, we'll have to set up something. Here." She got out her notebook and scribbled her number on a page, then ripped it in half. "OK if we trade numbers?"

"Sure," said Felice, writing her number on the other half and pocketing Melissa's. "Maybe we can even have a sleepover!" She looked up at Abby. "You could come and we could watch movies –"

"Slow down, Lice," said Marlon, patting her hand. "Don't get ahead of yourself."

"I think that sounds nice," said Melissa. "But will your parents be OK with it?"

Felice's smug smile said it all. "They'll have no problem at all."

Abby shook her head. The bell rang again and they all carried their trays to the trash and went their separate ways.

"Good afternoon, Aunt Gladys." Abby led Melissa inside. "I have a guest today; I hope that's all right?"

"A guest?" Gladys looked up from her chair and did a double-take. "Miss Hilary, long time no see. How are you, dear?"

"Just fine, Mrs. Lynde." Melissa curtsied. "Sorry to drop by unannounced."

"It's all right, Miss Hilary." Gladys smiled. "Though please do call next time. Are you girls study buddies?"

"Pretty much," said Melissa. She wrapped a strand of her hair around her finger. "Do you mind if we study in Abby's room?"

"Not at all, dear, just leave the door open."

"That was easy," Melissa said as they walked down the hall. "You made it sound like she'd flip out." She looked back over her shoulder. "This place hasn't changed much."

"You're a girl, and you're not Felice." Abby switched on her bedroom light. "Yeah, well, Aunt Gladys likes things just-so."

"That Samson girl's a lot nicer than I thought." Melissa put her books down on the trunk. "A bit... uh, what's the word?"

"Acts like she's on a constant sugar high?" suggested Dominic. He curled up in the corner and lay there snickering.

"Felice looks at the glass half-full." Abby put her books on her desk. She turned and sat on her bed. "Take a seat."

Melissa sat beside her. "So, what's the plan?"

What was *the plan?* She could tell Mel to change her style of dress, go to church with her and Aunt Gladys, stop flirting... "I don't believe I'm saying this…" Abby took in a deep breath before asking: "Have you accepted Jesus as your Lord and Savior?"

"You're kidding, right?"

Abby rested her arms against her knees and leaned forward. "I wish. There's a bible verse that pretty much says 'don't marry non-believers'. I..." She looked at her door and lowered her voice. "I don't really think it's my place to push religion on anyone. But that's a big thing in your cons column right now. And it's not something you can fake."

Melissa looked at her feet, kicking them slightly. "I believe in God, Abby. I just don't like listening to sermons." She sighed. "Even Drew's *dad* is a bit over the top. I don't like how nosy churches seem to be."

"I know that feeling," she admitted. "Still, you realize if you want Drew, his parents are part of the package, right?" When Mel did not reply, she added, "This isn't a fairy tale. He's not going to just dump his parents for love – that doesn't happen in the real world."

"I know if this goes all the way, I'm stuck with his parents. Given the way gossip goes, I'd end up a preacher's wife." Melissa blushed and covered her mouth. "I mean..."

"You meant what you said." Abby smiled. "And that's *exactly* the attitude you want to have." She looked around her room. "Your goal in life should be being a good wife and mother."

"Whoa!" Melissa threw up her hands. "Let's not get ahead of ourselves. I'm not even down the aisle yet. Too early for kids."

"We're not even in college yet and Drew's parents are hunting for his wife. You wanted to know what the Davidsons' are looking for," she replied. "That's it. A good Christian girl who is chaste, polite, and whose only life goal is being a housewife. Education not required."

Melissa looked at her for a moment. "They've only got two out of three with you, don't they?"

Abby nodded. "They just don't know it. Aunt Gladys would see me married this year if she had the chance."

"Geez. Guess we should actually do our homework." Melissa reached for her math book. "So what *do* you want, if not to be a housewife?"

"In layman's terms, I want to be a shrink." Abby got up and got her own book. She laid beside the other girl on the bed. "If you need any help, feel free to ask."

"I'll keep that in mind." Melissa started on the problems. "A shrink, huh? Well, at least you wouldn't have to see one again."

"That was a *long* time ago, Mel!" Abby's cheeks burned. *Some things never change.*

"I know," she replied with a grin. "And it still gets under your skin. Relax, I'm teasing you."

Dominic raised his head. "You need to toughen your skin, Abs. You take things far too literally."

Oh, shut up, you overgrown lizard! Abby made a face. "I know, it's just... I'm not crazy."

"Crazy people never think they are, remember?"

She rolled her eyes and tried to brush it off. "Very funny."

The girls worked in silence, moving on from math to science to literature. They finished within an hour.

"This was nice," said Melissa as she gathered her things. "We should do it again sometime." She smiled. "I think... I think I owe you an apology, Abby. Maybe we *shouldn't* judge by the company one keeps."

"Or at least get to know that company before making judgments." Abby smiled again. "By the way, my time spent with the Samsons is ministry work. Showing them another way."

Melissa burst out laughing. "You sure you don't want to be a comedian? Admittedly it doesn't pay as well..." She could not seem to stop snickering. "But I think you'd be good at it."

"Do you want to call your mom to come and get you?"

"No." Melissa's body language locked down at the mention of her mother. "She's going to flip enough as it is. I'll walk home."

Abby nodded and walked her to the front door.

"Headed home, dear?" asked Gladys. "A young lady shouldn't be out alone. May I call someone to pick you up?"

"I already offered, Aunt Gladys." Abby looked over at her aunt. "She does just live in the next building."

"And it's not that late, Mrs. Lynde. I'll be fine." Melissa tried for a curtsy. "Thank you for your hospitality." She escaped out the door.

"Such a nice girl," said Gladys turning her attention back to the preacher on the TV screen. "It's a shame how she's turning out though. Dressing like she does and getting the boys all worked up."

Abby debated for a moment then said, "She's planning on changing her behavior. That's really why she came over; she wanted my advice."

"Really?" Gladys' surprise was all too genuine. "Well, isn't that something? Abby dear, you really have a way with our Lord's lost sheep." She giggled. "Maybe I should start calling you a sheepdog."

"Maybe," said Abby. *But please don't.* She escaped into the kitchen to start dinner. She cooked on autopilot, barely aware of what she was fixing. *I don't know which is stranger. Mel wanting my help or her and Felice actually bonding.* She turned the heat down. *Mel's got an uphill climb going. Just hope she's ready for it… or at least she doesn't blame me if it doesn't work out.* Even if Drew and Melissa got together, it only solved half of the problem. *Aunt Gladys will just start looking for another suitor.* Abby got down two plates and filled them. *I can't wait until I'm eighteen.*

CHAPTER 27

"There we go! See, I told you they could become something beautiful!"

Melissa spun around, blushing. The A-line dress she wore was far more modest now – it had only taken sewing two together. The hem had been lengthened and now fell at her ankle, and Melissa's entire arms were hidden under blue-and-white fabric that reminded Abby of blue jays. They'd added a little white peterpan collar to the dress, too. It helped that her wardrobe revealed less than what the twins' mother's once had. "Thank you, Mr. Samson."

Wendel just smiled. "Not a problem, Miss Hilary. Not a problem. You did your part." He bowed and left the room, most likely headed for his office.

Abby had to admit he was right. Melissa had come over almost every day, following instructions, and helping to turn her old dresses into much more presentable attire. The results not only showed her new respect for her own body, but her willingness to work to change. *Hopefully Preacher Davidson will see it the same way.*

"So which one are you going to wear to church this Sunday?" Felice helped to fold the rest of the dresses, putting them in the box her mother had provided.

"I think the one I have on," said Melissa smiling. "What do you think, Abs?"

She looked the dress over. She smiled. "I think it'll do nicely."

"We just need to find the right earrings and –"

163

"I think what I have on will be best," said Melissa, interrupting Felice. She brushed her fingertips over the silver studs. "Don't want anything too flashy."

Felice nodded. "Oh, right."

Abby brushed against her own studs, silently reminding her friend that less equaled more in Preacher Davidson's church. "I'm just glad Aunt Gladys managed to talk Mrs. Davidson into letting you join us. That can only help."

"So long as I remember not to make a fool of myself." Melissa took off the dress and put her T-shirt and mid-length skirt back on. "The only drawback to 'modest' clothes is how *hot* you get in them."

"Just wait until next summer," said Abby. "Then you can tell me all about it. Thin fabrics are your friends, so long as you have a good bra."

Felice snickered. "Good bra meaning old lady types. Skin-tone or white only. Heaven forbid they be even *slightly* sexy. Literally."

Abby rolled her eyes. "The last time I tried a 'sexy' bra, I itched for days! Sorry, I'll stick with my granny bra."

"Abby's got a point. You tend to fall out of those." Melissa brushed her hair behind her shoulder. "Still... keeping a few on hand for special occasions doesn't hurt."

"Chastity, remember?" Abby shook her head. "I swear, Mel. I swear."

"No, you don't, or you'd owe Lice here a lot of money." She laughed. "Hey, you can dress sexy for yourself. Sometimes it's nice to know you're dressed up to the skin."

"If you say so. I still say it's just uncomfortable."

"You looked good though, admit it." Dominic's grin made her face heat up.

Shut up, Scales-for-Brains!

164

"Abs, you all right there?" Felice reached out and felt her forehead. "You look a little hot. You're not getting sick are you?" She looked closer. "Dang, girl are you getting any sleep?"

Abby rubbed at her eyes, knowing the shadows under them just got darker every day. "I try, Lice, I try…" She sighed. *How many times did I wake up last night?* Her sheets had come undone from all the tossing and turning she had done. "Just… nightmares." She didn't want to go into detail.

"Ouch," said Melissa. "Maybe you need to try listening to music before bed?"

"The kind of music I like I can't play around Aunt Gladys." Abby yawned. "Need help carrying those home?" She nodded at the box.

"No, I got it. You ought to get home and take a nap." Melissa picked up the box. "You look beat, Abs, seriously."

Felice nodded. "Yeah, go crash Abby. Maybe you won't have nightmares since it's day time."

Abby could not think of a good argument, so she nodded. She hugged her friends then went back to her apartment. She flopped on the bed, tempted to just drop where she lay.

"You aren't going to check the RP?" asked Dominic, leaping up beside her. "It's Saturday and if you crash now you might not get another chance this week."

They'll survive without me one week, she thought, really too tired to speak. But now that she'd been reminded, curiosity ate at her. She finally got up and got the laptop.

The laughter of the rest of the society ran in Ava's ears. She lowered her head, blushing. "How was I supposed to know?" she asked. "No one mentioned it to me, and since I work in a bookstore you'd think someone would."

The Wolf Among the Dogs was a fake. It had been written by undercover members to spread false information so they could move more freely in the city. Who cared if it meant innocent animals might be slaughtered? They had more power to spread their agenda now. More room to topple the government and end this charade of protecting the people from the monsters under the bed.

At least that was the gist of what they'd told her. Ava was not sure she bought it. Still, she was given her new assignment – to make sure as many of those books sold as possible. She nodded her agreement and sat back down, listening to the others report.

Abby sighed. There were plenty of members so it was understandable that it took a while for her post to be approved, but to approve it only to make a joke out of it seemed pretty petty. Then again, she supposed she was lucky it had been accepted at all. She followed along for the rest of the "meeting" and then signed off. *Great, now I'm awake again. I might as well do something useful.* She sat the laptop beside her as she picked up the driver's guide. *I have to pass. I can't afford not to.* She was doing better but would that hold up on exam day?

"If you don't worry so much you'll do just fine." Dominic was curled up beside her. "Just relax and have a little faith in yourself."

"That's easy for you to say." Abby skimmed the pages for what felt like the thousandth time. "You don't have to take the test."

"You worry too much, I swear."

Within a few pages, she felt her eyelids getting heavy again. Abby blinked then yawned. *I'm so tired.* She put the book on her nightstand, shut the laptop down, and put it away. Then she crawled under her covers. *Just a quick nap...*

"Tell me the truth!" The dragon roared, its hot breath filling the cavern. "You've come to destroy me! Admit it!"

"I have not! I don't even know how!" Abby backed up against the cold, rocky wall. Her throat was raw from the smoke and her shouting. "Please, I just want to help you! Let me help you!"

"Liar! Where were you when we needed you?"

She froze at the sound of voices she had not heard for years, save on old home videos. No... no... Please no! She looked up, pain filling her as she stared into the charred faces of her parents. Their clothing and skin crumbled to ash even as she looked at them.

"You left us! You let us die!"

"No! No I didn't! I didn't know! I couldn't know!"

"LIES!" roared the dragon. "You are to blame. Now you can share their fate!" It let out a bellow of fire, engulfing her in the flames.

She closed her eyes against the light even as she screamed and the flames licked the inside of her mouth and throat.

Abby bolted upright in the bed, breathing heavy as she struggled to push the dream's images away. She looked over at the dragon lying against her.

Dominic raised his head, a concerned expression on his face. "Another nightmare?"

"Yes," she replied. She sat up against the headboard. "How many times am I going to have that dream? I know it's just my subconscious, but..." She shuddered. "It feels so real." She rubbed her chilled arms.

He crawled up and lay his head on her stomach, allowing her to pet his mane. "I don't know. It's too bad you can't beat that game – maybe then the dreams would stop."

"The game gave Grandpa nightmares, too." She could almost feel real fur under her hand as she stroked him. "Maybe it's just too creepy."

Dominic snorted. "I doubt it was the *game* alone that gave the bad dreams to its creator. Then again, you're more imaginative than he."

"You might have a point there." Abby closed her eyes again, this time drifting off into simple darkness.

It was a welcome relief.

"How long are you going to keep up this childish behavior?"

"Oh, come on, Annie," the deceiver said, grinning. "They're just dreams. They never hurt anyone." He leaned against the wall as they watched their charge sleep. "Least of all a little kid."

She is no longer a child, and it is your mistake that you cannot see that. The guardian focused on keeping her rest peaceful. He could not protect her from all of Bjarte's mind games, but any solace he could offer, he would. Aeneas glared at his rival. "You are nothing but a coward!"

"Said it before, and I'll say it again – we aren't as different as you like to pretend."

"You are wrong about that and so much else." He flexed his hand, longing to summon his staff. "Though, it's no surprise you believe your own lies. Your master does it quite well."

Bjarte chuckled. "You're the one wasting energy keeping her bad dreams away, Annie." He bent over with mirth. "Next you'll be guarding against the monster under the bed!"

I'm more concerned with the beast in her head. Aeneas frowned but fell silent. There was no use in trying to talk sense into such a creature. Bjarte thrived on nonsense and chaos and was incapable of comprehending anything logical. Then again, one of the things deceivers understood the least was something that went against all logic. Love. It forever baffled them. Oh, they knew how to pull at its strings and make use of it, but they could never understand it. Many the best laid plan of both guardian and deceiver had been thwarted by it. *Such as my last failure. Nothing is ever certain; I've learned that lesson. Still... I will not stand aside.*

CHAPTER 28

Abby stole a glance at Melissa where she sat beside her in the backseat of Mrs. Davidson's car. She fought not to smile at the picture she made.

Melissa appeared as a pious young lady, respectful and devout. Her hair hung below her shoulders and she'd tucked it behind her ears. Her dress reached her ankles and wrists, the neckline high. In all honestly she had overdone it in Abby's opinion, but it was obvious she had made an impression on their driver.

"I must say, Miss Hilary, you look lovely today." Mrs. Davidson glanced back at them in the rear view mirror and smiled. "Such a treat to see young women who know how to respect themselves."

"Thank you, ma'am." Melissa smiled back, brushing at her dress. "I really appreciate the ride as well. I hope it wasn't too much trouble."

"Not at all, dear. I'm quite happy to help others keep the fourth commandment."

They arrived without incident and wasted no time seating themselves. They folded their hands in their laps and waited for Preacher Davidson to begin.

He stepped out to the podium, smiling like Christmas had come early. He opened his bible and gestured to the congregation. "Welcome, my brothers and sisters! Today I turn your attention to Luke chapter fifteen. Note verses four through seven, where the Lord speaks of a shepherd that goes out after his lost sheep, and how the joy over the return of that *one* sheep is like the Father's joy when a sinner returns to him to him at last."

"I wondered how long it would take him to take a shot at her," said Dominic, his tail lashing like a whip. "Should have known he'd get right to it."

Abby sighed. *Will you hush for once?* She snuck a glance over at Melissa, but the other girl showed no sign of being disturbed by the content. Either Mel didn't realize he meant she was the lost sheep, or she was a good actress.

"Now look to James chapter five, verses nineteen and twenty. This verse reminds us of how important it is to reach out to the sinner, and bring him home to the Lord. In this we become that shepherd, do we not? At the very least we become his dogs, guiding lose members of the flock back to our Master. Think of the Father's *joy*, brothers and sisters, when the lost sheep comes home. Think that you have the power to give that joy to Him!"

WHAT!?! Abby looked over at Gladys, whose proud smile made her cringe. She swallowed hard when she realized it wasn't Melissa he was talking about.

"In Jeremiah chapter fifty, verses six through seven, the prophet laments on how his people have gone astray. We today are like him, brothers and sisters! We stand and look at our fellow man, lamenting on how he has fallen away from the Lord. But remember those previous verses! We have the power to *change* that! It is not only our ability, but our *duty* to bring the lost sheep home!"

"YOU –" Dominic jumped to his feet, his next words so blistering Abby choked.

DOMMY! She cleared her throat as she felt her face heat up again. *I can't believe you said that! And DON'T try to tell me I did!* She couldn't believe that had came out of her head.

"I'm not *real*, remember? So where else would it come from?"

Abby kept her eyes on Preacher Davidson. She did her best not to let her feelings show. Her hands clenched together so tight they hurt. She tuned out the rest of the sermon. She had never felt so *dirty* in her life. She shifted in her seat, her skin itched as she longed for the shower. It was worse than what he usually did to people. This wasn't indirect scolding. This was *praise,* and it made her sick. *I'm not a sheepdog!* She closed her eyes, wishing she could hide. *I don't round up anyone. I just hold the door open and try to lead by example!*

"And there's nothing wrong with that," said Dominic, still growling Davidson's way. "You'll bring more 'sheep' home that way than if you dragged them kicking and screaming. People need to come to the Lord of their own free will, not be guilted into it."

She tried to believe that. Silently, she began reciting her prayers. She did not want to be like Preacher Davidson, whose door only opened to the few who shared his beliefs exactly and followed the path he walked alone. She had never believed that. She did not think even Jesus Himself had felt that way. Jesus who dined with tax collectors and prostitutes? Jesus, who went to the sinners when they did not come to Him? Her eyes narrowed as she looked up at Davidson. *I'm not you!*

Melissa reached out and squeezed her hands for a second. When Abby looked over, Melissa smiled then subtly reached up and brushed at her head. The signal they had established: *Remember where you are.*

Abby nodded just barely. *Remember where you are, Palmer. Open hostility will get you nowhere.* She didn't understand it. She'd successfully controlled her emotions all this time. Why was it suddenly harder? What had changed?

"You've gotten older, for one thing." Dominic pressed against her legs. "You are growing up. You know your own heart now, better than you ever have before."

She liked the sound of that, but somehow it felt off. She had been better at hiding how she felt when she was younger, yes, but... *I don't want to have to hide,* she realized. *I shouldn't HAVE to hide!* She bit her cheek as she fought for control. From somewhere in her memory the words *"I ain't into hiding the truth"* floated to the surface. She ran the rest of the song through her mind when she placed the lyric, raising her head as she took the words to heart.

After the service, Abby followed her aunt and Melissa outside. She braced herself for the ride home. *I really don't want to get in the car with Mrs. Davidson.* She felt like she needed a few minutes to herself. Just a few minutes to put her mask back into place. *It's not like anything has changed,* she reminded herself. *My life's been nothing but half-truths since...* Since she had made the choice to hide Dominic's existence. She looked down at the dragon at her heels. *You need to leave.*

He looked up at her, startled. "Why? I've always been here for you, haven't I? Why would you want me gone *now?*"

I'm a grown-up now. That's what you keep telling me. Abby moved her gaze back to her great-aunt. *Grown-ups don't have imaginary friends. I have friends, Dominic. I don't need you anymore.* The words hurt to think. *I don't want to lose anyone else, but I can't hold onto you forever.*

"Don't say that!" The fear in his voice cut like a knife. "You can't send me away! We don't know what happens to forgotten imaginary friends!"

So it's about YOU and not me, then? She took a step back as Gladys and Melissa spoke with the Davidsons. This had to be dealt with. *Are you really protecting me, Dommy? Because I'm not sure anymore.* She blinked as tears pricked at her eyes. *I trusted you, I always have. Now you need to trust me. You need to go. Please, go!*

"NO!"

The declaration erupted in her head along with a world of pain. She grabbed the sides of her head as she hit her knees. Someone screamed and it took her a moment to realize it was her.

"Abigail!"

"Miss Palmer!"

"Abby!"

She heard Gladys, she heard Drew and Melissa, but she couldn't move. She clenched her teeth against the pain. *What the heck is happening?* Then as abruptly as it started, the pain stopped. She opened her eyes to find the blue gaze of the dragon staring at her.

"Are you all right?" he asked, one paw on her arm. His ears were back and he looked so concerned.

"Abigail, what's wrong?" Gladys cupped her chin and made her look at her. "What happened, dear?"

What did *happen?* Abby fought to understand it. She could not remember much. *I was walking behind Aunt Gladys... then...* "I don't know, I just... headache," she said. "Really bad headache." She reached up and rubbed at her temples, trying to get the remaining pain to fade. Her head felt like it had just been released from a vice.

"This is what happens when the Devil sees one of God's children following his teachings so well," said Preacher Davidson solemnly. "He attacks the strong of faith, for they are the true prizes. Stay the course, Miss Palmer. Do not allow the Enemy to defeat you."

"She wasn't possessed, was she?" Gladys looked frightened. She stood up and faced Preacher Davidson. "I mean, that was so *sudden!*"

"If she was, Sister Lynde, then her faith in the Lord drove the demon off. Personally, I'd call this an isolated attack. Still, Miss Palmer, you should take care just in case another comes."

Melissa took Abby's arm and helped her up. "Maybe you should see a doctor, Abs."

"I'm fine," said Abby, stumbling slightly as she moved away. "Thanks Mel, but I'm sure it's just a one-time deal." She forced a smile. "I think I just need to get home and take a nap."

"Quite right," said Mrs. Davidson. "Come on, girls, let's get you three out of this cold and back in your nice warm homes!"

As she followed the others to the car, Abby's hand reached down and brushed against Dominic's mane. *Stay close, Dommy.*

He smiled. "Always."

CHAPTER 29

"Are you sure you're OK, Abby?" Melissa followed Abby to her room. "I really think you should see a doctor." She sat on the bed and watched as Abby got out a more comfortable dress.

"I feel fine, Mel, I just got a headache." Abby hung the dress over her arm and headed for the bathroom. "I'll be right back." Once safely behind the door, she turned on the shower and stripped off her church dress. She was about to step in when she heard a wolf whistle. *Dommy!*

The dragon sat by the door, grinning. "Looking good, beautiful."

You... She pulled back the shower curtain and stepped inside, dragging it closed more harshly than she needed to. As she let the warm water run down her body, she thought over the events that led to her headache. *I was walking with Aunt Gladys and Melissa, I stepped back to let them talk with the Davidsons... what was I thinking before it happened?* Trying to think about it made her head hurt again, but not quite as badly. *Come on, Abs, you're too young to have memory loss!*

"You just got upset over nothing," said Dominic from right outside the shower curtain. "Don't let it worry you. It's over now."

"This is what happens when the Devil sees..." How did Mr. Davidson put *that?* She snorted. *Great, now I'm taking* him *seriously?* Still, the idea stuck. Could it have been a demon?

"Don't be ridiculous," said the dragon. "This isn't biblical times! And as much as he likes to think it, that buffoon can't walk on water."

Abby didn't reply. She shut off the water and reached out, pulling her towel behind the curtain.

"Is there a reason you mind if a *figment of your imagination* sees you naked?" A slight laugh followed the statement. "That's almost as ridiculous as demon attacks."

He had a point. It wasn't like he was *real* and getting a thrill from it. Still, she felt more comfortable behind the curtain. Once she dried off she wrapped the towel around herself and stepped out. She snapped her fingers and gestured for him to turn around.

Dominic rolled his eyes and obliged, his tail tapping against the floor.

Pervert, she mentally snapped, dressing as quickly as she could. *I swear... Why do I keep you around?* She flinched as a slight pain near her temple hit. She rubbed the spot. *Maybe Mel's right and I should see a doctor.*

"You're just stressed from having to deal with too much bull–"

Language! She sighed. *You may have a point there.* Dressed, she headed back to her room. She found Melissa sitting on her bed, the frame off the nightstand in her hand.

"I pity that Samson boy."

"What are you talking about?" Abby sat beside her, smiling. "He didn't have to put up with Mr. Davidson's sermon."

"You don't see how he looks at you, do you?" Melissa handed her the frame. "The poor boy's got it bad."

Abby looked at the photos. She had bought the collage frame a couple years ago. Aunt Gladys, her parents, and her grandparents took up the biggest spots. An old photo of her and Mel at school took up another. One that Mr. Samson had snapped of her and the twins a year or two ago had the last one. She did not see anything special about it. Marlon and Felice were both giving each other rabbit ears; if anything, it was a silly picture. "He's my friend."

"It's best to start that way." Melissa smiled. "Thank you for all your help. Drew's parents were actually talking to me today." She giggled. "Poor Drew wouldn't take his hands out of his pockets."

"You know," said Abby, getting up and putting the frame back where it belonged. "If Drew likes *you*, he might not want you to change."

"I know," she replied. "I'm hoping I'll get a chance to talk to him at school. Let him know I'm still *me*, you know? Just... better behaved."

"Actresses on life's stage," said Dominic, jumping up on the bed and curling up on a pillow. "You two play the part well, I must admit."

Will you shut up for once? Abby patted Melissa's shoulder. "That's a good idea. I hope it works out for you two."

"Because you want a friend to be happy, or so the Davidsons will get off your back?" Mel's grin took the sting out of the words.

"Little of both, honestly." Abby kicked her feet. "Still, even if you two *do* get together, I'm sure Aunt Gladys will just start looking for someone else to set me up with."

"The boy next door maybe?" Melissa laughed and dodged the slap Abby sent her way. "Oh, come on! Once you get past the whole messed-up-family thing, the guy's kinda cute."

Abby felt her face heat up. She had never really thought about it before, but... *She's not wrong.*

"Aw! I knew it! You like him, too!"

"Not like *that!* For Pete's sake, Mel, grow up!" Abby shook her head. "Even if I did, do you *really* think Aunt Gladys would approve of *Marlon?* Heck, it wasn't too long ago *you* wouldn't give him a chance, either!"

Melissa's face fell. "Yeah... that was kinda... I don't know if I should apologize to them for that or just go on as we are. I should have known better; you're a good judge of character." She smiled sheepishly. "After all, you wanted to be friends with me."

"I'd just go with the flow. Today is what matters."

"I still can't believe Mr. Davidson called you a bitch."

"Say what now?" Abby raised her eyebrows in surprise. "When did he say that?"

"Sheepdog, same thing." Melissa brushed her hair back over her shoulder. "I'm surprised he didn't try to take credit for your 'successes' lately. That demon talk's such bull."

"Thanks for the reminder, by the way." Abby sighed. "I don't know what got into me. I can usually handle his..." She shuddered. "Anyway, I can usually deal with him. Today was just..."

"I don't blame you. He pretty much made it sound like you were some, I dunno. I forgot how holier-than-thou he is. My memory didn't do him justice."

"Just think: you get your way, he'll be your father-in-law."

"Maybe I can talk Drew into moving to another state..."

"Good luck with that."

After Melissa left, Abby got out her laptop. She didn't say anything to Dominic as she typed "demon attacks" in the search bar. Most of what came up just sounded like the same nonsense she saw when she read up on her favorite music. She glanced at the dragon. He seemed to be asleep. She stroked the keys a few times then typed "imaginary friends". She screwed up somehow though; she had meant to erase the previous search first but when she looked it was still in the box. *Dang it.* She was about to start over when one of the results caught her eye.

"Can an imaginary friend be a demon?"

Say what now? That was a possibility she'd never considered. She clicked the link and read the article. Some of it sounded a little... wrong.

"My child has an imaginary friend. That in and of itself isn't the problem. The issue is that he says it doesn't want him to do certain things – go to church, clean his room, etc. Now I'd brush it off as him just not wanting to do these things but supposedly the friend 'hurts' him when he does any of these things. Anyone else have this problem?"

Abby went back to the search results and read more of the articles. Some came off just like the previous ones – the kinds of thing Aunt Gladys or Preacher Davidson said. A couple though... *Could Dommy be a demon in disguise?*

"Don't be an idiot!" Dominic raised his head, growling softly. "I'm just in your head, remember? I can't do anything *you* don't make me. Why are you so worried all of a sudden? What did *I* do?"

I'm not saying you did anything, you're just... I'm sixteen and I still have an imaginary friend. Seriously, if I told anyone I'd either be locked up in a nuthouse or laughed at. She went to shutdown the laptop when the messenger window popped open.

RandomWord: Hey, Abs. You OK?

DragonflyGirl: Yeah, why?

RandomWord: Just... a little birdy told me you had something go down after church today. Mr. Davidson make you sick or something?

Dang it Mel! Abby shook her head. *Great, just great.*

DragonflyGirl: It's nothing, Mars-Bars. I just got a headache as we were walking out, no big deal. *rolls eyes* Tell Mel I said she's already gossiping like a church lady.

RandomWord: LMAO. Yeah, I'll do that considering her and Felice are over here playing dress up. Seriously what is it with girls and clothes?

DragonflyGirl: Says the son and grandson of a tailor.

RandomWord: Making 'em and wanting to try several outfits on for hours is two different things. How you feeling about the driving test?

DragonflyGirl: Like it's coming up too fast.

RandomWord: You've got it in the bag, you were doing fine last Friday. Looked a bit like a vampire though, seriously are you getting any sleep?

DragonflyGirl: Which of them told you to check up on me?

No reply came for a minute or two. Just as Abby was about to apologize, Marlon finally responded.

RandomWord: Neither, though they do care about you, you know. We're friends Abs, that kinda means I get worried about you. Goes with the territory. Look, why don't you log off and get some sleep, OK? You want to be rested when you get behind the wheel after all.

DragonflyGirl: Love to, but can't. I gotta fix dinner

RandomWord: I'll take care of it. Mrs. Lynde likes that take-out place right? I'll pick up something and bring it over. Problem solved.

Abby stared at the screen. She didn't know what to think.

"Marlon and Abby, sittin' in a tree," said Dominic, grinning. "K-I-S-S-I-N-G."

"Oh, shut up!" She shook her head at the overgrown lizard and typed, "You don't have to do that. I'll be fine."

RandomWord: Doing it anyway, so suck it up, buttercup. Now log off and crash before I come over and knock ya out myself.

DragonflyGirl: You are simply incorrigible.

RandomWord: You are simply incorrigible. I know, now get some sleep, I mean it.

DragonflyGirl: Yes, sir, right away sir!

Abby laughed as she shut down the laptop and put it away. "Thank God there's only one Mars-Bars. The world wouldn't handle two... He really is... kinda... cute." She curled up under the covers and fell asleep almost the moment her head hit the pillow.

"I cannot believe you had the gall to harm a child like that!"

"She ain't a child anymore, Annie, ain't ya noticed?" The deceiver grinned and licked his lips. "That's a body that'll lead a good man to ruin."

"Good thing neither of us is a man at all." Aeneas glared at his counterpart, once more longing to summon his staff. "You are *slime*. The lowest of the low. A mockery of kindness and compassion!"

Bjarte bowed sarcastically. "Why, thank you! It's so nice to be appreciated for one's talents!"

"You self-centered, selfish, two-faced–"

"Hey, I did us both a favor!" His grin just got wider. "She was about to get rid of that overgrown gecko, and then where would we be? Be a lot of ground to make up."

"Coward," Aeneas bit out. "You've only done *yourself* a 'favor'. I'd lose no ground, though you would have a hard time appealing to her conscience without the trust she places in that beast... trust your actions that are already weakening."

Bjarte shook his head. "Get over yourself, Annie. I'm not the one playin' with the computer to try and tell her stuff we're not supposed to, after all."

Aeneas finally smiled. "Revealing ourselves is *encouraged*, last I checked. What is the matter? Afraid once she sees what she is really dealing with you'll lose your hold?"

The deceiver's expression hardened. "You don't want to play hardball with me, Annie."

"Give me one good reason why I should not? After all," he replied, his voice as cold as steel, "if she falls, so do I. You creatures value your own existence above all else... and you are always telling me how alike we are, after all."

"Fine, then." Bjarte smirked. "Let's see what tomorrow brings... after tonight's little game."

The guardian watched, face showing no sign of the horror or the fury he felt as Abigail's nightmares began anew. *I cannot waste what power I have now,* he thought, *knowing he's got something far darker in store...*

The possibilities were endless, considering what lay at his disposal. He needed every bit of strength he could summon. *You will not win. I will not let you destroy such innocence.* Aeneas refused to remember how he had made such vows before... and had broken them one by one.

CHAPTER 30

The next day at school, Drew reached out and caught Abby's elbow for a second. "Miss Palmer? May I have a word, please?"

Abby figured her expression matched Mel's and the Samson twins': surprised, confused, nervous. She shrugged and nodded. "We'll catch up in a second, guys." Once they disappeared into the cafeteria, she turned back to Drew. "So what is it?"

"What's going on with you and Miss Hilary?"

"Going on?" Abby leaned against the wall, covering her mouth as she yawned. "What do you mean?" *Dang it, I wish I could take a nap.*

"Don't play dumb, Abby." Drew put his hands in his pockets and looked at her sternly. "Out of the blue you two are friends and she's playing the part of reformed sinner. What are you up to?"

"We're not friends *out of the blue*," she replied. "I've known Mel since I started school. She quit talking to me a few years ago, though..." She narrowed her eyes. "Like almost everyone else, she didn't like the company I kept."

"Yet, now she's all buddy-buddy and dressing like *you*... what's going on?"

"I don't know what to tell you." She really did not. She wasn't going to out Melissa on her attempts to gain the Davidsons' approval. "I just know Mel picked up my pencil the other day and asked for some advice."

"Advice on what?"

"You're not going to be able to beat around the bush forever," said Dominic as he pressed against her leg. "Might as well tell him."

"She wanted to turn over a new leaf, that's all."

"And this has *nothing* to do with the fact she and I broke up last summer?" Drew glanced at the people passing them in the hall and lowered his voice. "*Nothing* to do with your aunt and my parents thinking *we* make a good match?"

"Huh," said Dominic, chewing on a claw. "Boy's not as dense as I thought."

Abby pushed away from the wall and stood up as straight as she could. "Look *Drew*." If he could use her first name, she could his. "I'll admit you're not the jerk I thought you were. I'll give you that. But contrary to what Aunt Gladys thinks, I'm not looking for a suitor. I have no intention to be nothing but a housewife."

"I'm *so* happy to hear you no longer have such a dark opinion of me. And just what would you rather do than your Christian duty?"

She ignored the term and folded her arms. "I'm going to be a psychologist. There's nothing stopping me from getting married and having a family, too."

"Women are not supposed to work outside the home." Drew sounded like he was telling a child the sky is blue. "I won't marry a woman that even thinks like that."

"Then I guess we're not as good of a match as they think, are we?" Abby fought to keep her voice level. "Because I wouldn't marry a man that thinks *that* way, either."

"Then you won't marry a good man," he paused, swallowing hard, "though I'm sure you'll have no trouble finding someone with looser morals... considering the company you keep."

Abby froze. She literally could not move. "What did you just say?"

"Don't play dumb, it really doesn't suit you." Drew jerked his hands from his pockets and leaned back against the wall and folded his arms across his chest. "Anyone can see how Samson pants over you. Can't help wondering what he's getting out of it."

"Hmm, I guess even he's noticed your appeal to the little wasp," said Dominic. He chewed at another claw. "Though that was a roundabout way to put it."

"If I didn't know better I'd say I was talking to your father." Abby clenched her fists. *Do not hit him, you should not resort to violence,* she told herself. "Marlon's my *friend.* That's *it.*"

"Sure, and Melissa just decided to 'turn over a new leaf.'" He looked at her coldly. "What did you say to her? 'Here, I'll teach you how to deceive everyone so –"

"I'm not a liar." Abby bit the words out. "Melissa came to *me,* not the other way around. And if you really want to know what she's up to, maybe you should ask *her.* Now, if you don't mind I'd rather not miss lunch just so I can be judged just because I tried to help someone who asked for it." She turned and headed into the cafeteria. She ignored Drew when he followed her and got in line behind her. She took her tray over to the table and sat with her friends.

"So what's up you two?" asked Felice. "Why the one-on-one? There a surprise we're missing?"

"Mr. Davidson just had some concerns he wanted to address privately," Abby replied. She took a bite of her cheeseburger and considered the subject closed.

Drew sat down and started talking with Marlon as if nothing had happened.

"Two-faced, traitorous rat!" Dominic growled as he curled up at her feet. "If anyone's playing a part it's *him.*"

Dommy, with all due respect... SHUT UP!

"You OK, Abs?" asked Melissa. "You look … uh..."

"She looks like a vampire," said Marlon. His concern showed in his eyes. "Nightmares still getting to you?"

"Nightmares?" repeated Drew, frowning. "You're having nightmares?"

"I've been having them for over a week now, yes." Abby rubbed the side of her head as she tried to block the images that just *talking* about it brought to mind.

"Maybe the Lord's trying to tell you something."

"Or maybe she's just under a lot of unnecessary stress," Marlon snapped.

The bell rang before anyone could say anything else. They all got up and dumped their trays before heading to their next class. *Marlon is too perceptive for his own good.* Abby glanced around at the throng of students rushing to their classes. *Good thing everyone else is too busy to notice.*

Melissa fell in step beside Abby, one finger playing with her hair. "Are you OK?"

"I think so," Abby replied. "You need to talk to Drew. He's suffering under some *severe* delusions." She sighed. "But I think he's just worried about you, if that makes sense."

"Worried about me?" Melissa smiled. "Sorry, but... Right now that sounds nice."

Dominic snorted. "Bully for you."

Dominic, I said hush! Abby nodded. "Just do me a favor and talk to him as soon as you can, OK? We don't need any misunderstandings." Melissa tilted her head. "What did he say?"

"Ask him yourself, please." Abby blinked as she settled into her seat for English. "He said she said causes way too much trouble."

"You've got a point there," said Melissa then she fell silent as the teacher called the class to order.

Abby yawned again and folded her arms on her desk. She rested her chin on her hands and blinked. *Can't fall asleep... need to … pay attention.*

CHAPTER 31

"Abby. Abby! *Abby!*"

Abby jolted so fast she smacked her back against the chair. "Huh? What? Where…"

"You crashed about three minutes into class, Abs." Melissa looked at her with a worried expression. "It's a good thing Mr. Mathews let you sleep when I told him you haven't been sleeping right lately." She held out a stack of paper. "Here, I took notes for both of us."

"Thanks," said Abby, taking them as she felt her face heat up again. *I'll be so glad when this day is over.* She followed Mel out of the classroom and down the hall. "I wasn't snoring, was I?"

"No, thank goodness." Melissa giggled. "That would have been something."

"Maybe you should see the nurse," said Dominic. "Or go home for the day."

I'm not skipping school, the driving test is today. She bid farewell to Melissa outside her next class. She sighed as she saw Marlon in his usual spot at the science table. She slid into her seat beside him, setting her books on the table.

"Abs, no offense but you look like death warmed over." Marlon's worried expression touched her. He reached out lay a hand on hers. "What the f —" he caught himself "fudge are you dreaming about?" He squeezed her hand. "You… honestly look like you've been through Hell."

"How charming," said Dominic as he curled up under her chair. "Seems *both* boys in your life want to know what's going on in that pretty head of yours. OW!"

Abby smiled to herself as she kicked her feet, subtly kicking the mouthy dragon. Then she looked at her friend. "You don't want to know." *And I don't want to tell you.* The images flashed again. Fire. The game's dragon. Her parents. The feeling of helplessness... *No one else should have to live with this in their head.*

"Yes, I do. You shouldn't have to deal with this alone. Whatever *this* is. Abs, you've been –"

"Mr. Samson?" called the teacher. "Do you and Miss Palmer have something you would like to *share* with the rest of the class?"

"No, sir." Marlon pulled his hand away and sat up in his seat. "Sorry, sir."

"Now, who can tell me the proper application of ..."

Abby stared at her hand for a moment, then lay her other one on it. Something felt different. She glanced up at Marlon and he winked at her. She couldn't help smiling at the warmth that settled in her chest. She pushed the difference from her mind. *Just one more class,* she told herself. *Then you just have to pass the driving test. How did I manage to fall asleep in class? Study hall I could understand but...* She shrugged. Water under the bridge. She got out her notebook and tried to keep up with the lesson.

"OK, Abby, buckle up."

"I've already got my seatbelt on, Mr. Samson." Abby gripped the wheel but this time her hands remained loose. She nodded and started the car when told to do so.

"Doing good, girl. Now make a left."

They followed the familiar streets as Bryan marked things down on his clipboard. Abby didn't ask how she was doing, and he didn't say. He just gave directions and she followed.

"Told you you could manage this," said Dominic from the backseat. "Straighten up, you're doing just fine. You own this."

Abby smiled even as she blinked rapidly. The warm car felt nice. Cozy. She found herself blinking more and more. *I can't wait to get home and crash.* Then again, if her nightmares were waiting... *Still I need the sleep. Might have to break down and take something.*

They were on their way back to the school when Bryan's cell phone rang. He looked at the I.D. and dropped the f-word as he snapped the phone open. "Missy, you better have a *good* reason for not calling for over two weeks! Are you OK?"

She tried to tune out the conversation. It wasn't any of her business.

"You're doing so well. So very good. Steady now, steady..."

Dominic's voice was soothing, and besides, it gave her something focus on. She blinked again. She could see the school up ahead. *Almost over.*

"Yes, it is."

The hum of the car and the sound of Bryan's voice began to fade as her eyes drifted closed.

"What are you doing?" Aeneas looked from Abby to Bryan and back again. While the bumbler was on the phone with his headstrong daughter, their charge had fallen asleep at the wheel. "Are you *trying* to get her killed?" He froze at the grin on his rival's face. "You –"

"Come off it, Annie." Bjarte leaned back in the car seat. "*This* makes everything so much easier. No more fighting, no more challenges. Just her soul's fate... finally decided."

"Abby!" shouted the guardian. "Abby, wake up!" He thought of the other pair present, but there would be no assistance from that end. Aeneas reached out and shoved her shoulder. "ABBY!"

"Yell your head off all you like, brother." The deceiver's grin just widened. "She doesn't hear *either* of us anymore unless it's through that lizard of hers."

"You selfish monster." The guardian glared at his counterpart. "Abby wake up! Abby!" It was pointless. As much as he hated to admit it Bjarte was right for once. She did not hear either of *their* voices any longer. Still he had to try. *"ABIGAIL!" Please let her wake. Please!*

There was shift in the air and the guardian tried to place the disturbance. *That's... I've felt that before. Haven't I?*

Before he could think on it much farther, his request was granted.

Abby snapped her head up at the sound of Dominic shouting her name. She gasped when she saw the car was headed straight for one of the trees that lined the sidewalk. She slammed on the break just as Bryan reached out and grabbed the wheel. The car jerked to a stop halfway on the sidewalk next to the tree. Her heart raced and her breath came in gasps.

"What the Hell just happened?" Bryan stared at her, his expression torn between furious and frightened.

"I..." She fought to catch her breath. "I think I fell asleep." Her heart hammered in her chest. She looked around and tried to place the last thing she remembered seeing. *Holy crap!*

"DAD! YOU PICK UP THE PHONE RIGHT NOW! DAD!"

They both looked down at Bryan's phone where it had dropped on the floor. He reached down and grabbed it. "Sorry, Firecracker, I'm gonna have to call you back. I've got a bit of situation here." The voice on the other end was too soft to hear. "Yes, I'm OK, I love you too." He snapped the phone shut and pocketed it.

"I... I'm sorry." Abby rubbed at her eyes. "I don't have an excuse I just... I don't..."

"Your head's been screwin' with ya," said Bryan. "And I'm an idiot for bein' on the phone when I knew that." He sighed. "We both screwed up. I'm old enough to know better."

Abby finally got her heart rate under control. She glanced in the mirror at the concerned face of the dragon. *Dommy...*

"Are you OK?" He hung his head. "I tried to wake you the whole time, I just couldn't –"

I'm fine. She blinked and replayed everything she could remember. *Wait...* Her eyes narrowed and she looked back into the mirror. *I heard you. You woke me up.*

Dominic shifted sheepishly. "So?"

"Abs, I'm sorry, but I can't pass you after this." Bryan hung his head. "I know it's as much my fault as yours but... look, you can retake the test next week. I'd say Friday but I can't do that legally. I know how much this means to you."

"I'm just glad I didn't kill us both, sir." Abby looked up at him. "You want to take the wheel back to the school? I don't –" A yawn stressed her point.

"Sure, Abby, sure." Bryan unbuckled his seatbelt and got out of the car. He closed the door, walked around to the driver's side and opened the door. "Slide over, Dragonfly."

"Dragonfly?" she asked, unbuckling her belt and dropping into the passenger seat. She put the seat belt on and looked at him. "Marlon, right?"

"Marlon... and you *are* the Dragon's granddaughter." He smiled as he reached out and ruffled her hair. He nodded and backed the car up onto the road. "So I think it fits."

Abby shook her head. "Well, he is the Little Wasp; guess it only makes sense I'm the Little Dragon."

"Who called him *that*?"

"Grandma."

He laughed. "Figures."

Speaking of dragons. Abby's eyes went back to the mirror. *I heard you. You WOKE me up.*

"Would you rather be dead?" he snapped. "How about a 'thank you'?"

Thank you, she thought sharply. *It's not that I'm NOT grateful, it's just... I heard you!*

"So you've said. What's your point?"

You're not real... remember?

CHAPTER 32

"How did the driving exam go, dear?"

Abby walked to the dining room and put the chicken dinner on the table. She had bought from the take-out place down the street on the way home. She waited until Gladys followed her into the room then said, "I failed." She set the cutlery and the napkins out. "I'll have to retake it next week."

"You... what happened, Abigail?" Gladys' concern showed in her voice. She sat down and noticed Abby had only laid one plate out. "Aren't you eating, dear?"

"I'm just tired," she replied, not wanting to explain things to her aunt yet. She picked up the bag with her dinner still in it and put it in the refrigerator. "And I'll eat when I wake up. Right now I'm so tired... I'm going to bed, Aunt Gladys. Good night." She heard Gladys murmur the phrase. She headed for the bathroom and opened the medicine cabinet.

"What are you doing?" Dominic stopped at her side, looking up with his ears back.

I need sleep. Abby took out the bottle of cold pills. *Without nightmares.* She opened the bottle and dropped two pills into her palm. She tossed them in her mouth and followed with tap water before she could change her mind. Then she put the bottle back, headed for her room and crawled into her bed. Snuggled down in her covers, she silently prayed. *Please... just let me sleep.*

Aeneas watched as she fell asleep. Between the medicine and his own efforts, no nightmares came, in fact no dreams at all. He stood there silent, daring his rival to speak first. *She suspects... she finally suspects there's more to the dragon than just a child's game. Now if that will be of any help or not...*

"I can't believe you pulled that off," said Bjarte. The deceiver eyed him with grudging respect. "You actually managed to get through to her." He clapped sarcastically. "Well done, Annie."

Did I? The guardian considered the presence he had sensed when she awoke. It was familiar but... *Impossible. Each charge only has one guardian.* Still, he had felt it.

"You bought yourself some time. Good for you." The deceiver grinned. "You've already lost, though. The more those holier-than-thou idiots push, the further she falls."

"You understand nothing, thus it is pointless to discuss anything with you."

"Keep telling yourself that, Annie. Keep telling yourself that. Game over."

Not yet. Aeneas stared down at Abby. *She is stronger than any give her credit for.*

"You doing OK, Abs?"

"I'm fine." Abby shot Melissa a reassuring smile as she sat beside her in studyhall. Three days had passed since her failed test. She *was* "fine." She had continued to take the cold pills before bed and so slept through the night. The day before she had combed the school library, too, but not surprisingly it lacked in books about demons.

"Like it matters," said Dominic, curling up at her feet as usual. "I'm not a 'demon'. Sheesh, you sound like that know-it-all Davidson. I'm just an imaginary friend."

Abby kept her eyes on her English homework. *I'm not buying that.*

"You know, when someone saves a *normal person's* life, there's usually some gratitude and *trust.*"

I am grateful. That was the truth. *But trust is earned. If you were just an 'imaginary friend', there would be nothing to be grateful for, since you wouldn't have been able to do anything.*

"When are you going to quit over-thinking this?"

When I find out what you are. She moved on the next assignment.

"So... I talked to Drew yesterday." Melissa wrapped her hair around her finger. "Apparently you were right... it was his parents." She paused, clearly waiting for a response. When none came, she went on, "He... told me what he said to you."

"And?" Abby said sharply, but then took a deep breath. *Just because you have a mess on your hands is no reason to be rude, Palmer.* "Sorry, I'm a little stressed out right now. I'm listening."

Melissa shook her head. "Well, for one thing I set him straight real fast. Told him I want him back, what we *had* back, and I went *to you* for help with that. I also pointed out this isn't an *act*; I get I wasn't ... girl-you-bring-home material." She sighed. "I can't believe he actually thought... why are men so dumb sometimes?"

"Everyone is once in a while, Mel. So you got everything straightened out?"

"Define 'straightened out'," she replied. "We talked... and he um, said..."

"He told that girl it couldn't be true, that it was just a trick and –"

Dominic will you SHUT UP! "I don't need to know what he said," she told Melissa, fighting to keep her voice level. "I'm just asking if you two worked things out or not."

"All the cards are on the table now. I honestly think his pride took a hit, you know?" Melissa sighed. "What with being God's gift to women the way he acts sometimes..." She smiled. "And *you* didn't want him. Still, I think I got him to cash his reality check."

"How hard did she have to hit him over the head for it to sink in?"

Abby subtly kicked the dragon. "Good. Now we just need to convince his parents *you* are the better option." She took out her math homework. *And that I'm not even close.*

"*We* don't," said Melissa, reaching out and putting a hand on Abby's shoulder. "You've done your part, Abs. The rest is on me and him."

"You could always tell them about your future plans," suggested Dominic. "I'm sure the fact you *don't* want to be a good little bit– "

Enough! Hush, you overgrown gecko! Abby smiled. "Good luck, Mel. I hope you can pull it off. And *not* just 'cause it means *I* don't have to deal with it. Drew's not a bad guy." *Even if his opinions do seem to bounce around like a yo-yo.*

"Neither are the Samsons," said Melissa. "Never thought I'd hear myself say *that.*"

When the bell rang they gathered their things and headed out the door into the hallway.

"Good day, Miss Palmer, Miss Hilary." Drew was leaning against the wall as usual. He fell into step beside them and started up a conversation with Mel, which Abby tuned out.

Abby noticed how he stood on *Melissa's* side this time and smiled.

"Looks like she yanked his leash," said Dominic. He nodded. "One less worry on your plate."

"A word, Miss Palmer?"

"Of course," she replied automatically. She saw Melissa wink and disappear into the cafeteria. "What can I do for you, Mr. Davidson?"

Drew scuffed his feet and put his hands in his pockets. He couldn't look at her face. "I'm sorry."

"Say what?"

"Don't be a jerk, OK?" His head shot up and he looked her straight in the eye. "I'm sorry. I jumped to conclusions and... Look, I was out of line. I apologize." A small smile appeared on his face. "I wouldn't blame you if you slugged me again."

"I considered it, but I'm pretty sure Mel prefers you intact." She shifted her books against her chest, smiling back. "Apology accepted. May we get lunch now?"

Drew laughed. "Yeah." He followed her as she got in the lunch line. "Oh, and... thanks. Still don't know why *you* didn't just tell me yourself."

"I did say *she* came to *me* remember? Besides, would you have *believed* me?" Her eyes narrowed. "It didn't seem likely."

Drew hung his head. "I... yeah, you're right. Again, I'm sorry."

"Don't mention it." Abby chose a sandwich and a bottle of water, pocketing the rest of her lunch money. *Going to need it later.* She was glad to see Mel and the twins talking before she sat down at their table. She nodded, said grace, and started in on her meal.

"That's all you're getting?" Marlon looked confused. "Abs... are you OK?"

She swallowed quickly. "I'm fine, Mars-Bars." No one needed to know her plans. She didn't need to be sent back to the shrink.

"This whole idea is a waste of time and you know it." Dominic took his place at her feet. "Still, if it's what you feel you need to do... I'm right beside you."

I'm sure you are. Abby was grateful when Drew got Marlon back onto the game track. She couldn't lie and her friend was one of the few who would push. *I just have to get through the rest of the day. Then...* She went over her plan one more time. If there was *any* chance she did have a demon on her hands, she knew only one place to go. *It's just a matter of getting there.*

CHAPTER 33

Marlon wasn't as easily distracted as Abby would have liked. He fell into step beside her and kept pace the whole way to their next class. He started to speak at least three times but each time he hesitated. He finally got his chance when they sat at their table. "Abs, seriously, what's going on?"

Abby sat her books down and busied herself with finding the page number the teacher had written on the board. "We're in science class, Mars-Bars. And we're *supposed* to have our books out."

"That's not what I meant and you know it." Marlon got out his book and notebook anyway. "I've known you too long not to know when something's up. Spill it."

"Mr. Samson, please keep your conversation *outside* my classroom."

"Yes, sir." Marlon leaned over his book and hissed, "After class."

Abby forced a smile. *This isn't something you can help with Mars-Bars.* She took notes carefully, forcing her mind onto the task at hand.

"You could always call this foolishness off," said Dominic. "Or tell him your fears; I'm sure he could lay them to rest."

Marlon doesn't believe in God, never mind demons. There was no way she could tell him. No, this was something she had to do on her own.

Abby made a point to get Drew and Marlon talking when school ended, and she slipped away while they debated about game systems.

She headed home as quickly as she could. To her relief Gladys was already gone. She locked the door behind her and went to her room to change... and prepare for battle. She hummed an old Stryper song under her breath.

"Quit being so dramatic," Dominic sat in the corner watching her. "You're not waging war here. You're wasting time and money to prove a non-existent point."

"I find it funny how against this you are." Abby reached up, undid the clasp of her cross necklace, and stretched it on her nightstand for a moment. She opened the drawer in the stand and pulled out the book safe she had stashed her grandfather's rosary and her mother's crucifix inside. After removing the cross charm, she slid the larger crucifix onto the chain before securing it around her neck. Next, she took the rosary and looped it through one of the belt loops in her skirt. "I think the dragon protests too much." She got out the laptop.

"It's not that," he replied, growling slightly under his breath. "If this is what you have to do, fine. I just think you're wasting your time."

Abby ignored him and did a search for directions. She hadn't been to the place in years, though she'd heard the neighborhood had grown since she'd been gone. She wrote them down in a matter of minutes. She shut the laptop down and put it away. She got out her purse and made sure she had everything she needed. Along with her wallet and phone, she had tucked inside her purse a lighter, a packet of incense, and a burner. She swung the strap over her shoulder. She straightened her bed and made sure her room was in order.

"Will you quit acting like you're leaving forever?" Dominic's tail lashed. "Unless you get hit by a car on the way or the bus crashes, you'll be back."

"You're not going to scare me, *Dommy*," she said. She headed outside, locked the door behind her, and got on her bike. *This is the only way I know to deal with this.*

"I am *not* trying to scare you," said the dragon as he ran alongside her. "I just think this is ridiculous. I saved your life, yet somehow I'm a demon? Where's your logic?"

A small smile appeared on her face. *The fact you keep bouncing back and forth between 'I'm with you!' and 'This is stupid!' kind of proves my theory.*

"I – That's – I don't believe –" He fell silent the rest of the trip to the bus stop.

Abby handed her money to the driver and locked her bike on the bus's rack before climbing aboard. She took a seat by the window and watched the familiar streets pass by. Dominic sat on the floor at her feet and rubbed his head against her legs.

"ABBY!" Marlon pounded on the door. "ABBY, DAMN IT, OPEN UP!" He fought to catch his breath. *This isn't good this isn't good, what the heck is going on?*

"Samson, *what* are you *doing?*"

Marlon did not answer. He looked at Drew for a moment then said, "Screw it!" and jumped to reach the top of the door frame to grab the spare key. He unlocked the door and walked inside.

"I do believe this qualifies as breaking-and-entering," said Drew as he followed. "What the heck is wrong with you?"

"ABBY!" Marlon went straight back to her room to find it neat as a pin. Nothing seemed out of place, except... A glint of metal caught his eye and he saw her cross charm laying on the nightstand. *Why would she leave this behind?* He grabbed it and held it a moment before pocketing it. He pushed past Davidson and turned down the hall into the kitchen. He looked on the fridge, by the phone, anywhere in plain sight. He turned and glanced at the other boy before walking back out of the apartment. "No note, she's not home, *crap!*"

"Samson will you slow down?" Drew reached out and took the key, locking the door again and hiding the key away. "What has gotten *into* you?"

"Abby's missing," he said, turning and heading for his own apartment. "I don't know where she is – she never goes anywhere and doesn't leave a note."

Drew rolled his eyes. "She has a cell phone, just call her." He followed at Marlon's heels. "You're having a panic attack over nothing. We saw her only a few hours ago."

"Great idea... if her phone took incoming calls..." Marlon went inside, not caring if Drew followed or not. "Dad!" He pushed into his father's office, startling both his father and grandfather, and repeated what he had already said to Davidson. "I don't like this I don't know what to do how do I –" He rambled on, not even sure what he was saying anymore as he paced.

Wendel did not say a word. He just started typing, and a few seconds later the printer ran. He snatched the paper and handed it to Marlon. "Here, she's at a church in Reynoldsburg, so relax."

"Thanks Dad!" Marlon snatched the paper. *What the heck is she doing out that way?*

"Boy's got it bad," he heard his grandfather say as he bolted out the door.

Wendel's tone went dry. "You're just now figuring that out?"

Marlon went straight to his bike and started to unlock it when a car horn blared nearby. "Hey, what the –"

The passenger door swung open and Davidson jerked his thumb at him. "Get in, idiot. Wherever you're going I can get there faster."

He didn't know what to say. He strapped in and handed Davidson the directions.

Davidson looked them over in confusion. "A Catholic church? Where did you get this anyway?"

"Dad. And your guess is as good as mine, but all I know is Dad's got the world wired. If he says she's there she is, and if she's –"

"OK, OK, take a chill pill." Drew pulled into the road. "We'll get there as fast as we can. But don't have a heart attack."

"You don't get it. Abs has been acting real weird lately and she *never* leaves without leaving a note and this is just wrong on every level." Marlon started scratching at his hair. "I don't like this."

"Just try to relax. God grant me the – "

"Don't throw the serenity prayer at me right now, OK?" Marlon. His hand went to his pocket and he rubbed the cross through the cloth. *I'm doing enough praying on my own... Look, uh, Sir, I don't know if I believe in You or anything but Abs does so if you could take care of her until I get there I'd appreciate it.* He paused. *If... if she's OK I'll even join the church with her. Just PLEASE let her be all right!*

CHAPTER 34

"Thank you, sir," said Abby as she got off the last bus. She retrieved her bike and looked up at the driver. "Sir, which way is Main Street, do you know?" He pointed behind her and she nodded. "Thanks again." She mounted her bike and headed up the road. *This is so... this feels weird.*

"Yeah, cause you haven't been here in how long?" Dominic kept pace beside her. "This isn't necessary you could have done this at home."

"No, I couldn't." She did not worry about being heard. The few people she saw were too caught up in their own lives to notice her. "For one thing, if Aunt Gladys caught me, I'd be in a world of trouble. And this is best done on holy ground."

"Why don't you just say 'sacred ground' and be done with it?"

"Because this isn't a movie or a TV show." Abby looked around as she rode, on the lookout for the turns she needed to take. The first one came up before she expected it. "I figured this would take longer. Maybe I need to study harder in math."

"Or slow down. You'd think the hounds of Hell were at your heels."

She glanced down at the dragon, whose head was level with her seat. "Very funny."

The road changed a lot since she'd last been down it. Buildings were in places that had once been vacant. She watched the street signs and turned onto the last road. Then she saw it, and stopped short.

Saint Pius X looked the same as she remembered. The black roof was sliced by white supports, looking like an accordion or a cake. The stone walls were a bleached out gray and brown. Trees grew around it and the school she had almost attended lay across the drive. *I guess not everything changes.* She rode up the drive and around to the parking lot and the doors she and her parents had always used. She locked up her bike then passed the white square pillars to the wooden doors.

Dominic stayed at her heels, looking at the building like it was a dungeon. He shivered. "They haven't changed *anything* here, have they?"

Abby looked over her shoulder. The statue of the church's namesake stood where she remembered, the ashtrays were in place, the benches too. She shrugged and put her hand on the door, pushing it open and walking inside. She half-expected Dominic to refuse to cross the threshold.

"I told you before, I'm *not* a demon." He walked over the doorway with no problem, then sat beside the doors that led into the sanctuary. "Gee, no bursting into flames. Amazing."

"You are such a smart-alec." Abby crossed over to the doors and pulled one open. She took a deep breath, dipped her hand into the small basin of holy water, and crossed herself before she stepped from the vestibule into the sanctuary. She looked around. *Same pews, same altar...* she walked toward the tabernacle and felt the downward slope in the floor. *It's still the same.*

"I don't know what you think you're going to accomplish here," said Dominic as he followed her. "Catholic church or not, you are not a priest. You can't perform an exorcism."

"I thought you said you aren't a demon." Abby genuflected before the tabernacle and crossed herself a second time. "Father... Son...

Holy Spirit... Amen." She shifted to her knees and drew out the incense, the burner and the lighter. She lit a single stick of incense and the smell of sandalwood filled the air. She repeated the Sign of the Cross with it, then tucked it into the burner she'd set on the floor in front of her. She took a deep breath, letting the scent soothe her frayed nerves.

"I'm *not*, anymore than this incense nonsense is *Catholic*." Dominic sat beside her, one paw swiping through the smoke. "You look like some witch in a fairy tale."

"I guess that makes you my familiar."

"Why is everything negative with you?" He shook his head. "You need more sleep. You've always been a grouch when you're tired."

"I am tired. I'm tired of lies... tired of wearing a mask..." Her voice echoed in the empty building. The only light came from the stained glass windows. Abby got to her feet, walking over to stand beside the tabernacle. Head held high, she looked the dragon in the eye. "In the name of the Father, the Son and the Holy Spirit..."

"You don't have to do this." Dominic's voice cracked. The smug tone disappeared. His eyes grew wide as he cowered down like a whipped dog. "You *know* you don't have to do this. I saved your life – what *more* do you want from me?"

"Just the answer to one question." She forced her voice to stay firm. *I have to know. Can I trust you anymore?* "In the name of the Father, Son and Holy Spirit – *whose side are you on?*"

Her question echoed off the walls as Dominic roared in pain. He hit the floor, his body shaking as he thrashed, snapping at empty air.

Abby's jaw dropped. *Dommy!* She flinched as she watched her friend suffer. Her heart sank. *I was right.* She wanted to cry, but she didn't get the chance.

Two humanoid forms were ripped from the dragon by an unseen source. When they were free of his body, Dominic wheeled around, crouching between her and the beings, snarling.

Two men, it seemed. One blond, the other brunette. One dressed in black, the other in red and white. The brunette walked over and joined her dragon. A staff materialized and stretched out from his palm as he crouched at Dominic's side.

The two from the game?!? Abby backed up until she smacked into the wall behind her. Why would those two have come from *Dominic?* Her eyes ping-ponged between the pair, then locked on the brunette. Old photos of her grandfather flashed through her mind. But the face wasn't quite the same. Still the resemblance struck her. In a shrill voice, she asked, "Who are you?"

"You are not welcome here," said the dark-haired man and the dragon in unison to the other being, their voices echoing in the empty building. "Be gone!"

"That's not for you to say," the lighter haired man replied. He looked at Abby and smiled. "Surely you don't mind me sticking around, Abs? What fun would hanging with this," he waved a hand at the dark-haired man in front of her, "stick in the mud be?"

What's going on? None of this made sense. Abby closed her eyes, then opened them, expecting the pair to be gone. When they weren't, she reached her hand back to touch the wall and ran her hand over the surface. *I guess it* is *real.* "I asked a question." She tried to sound strong. To sound like she was in control. "I expect an answer."

"I am Aeneas, your guardian," said the dark-haired man. He narrowed his eyes at the blond. "And the deceiver is Bjarte. We have been with you since birth."

Dominic growled and shifted so the length of his body blocked the path to her. "You are their charge." The scorn in his voice was palpable. "The *toy* they are fighting over."

"What does that make you?" she asked, looking at the dragon, confused by his presence and his actions. *If I'm not controlling him, and they aren't, then what is he?* "Their..."

"Mask," said the blond with a smirk she'd seen before on Dominic's face. "Come on, Abs, relax. We're friends, remember? And friends stick together."

"You are not my friend – a friend wouldn't lie to me." Abby narrowed her eyes. *So this is where all that creepy stuff came from.* She remembered the soothing words just before she fell asleep at the wheel. "A *friend* wouldn't almost kill me. A friend wouldn't make me doubt myself!" She took a deep breath, stepped forward to stand alongside the dragon, and held out her hand. "In the Name of the Father, the Son and the Holy Spirit – be gone! You are not welcome here!"

The demon laughed. "I already told you! You aren't a priest, you can't –" His laughter cut off when a light shone behind Abby and crept across the floor toward him. Bjarte gasped as the bright white light grew stronger. "No fair! This isn't in the rules!"

"All's fair in love and war," said Dominic. He moved forward with a snarl. "Just admit it. She's stronger than you. Stronger than I. You have no power here."

Dim memories flashed through Abby's mind at the sight. Her parents' voices, telling her to picture the Lord's presence around her when she was afraid of the dark. Whenever she had, it'd been this light that could chase away every shadow.

The light continued to fill the room as the demon scrambled backwards. He glared at the dragon. "Annie, give it up! That *beast* is the one without power – nothing but an empty shell." His back hit the wall the behind him. He waved a hand at the light. "Back off! You aren't allowed to – *AHH!*" The demon's pain-filled screams echoed off the walls as the light washed over him.

Then, nothing. The screams were gone. Abby took a deep breath and hit her knees. She dug her hands into the carpet, fighting to ground herself. *Is it over? That easily?* It seemed too simple.

"One should not speak of things they do not understand." Dominic came alongside her, pressing against her shoulder. "Wouldn't you agree?"

The angel nodded at the dragon with a small smile of his own. "I would."

Abby reached out a shaking hand toward Dominic. "How are you still —" The light continued to fill the room, blinding her. "Ow!" She closed her eyes but still the light pressed and stung. "STOP!"

"Abby! Abs!"

She opened her eyes to find Marlon shaking her shoulder. He was as white as a ghost. She looked around in confusion. She was laying on her side and the incense stick was now a line of ash. *Did I just imagine all that?* "What... Mars-Bars, what are you doing here?"

"Oh, thank *God*," he said, helping her sit up. "Don't you *ever* pull something like this again! I don't think I've ever been so scared in my life."

"Do what?" She was still confused. She sat up, picked up the burner and dropped it back in her purse. She saw a flash of black out of the corner of her eye and gasped.

At her side, his expression concerned as ever, crouched Dominic. "He was worried about you," said the dragon. "Worried enough to beg your protection from Someone he thinks is not real."

Marlon prayed for me? She shook her head. *How do you even know...*

"Do what?" Marlon repeated Abby's question, his voice going up a couple octaves. He put his hand on her cheek and made her look at him. *"Do what?* Not telling me what's bothering you when it's clear as day you're upset, then sneaking off on your own and *not leaving a note behind*. Want me to go on? You scared me out of my wits!"

208

"How did you even find me in the first place?" She got to her feet and bowed to the tabernacle then headed for the doors. But Marlon pulled her back by the arm and set her into a pew.

"Geez, Abs, you were out cold when I came in. Sit down for a bit." He stood over her. "Dad – how else? I don't know if he tracked your phone or what but he knew where you were. What the heck were you even doing here?"

"Something I had to do on my own." She glanced down at the dragon sitting in the aisle. "You couldn't have helped with this. I'm sorry I worried you though. I thought I'd be back before anyone noticed I was gone."

"You could have left a note."

"And said what? 'Went to Catholic church, be back soon'? Do you *know* what Aunt Gladys would have – wait." She looked at him. "How do you know I didn't leave a note?" Granted, she *always* left notes, and it was such a running joke that one year her Christmas gift had been a box of sticky-notes.

Marlon's face turned seven shades of red. "I... kinda grabbed the spare key when you wouldn't open the door. Which reminds me." He dug in his pocket and pulled out her cross. "Why did you take this off?"

Abby reached under her top, pulled out the crucifix and showed it to him. "I …" She wasn't sure how to explain.

He looked at it for a second then pulled on the chain he wore so the clasp came to the front and unhooked it. He slid the cross onto the chain, letting it rest beside the pendant he wore showing his family's crest. Then he put the chain back on and smiled at her. "If you don't mind, I'll hold on to it."

"Who are you and what have you done with Marlon Samson?" Abby couldn't believe her eyes. *Marlon wearing a cross?*

"*Your* cross," said the dragon. "And he made a deal..."

"You really scared me, Abs." Marlon scratched at the back of his head. He sat down on the pew next to her. "So much that I kind of... got desperate. I *might* have made a bargain with the Man Upstairs."

"You did what?" Abby blinked. She rubbed her head. "Help, I'm slipping into the Twilight Zone...," she paused and sighed, "...again." *Nothing's making sense today.*

"Can I help you, children?" A priest walked into the room. He smiled at them. "I'm afraid Mass is over for today."

Marlon ducked his head. "Uh, we were just..."

"Hello, Father," said Abby smiling. "Is there any way I could arrange to attend first communion and go through confirmation?" *Maybe Marlon will write this off as me trying to decide if I should rejoin the Catholic church.* Besides, she *did* want to finish the sacraments.

"You're not a member of the parish," he said. "Are you thinking of joining?"

"Yes, sir." Abby nodded. "I *was* a member when I was a child, though, and I'd like to be again. Can you help me with that?"

"Of course, let me give you my number. May I suggest RCIA classes? If you've been away for a long time and that would be a good start."

"That will be fine." She got up from the pew and followed the pastor out, Marlon and Dominic on her heels. She waited as the man took a pen from his pocket and wrote his number on a pamphlet on a table in the entryway. "Thank you, Father." She curtsied, caught Marlon's hand and led him toward the doors. When he closed his hand around hers, her face warmed. Then, when she saw who was standing in the parking lot, it felt like she had just opened a hot oven's door. "What in the world?"

Drew Davidson leaned against his car, hands in his pockets. "Hey, Miss Palmer," he said with a smile. He pushed away from the car and opened the door. "Need a ride home?"

"What?" She looked up at Marlon in confusion. "How who... *someone* explain please."

"Samson had a panic attack and I gave him a lift." Drew popped the trunk. "Mind unlocking your bike?"

Abby did so automatically. She looked back at the church then climbed into the backseat, the dragon close behind. She slid to the other side, putting as much distance as she could between herself and Dominic. She stared at him. *Why are you still here?* Now that she was paying attention, she realized she had no control over the dragon at all. Had the angel reclaimed the mask?

"Where would I go? You still - HEY!" Dominic dropped to the floor as Marlon took the seat beside her. He sighed and curled up at her feet.

Drew got in the driver's seat and looked back at them in the mirror. He shook his head and started the car. "I'm glad to see you in one piece, Miss Palmer. I think you took a couple years off Samson's life with your disappearing act."

Marlon didn't take the bait. He glanced at Drew for a split second then back to her, concern written all over his face. "You all right, Abs?"

Abby nodded then leaned against the door and watched the church fade into the distance. She tried to ignore the dragon at her feet, but it was hard to do. Nothing made sense. *Since when do guardian angels masquerade as imaginary dragons?*

"Since a little girl put all her trust in an imaginary friend." Dominic lay with his head on his paws. "Sometimes you have to use what's available to you."

That still doesn't explain why you don't take your true form. Abby straightened up in the seat, her shoulder brushing against Marlon's. She looked over and tried to give him a reassuring smile. She leaned back in the seat. The car felt warm, and she found her eyes drifting closed. *You're going to have to… explain…*

CHAPTER 35

"Wake up, Sleeping Beauty."

Abby blinked her eyes open. She was lying across the backseat, her head on Marlon's lap. She jerked up. "Dang it. When did I fall asleep?" She rubbed her eyes and looked around.

"You're home now, so relax," said Drew as he shut the car off. He unbuckled his seatbelt and got out, coming around to open her door. "Nothing inappropriate happened... unless you wanna count Samson playing with your hair."

Marlon's face went red and he shot a one-fingered salute at Drew.

"Boys," said Abby, getting out of the car. "Behave and you can come in for something to drink." She shook her head. "I don't know if I should thank you or slap your heads together."

"How about both?" Dominic leaped out of the car to land beside her. He yawned. "Seems like a plan to me."

Why are you still using that form? Abby sighed. Comments like that made her doubt the demon was truly gone. *Should an angel be suggesting violence?*

The dragon smiled innocently enough.

"I thought you couldn't have anyone inside when your aunt's not home," said Drew. He put his hands in his pockets. "So what's changed?"

I don't want to be alone with my imaginary friend. Abby rolled her eyes and headed over to unlock the door. "I'm not supposed to be alone with anyone... but you two are here *together* so I think that qualifies as 'not alone'." She pushed the door open and stepped inside, holding it open for the boys. "I hope so, anyway."

Drew wandered over to the shelf in the corner that housed her yearly Christmas photos. "Cute cat, Miss Palmer. Not that you aren't too – OW! Hey!" He looked at Marlon as he rubbed his head. "What was that for?"

Marlon just put his hands behind his back and grinned. "You had a fly back there."

"Don't start fights, Mars-Bars; you'll get blood on Aunt Gladys' carpet and I'll never hear the end of it." She turned toward the kitchen. "That's Troubadour – True for short."

"Troubadour?"

Marlon reached out and caught her arm. "No offense Abs, but you look like you been ridin' with Grandpa. Why don't you comb your hair before your aunt shows up?" He turned back to Drew. "Surprised you don't remember him. She took that cat everywhere she could."

As Marlon told Drew how she'd tried to take True to church, Abby headed to the bathroom. She braced her hands on the sink, taking deep breaths. The demon's words played through her mind. *He's gone,* she told herself. *He's gone.* Maybe if she repeated it enough, she'd believe it. She glanced down at the dragon at her heels.

Dominic just watched her, eyes full of concern. He tilted his head, much like a dog, and his tail swished for a moment. But he said nothing.

That wasn't comforting. Abby picked up her brush with a shaking hand and did her best to put her hair in order. *Marlon's right, my hair looks like a cyclone hit it.* When she walked back into the living room she found Drew still staring at the pictures while Marlon sat on the loveseat. A tray with three glasses of lemonade was on the coffee table. Abby sat beside Marlon.

Dominic curled up at her feet, same as always, and remained silent.

Marlon handed her a glass then held one out to Drew. "Are you going to sit down or what?"

Drew took the glass and sat in the armchair. He took a sip. "So I take it your cat doesn't like strangers?" He looked around the room. "Since I've never seen him."

"Boy is denser than a rock," said Dominic, his tail tapping the carpet much like True's had when he was annoyed.

I should have known you couldn't keep quiet for long. Abby sighed. "True died two years ago." She sipped her lemonade and pushed the memories aside.

"Ouch. Sorry," said Drew. He frowned as he swished his glass. "That sucks, considering you must have had him for a while."

"Ten years," said Abby. She struggled to come up with a way to close the subject. *This has been the day from Hell. Literally.*

"So what were you doing here, Davidson?" asked Marlon, tilting his head. "Earlier, I mean."

"When you were trying to knock the door down?" he replied with a smirk. "I came over to see if you all were doing anything next Friday." He suddenly became interested in his glass. "I heard about this concert and Mel thought we could go together."

"A concert?" Abby blinked. "Uh, I'd have ask Aunt Gladys..."

The lock clicked and they all looked up as Gladys walked in, followed by Drew's mother.

"Well, well," said Mrs. Davidson, eyes darting from her son to Abby and Marlon. "Gladys, looks like Abby has some company. I hope we aren't interrupting anything."

"Speak of the Devil," said Dominic with a slight growl.

Hush! "Hello Aunt Gladys, Mrs. Davidson. May I get you some lemonade?"

"That would be lovely dear," said Gladys as she hung up her coat then offered to take Mrs. Davidson's. She smiled at both boys. "Hello Mr. Davidson, Mr. Samson. And how are you today?"

"I'm just fine, Mrs. Lynde," said Marlon, getting to his feet. He reached out and patted Abby's shoulder. "I'll get their drinks, Abs, relax."

"I swear the more I see of that boy, the more I am impressed by his manners. Dolores, do sit down. I'll get a few more chairs." She pulled two folding chairs from the closet.

"Gladys, now you know that's too heavy for you," said Mrs. Davidson, putting her hand on the other woman's arm. She looked at her son. "Drew, dear, aren't you going to offer to help?"

Drew sat his glass down and got up. "Of course, Mother. Let me get it Mrs. Lynde."

"Thank you, Mr. Davidson." Gladys sighed and sat in the other chair while Drew's mother took the seat he vacated. "So what did you do today, dear?"

Abby took a drink to buy time. She couldn't lie. *But what am I supposed to say?*

"Got me into a church," said Marlon. He came back into the living room with a glass in each hand. He smiled as he held them out to the older women.

"Thank you," said Gladys, taking the glasses from him and passing one to Mrs. Davidson. She took a drink of hers then jerked her head up. "Wait, Abby got *you* into a church?"

"Yes, ma'am," said Marlon, smiling. He reclaimed his seat beside Abby. "I was wondering if you'd allow me to accompany you next Sunday?"

Abby almost spit out her drink. *What the heck is he up to?* She stared at Marlon in confusion. *Marlon in Preacher Davidson's church?*

"I told you – he made a deal." Dominic eyed Marlon with respect. "He intends to honor it."

"I... uh, well, you see, Mr. Samson, I don't drive and..." Gladys was clearly just as stunned.

"And the car is already full with Miss Hilary now in our carpool," said Mrs. Davidson, sipping her lemonade. "Though surely your parents could make sure you get there."

"I'll take you," said Drew. He unfolded the chair and sat it beside Marlon and sat down. He smiled at the other boy. "I've got plenty of room."

Abby took a drink to hide her own smile at the expression on Mrs. Davidson's face. *She can't object and she knows it. This ought to be good.*

Dominic snickered. "Amen."

"That's very nice of you, dear, but surely Mr. Samson's parents –"

"Mother, please be reasonable. This makes things much easier for everyone." Drew turned his attention back to Marlon. "You can ask your parents about it, but this way you know you have a ride even if they have plans."

"Works for me," said Marlon, grinning. "Thanks, Davidson."

"No problem. I'm always happy to aid someone in finding their way home. Right, Mother?"

"This makes two lost sheep you've managed to return to the fold, Miss Palmer." Mrs. Davidson finished her drink. "Drew, dear, it's late and we really must be going." She smiled and nodded to Gladys then Marlon and Abby. "Good-bye, dears. I look forward to seeing you Sunday, Mr. Samson."

"Thank you, Mrs. Davidson, and thank you, sir, for the ride." Marlon's grin threatened to split his face. "I'm sure you'll soon be sick of me."

Abby bit her tongue to keep from laughing. *What a day...*

CHAPTER 36

"So the parrot says, 'same idiot who named the Rottweiler Jesus."

Ava chuckled at "Jenner's" joke and passed out drinks. "So why my place for a meeting?" Her gray cat Troubadour curled up in her lap when she sat down.

"You're the new kid. No one's watching you." Jenner took his drink. "Hey, cute kitty..." He chuckled. "Remind me not to shift around him."

"Noted," said Ava, stroking the furball. "So what's the plan?"

"We're going to have to evacuate. You need to make sure the shop's open so we can get to that passage."

WaterHorse looked at the window as headlights flashed by. "OK, gang we need to be going. Just be there, Dragonfly." She smiled. "We're counting on you."

"I'll be there," said Ava, smiling back. "Promise."

Abby shook her head as the scene wrapped up. She glanced down at the forum's chatbox and shook her head. Jenner and WaterHorse were at it again. *Those two I swear...*

"You have strange friends," Dominic noted, cranking his neck to better see the screen.

"You're a strange angel," she countered and then typed, "Do you guys ever quit?"

JennerTheRat: Lighten up, Dragonfly. We're just teasing. :)

WaterHorse: We're good. As soon as Jenner admits Nickelback is better than Skillet.

JennerTheRat: Never!

RandomWord: This is so ridiculous. G N' R tops both of 'em. There. "Fight" over.

JennerTheRat: So mature, Rand, so mature.

RandomWord: Like you're doing any better. You're arguing over bands that I'm pretty sure your parents listened to.

WaterHorse: Oh, and you actually listen to Guns N' Roses? *snorts* Yeah, right.

DragonflyGirl: I could knock you all for a loop and say Stryper beats them all. Of course you'll all jump me so…

RandomWord: At least you didn't say DC whatever.

JennerTheRat: DC Talk, I'm guessing? Hey Dragonfly, cool name for Ava's cat. Where'd you come up with it?

DragonflyGirl: My cat. He died a couple years ago though.

JennerTheRat: Sorry I asked.

GreenQueen: Do you people not have Instant Messenger or something? This chat is for the GAME not you're petty arguments. Now knock it off or take it Private Messages.

DragonflyGirl: I need to crash guys, see you around.

Abby started to close the window when the Private Message Notice popped up. She clicked the inbox. *Who would…?* The message was from WaterHorse.

Don't be a coward. There's no rule that says we can only talk about the game.

She stared at the words. She didn't know what to say. Another message followed WaterHorse's. And another. Even Jenner got in on the act. The gist was "don't back down." Abby sighed. She replied, "I don't do confrontation well. And I really do need sleep. See ya," to all of them. Then she shut the laptop down, put it away, and headed into the kitchen to start dinner.

"Amazing," said the dragon as he followed at her heels. "You can face down B –"

Don't say the name, she snapped. She got out a box of spaghetti and a jar of sauce. *I still don't get why you're still around. Or at least why you don't take your real form.*

"You still need me around, and you're used to this form." Dominic sat at her feet. "Still, you can stand strong against a dark creature, yet not against someone on the other side of a computer?"

It's more... She sighed. *I don't want to get kicked out. My friends don't have my messenger account.*

"Wouldn't take much to find you, *Dragonfly*." Dominic smiled. "And besides, I'm sure Little Wasp would pass on the info if you asked."

You have a point. She put the noodles on to boil. *I'm still trying to picture Marlon in CHURCH!* Abby shook her head. *Tomorrow is going to be interesting.*

Abby jerked when Gladys nudged her side. She tore her eyes from the congregation and back to the pulpit. *I don't think this many people stared when I came here with Bryan.* She snuck a glance at Melissa with Drew and bit her cheek to keep from smiling.

"Looks like you're off the hook there," said Dominic. He pressed against her leg, tail swishing. "Need shades for the love-dovey glow they're giving off."

"Brothers and sisters, I draw your attention to Matthew Chapter Seven, Verse Fifteen." Davidson smacked his bible against his hand. "Our Lord warns of false prophets and these days we are *surrounded* by them! The dens of these wolves are deeply entrenched in our community. Our flock is in need of protection and guidance – I call on each of you to stand guard, to be sheepdogs for your fellow Christians. Do not let them fall victim to the sweet song of these wolves."

Dominic began growling. "Dogs are kin of wolves, you idiot!"

Don't go there. Abby reached up and rubbed the crucifix under her dress. *I guess we're due for the "don't trust Catholics, etc." lecture.* She sighed. *Perfect timing.*

Aunt Gladys nodded along, shouting "Amen!" She was the loudest of the crowd.

Abby dropped her hand and tugged at her dress. *Hail Mary, full of Grace...* She jerked when she felt a hand rest on hers and looked down then up to find Marlon had laid his own upon hers. She returned her gaze to the preacher. *If Aunt Gladys notices...* She felt her face heat up when he squeezed her hand for a moment. The silent support meant more than she would have thought.

Marlon's expression betrayed nothing. He watched Davidson move around the pulpit as if it was the most fascinating thing he'd ever seen.

Abby calmly got through the prayers. *I guess the demon was responsible for my self-control issues.* She shook her head slightly. *No, it was me. Still...* She turned her hand under Marlon's and laced her fingers with his. *Mars-Bars helps.*

Dominic wrapped his paw around their hands and nodded.

After the service, Abby leaned against the outside of the church. She drew a deep breath and let it out slow. She looked up at the clouds. She nearly jumped out of her skin when she felt a hand brush hers.

"Sorry, Abs." Marlon shot her a sheepish smile. "Are you OK?"

She didn't know how to answer that. *I'm used to disappointment.* She smiled. "Better now." She hesitated, then reached out and took his hand in hers. "Thanks for being here."

"I made a promise." Marlon looked at their hands then closed his around hers. "And I'm going to keep it." He tilted his head and she realized yet another thing he had inherited from his grandfather. "If you switch churches I'll follow."

"I doubt that's going to happen for a while." Abby kicked her feet. *I was so...*

"High on victory," said Dominic. He sat beside her, his tail tapping the ground. "It's only two years. In the meantime you've got me and the Little Wasp."

"That's OK, Abs. I'll follow when you're ready," Marlon said, as if to add to Dominic's sentiment.

"Well, will you look at the lovebirds." Drew came over to them, the sting taken out of his words by his smile and the fact Mel's hand was tight in his. "Seriously need a camera."

Marlon blushed but reached up and scratched his face with the middle finger of his free hand. "This okay for the camera, too, Davidson?"

Melissa rolled her eyes. She pointed to her temple and spun her finger in a circle. "You two are nuts." She winked at Drew then went over to his parents and Gladys.

"Hope the sermon wasn't too painful," said Drew. He looked from Abby to Marlon and back again. "Do you ever think about getting another cat, Dragonfly?"

"Aunt Gladys would have a fit," said Abby. Then she looked at Drew. "Wait, what did you call me?"

Drew put his hands in his pockets and grinned. "Dragonfly. Girl, if you create a character and want to hide, don't give her cat the same weird name yours had."

Abby froze. *How does he know my username?*

It was Marlon that put two and two together. "Andrew Lawrence. Harley Davidson. Crap, how did we miss that?" He glared at Drew and let go of her hand. "If you breathe a word about Abby —"

"Relax, Samson." Drew nodded at Abby. "I didn't get ratted out, so I won't *do* any ratting out. Even if I am a rat." He snickered.

Abby finally got her mouth to move. "*You're* Jenner?" She pinched her nose. "I don't believe this!"

"Might as well, *Ava*." He looked up at Marlon. "So what's your user?"

Marlon bowed with a smirk. "Brock Dent, at your service."

"RandomWord?" Drew laughed out loud. "Man, you *suck* at names!"

"Like you're any better, Mr. Name-From-A-Book-You-Read-In-Fifth-Grade." Marlon's eyes sparkled. "I'm with Abs. I don't believe this. It was *you* this whole time?" He shook his head. "Well, gotta say you're a dang good actor."

"Is everyone cool now?" asked Dominic. "Because here comes Mr. Holier-Than-Thou."

"It's good to see you, Mr. Samson." Preacher Davidson's smile made Abby shiver. "I hope you enjoyed the service."

"You are very passionate about your faith, sir, and it shows." Marlon nodded. "I hope you don't mind if I continue to attend?" He looked at Drew. "If I pass the driver's exam tomorrow I'll be able to borrow Dad's car and save you the trouble, but thanks for today."

"Of course, Mr. Samson, we'll be happy to have you." Preacher Davidson leaned down slightly. "Though, I must ask: have you accepted Christ as your Lord and Savior?"

Marlon reached out and carefully took Abby's hand in his once more. "I follow the same Lord Abby does, sir. Where she goes, I follow."

"The Lord works in mysterious ways." Preacher Davidson looked over at his son and Melissa then at Abby and Marlon. "Love covers a multitude of sins, my boy, and it conquers all. I look forward to seeing you next Sunday. Behave yourselves, children."

Once he'd left, they all sighed in relief.

"I love my father," said Drew, "but if I *ever* act that heavy-handed when I become a preacher, one of you slap me." He shook his head.

"You got it, Davids – Drew." Marlon smiled. "In fact it's a promise."

Drew snorted. "Thanks, Marlon. I knew I could count on you."

"Melissa," said Mel, touching her chest then waved a hand at Abby. "Abby. There, now we're on a first name basis. Maybe now we can talk like we were born this century."

"Hey," Drew said, smiling. "Good manners never go out of style."

Marlon folded his arms and leaned back against the church. "Yeah but acting like a pompous p-"

"Mars-Bars!" Abby rubbed her temples. *One day they'll get along. One day.*

Dominic chucked. "I wouldn't count on it."

CHAPTER 37

"Ready for this?"

Abby buckled her seatbelt and smiled at Bryan. She put her hands on the wheel. "As I'll ever be." She glanced into the rear view mirror. "I got this."

"Don't over-do the confidence," cautioned the dragon from his place in the backseat. "Pride comes before a fall." He nodded and put his head down on his paws.

"Don't get cocky," said Bryan. He picked up the clipboard off the dash. "You're more likely to screw up when you're cocky."

You two are on the same wavelength for once. Abby nodded and started the car. "I know." She pulled out of the parking lot and started around the block. *Dominic keep your mouth shut, please.* She followed Bryan's directions, fighting against the nervousness. *I don't want to try and retake this with snow on the ground.* They were back near the school before she knew it. The sight of the tree she'd nearly hit made her heart race. *OK Palmer... almost there.*

"Steady now," said Bryan. His fingers tapped against the clipboard. "Steady."

"Relax, Wasp." Dominic raised his hands and smiled at her. "She's doing fine."

Thanks, but please be quiet. Abby swallowed the lump in her throat. She did not draw an easy breath until they were safely past the tree. She pulled into the parking lot, brought the car to a stop and shut it off. Removing her seatbelt, she looked up at Bryan.

"Well done," he said, grinning. "You passed."

"Thank You, God!" She hugged him, then pulled back, her face seven shades of red. "Sorry."

"No need, Dragonfly. No need." He snickered and ruffled her hair. "You earned it." He unbuckled his seatbelt and got out of the car. "And I think a couple people are waiting to congratulate you."

She followed his gaze to where Marlon and Felice stood alongside Drew and Mel. Her four friends were smiling. She got out of the car, flanked by the unseen dragon. She kept her head down until she reached them. "Well..." she said, then looked up. "I did it."

"Way to go, Abs!" Marlon grinned.

"Awesome!" Felice clapped. "So much for 'women' drivers."

Melissa was calmer than either of the twins. "Knew you could do it."

"Nice work, Dragonfly." Drew put his hands in his pockets. "So you want to drive to the concert Friday?"

"Let's take baby steps with that, shall we?" Abby laughed. "You never told me who's playing."

"That's for me to know, and you all," said Drew, waving a hand at them all, "to find out. It's a Christian band, and that's all you get to know."

"Still say you're lucky *your* parents agreed to this, never mind Aunt Gladys." Abby reached up and adjusted her crucifix. "How did you even talk them into a Christian rock concert?"

"Ministry work. Got to go where the lost sheep are if you want to bring them home." Drew smirked when they all laughed. "Hey, if it's not broke don't fix it."

"What's so funny?" Bryan came over then made a show of inspecting his outfit. "I'm not wearing blues with blacks again, am I?"

"You're fine, Grandpa." Marlon rolled his eyes. He fidgeted with his own shirt and jacket. "I don't think a t-shirt, jeans and a leather jacket can *not* match."

"I'm just glad everyone passed today," said Bryan. "Otherwise I'd have to scramble this Friday." He smiled and bowed. "Now if you'll excuse me I've got other obligations to meet." He turned, got on his motorcycle and rumbled off.

"Delightful scoundrel," said Abby, shaking her head as she adjusted her purse strap. She carefully reached out and took Marlon's hand. "We ought to get home, too."

Marlon smiled. "Yeah, need to study for that science test."

"Good plan," said Felice, "or you'll be repeating tenth grade."

"I am *not* that hopeless." Marlon stuck his free hand in his pocket and gave his sister a "get real" look. "You of little faith."

"You forget I've seen your report cards."

Drew shrugged. "You want a ride home? Someone would have to sit in the middle but it's doable."

"I'm fine," said Abby, fighting to keep the amusement off her face, "besides, I don't think all three bikes would fit in your trunk."

The Samsons seconded her statement but thanked him anyway.

Abby watched as Drew and Mel left to unlock the latter's bike. "I can't believe all that's left is to take this paper in to the DMV." She tucked the slip into her purse. "You up for a bus ride, Mars-Bars?"

"Dad's gonna take us to get ours later. You can just come with us." Marlon and his sister got their bikes. "I'm just glad it's over... almost. I'm gonna have to find a motorcycle before I can get that license, too."

"Determined, isn't he?" Dominic took point between Abby and Marlon. "Well, where there's a will, there's a way..." He chuckled. "In almost everything. It's just a matter of finding the right path."

"So when are you going to tell us who's playing tonight?" Abby adjusted her purse strap and stepped out of the car after Marlon. She looked at Drew and raised an eyebrow. "You made us cover our eyes so we wouldn't see the signs on the way in."

Drew smiled. "You'll see." He led the way to a shelter at the park. Once they reached the door, he pointed to the poster on the wall. "There you go."

The poster showed two men in black duster jackets with their wide-brim hats pulled over their eyes. It read *Bonfire and Brimstone.*

Abby had to bite her tongue to keep from laughing

"They look like Undertaker impersonators," said Melissa. She reached up and wrapped a strand of her hair around her finger. "'Bonfire and Brimstone'? Is that their names or the band?"

"The band," said Felice. "So, Drew, what made you pick them?" She was having just as much trouble keeping a straight face. She kept snickering and tried to muffle it with her hand.

"They were in town, so I thought why not, considering how much Abby talks about Christian rock. Figured this was a good introduction for the rest of us." Drew looked from Felice to her brother. "What am I missing?"

Marlon looked like he was biting his cheek and shook slightly. He walked over to the poster and tapped the names on the bottom. "What do you think?" he asked then started snickering with his sister.

Truman Samson. Bryan Samson.

Drew looked embarrassed. He scratched at the back of his head and gave them a sheepish smile. "Oh. Uh... well I guess we know the show will be good, right?"

They took their seats but the twins never stopped laughing. Abby smiled as she looked at her friends, then the smile hurt her face as she recognized the first song. *This is wonderful.*

Abby sat on her bed that weekend, tapping out a reply to allow the "evacuation" to proceed while she waited for Marlon to come over. He had already done his part and just had to clean up his room, far as she knew. Once the scene ended, she bid her friends farewell and closed the window. "I still can't believe Drew didn't realize that it was *Bryan* playing."

"No one said that the boy plays with a full deck." Dominic stretched then curled back up on the end of her bed. "Wasp does put on a good show though."

"I don't get why you insist on keeping that form," said Abby. She started a chess game to pass the time. "Maybe I should start calling you by your real name." She took a deep breath. "Aeneas."

"You can," said a voice then from behind her, "if you like."

Abby looked over to find the angel leaning against the wall. She blinked. "Good, you finally took your real form. Now maybe we can move past having to use the drag –"

"This form suits me just fine, thank you," said Dominic. "You're more comfortable with it, anyway."

Her eyes narrowed and she locked eye contact with the dragon on the bed, who tilted his head to the side. "You know, this is ridiculous. The demon is gone, so there's no need for a mask anymore."

"Bjarte was not destroyed, Abigail," said Aeneas, still visible against the wall. "He is only licking his wounds. He will return eventually. You are his charge as much as my own."

She tried not to show how much that worried her. "So he's not gone for good..." Abby shook her head. "My point stands. I don't need a mask he can put on." She kept her gaze on the dragon. "So this form needs to go."

Dominic rolled his eyes and began tapping his tail. "Start up *Path of the Dragon*."

"Don't change the subject. Besides, I'm not playing the game again - if Marlon and I *both* can't figure it out, there's no point in it..."

"I didn't say play it, I said start it up. A new game... just don't save."

Abby sighed. "If I do this, you give up that form." She started a new game, shaking her head as the first cutscene started.

"If you still want me to, I will." Dominic nodded at the screen. "Pay attention."

Abby shook her head as it got to where the younger brother vowed to find another way to free his brother. "I've seen this before, what's your point?"

"Pay attention!" repeated the dragon, nodding at the rest of the scene.

Years before, the brothers discussed the possibility of one falling prey to these dark creatures. The younger had asked the elder, "Will you hunt me down, if I become one of the fallen? Will you slay your own flesh and blood?" The elder had smiled and ruffled his brother's hair. "Sooner myself than you." And so now the younger bore that promise in his heart. He would sooner end himself than his brother.

"That's what the dragon asks," said Abby, her mouth hanging open. "'Will you slay your own flesh and blood'. That means..."

Dominic grinned. "So simple and yet not."

"You knew that this whole time?" Abby rubbed her head. "Or did I know?" She leaned back against her headboard. "I think I'm getting a headache."

"The creator always knows everything about his creation," said Aeneas. He folded his arms and crossed his feet at the ankles. "Does not matter if he is Creator of All or just a man."

Abby stared at the grinning dragon. The angel's words could only add up one way and yet... "It can't be. I just... forgot about it until now."

Dominic snorted. "Don't be dense, Abigail it doesn't suit you."

She reached out her hand and brushed it through the dragon's mane. Tears pricked her eyes. "Grandpa Nick."

"In the scales." Dominic chuckled. "Now, if you still want me to drop this form I will. But honestly I've gotten used to it."

"You could have informed me of your presence," said Aeneas, scowling.

Dominic glared at the angel. "Surprised it took that –" Abby flinched as he used Bryan's favorite cuss word "– near accident for you to even notice there was someone else wearing the mask besides just you two idiots."

They started bickering and Abby stopped paying attention to their words. *"Took that..."* Her eyes widened. "It was *you* that woke me up when I fell asleep at the wheel."

"Damn straight," replied Dominic. He growled in the angel's direction. "Someone had to do something since hotshot over there wasn't doing his job."

"I am a guardian, not all-powerful!"

Are my guardian angel and dead grandfather really bickering like an old married couple? Abby shook her head. *Maybe I do need to see a shrink instead of being one.*

A tap at the window cut the argument short, and Aeneas disappeared. Abby got up and let Marlon in. "Do you think you're a monkey or something?" she asked as she shut the window back. "I have a door."

"This works better." Marlon smiled, pulled his *Pokémon* deck from his pocket and fanned the cards from one hand to the other. "Wanna see if you can beat me yet?"

"Maybe after..." Abby sat back on her bed and brought up their saved game on *Path of the Dragon*. "I got something to show you." She patted the bed next to her.

"Aw, man, Abs, come on." Marlon sighed but joined her anyway. "There's just no beating that thing."

She didn't reply, just worked her way back to the final chamber. The dragon appeared and made its demand. She took a deep breath then typed, "Sooner myself than you."

The scene began to shake again, but this time the dragon hit the floor, roaring in pain. Behind the player, the blond man appeared. Unlike all the other times they'd seen him, he was somber. A text box appeared. *"You cannot save him."* He drew a sword and moved forward.

"Holy crap!" Marlon stared at the screen in shock. "You got it right!"

Abby hit the keys as fast as she could, making the player slam his staff into the sword. She remembered the journal entry about the nightly battles between the men her grandfather had seen. *So this is where that fits in.* She swallowed hard when the demon fell. *If only it was this easy for real.* "Now what?"

On screen, the dragon form melted and oozed away, and the elder brother materialized in its place. The two characters embraced and a familiar verse appeared on the screen.

"Seriously?" said Marlon. "That lost lamb verse again?" He started laughing. "All that trouble for a bible verse! Oh, man, the Dragon sure knew how to screw with people."

"More," said Dominic in a smug tone, "like I knew the value of something lost being found."

"You could say that," said Abby, grinning as she answered both.

CHAPTER 38

Abby sat in the backseat of Bryan's car with Marlon and watched the Christmas lights flash by. The snow reflected reds, greens, blues, and purples, and everything shined. She ran her hand over the charm bracelet Felice had given her. The chain only held a single charm – a silver dragonfly. "Thanks for the lift, Mr. and Mrs. Samson."

"Not a problem," said Bryan, pulling into the parking lot of Gail's apartment complex. "It'll be nice to see the Dragon's old lady again. OW!" He rubbed at his shoulder where his wife had slapped him.

"Never refer to a woman by her age," scolded Vera. "Honestly, Bumbler." She rolled her eyes. "Just when I think you've finally learned your manners."

"You can take the stray off the street," he replied with that grin as he shut the car off, "but not the street from the stray." He reached on the dash for two gift boxes. He walked around to her side of the car and opened the door for her. "After you, my lady."

Marlon mimicked his grandfather when he got out first and opened the door for Abby.

"Little Wasp got it bad." Dominic moved to Abby's side and stretched. "When are you two going to make it official? The song and dance routine is getting old."

No one asked you! Abby took Marlon's hand and followed his grandparents to her grandmother's door. She bit her cheek when Gail looked out the window and saw who was with her.

233

Her grandma came out to greet them, wearing a sweater that read "Jesus is the reason for the season". "Well, will you look what the cat dragged in," said Gail, smiling. "Long time, no see."

Bryan bowed and smirked. "You're looking lovely as ever, ma'am."

"Can it, Wasp," she replied, pointing a finger at him, "don't waste your questionable charm on me." Gail laughed and hugged Bryan. Unable to hug her back, he held his arms out with the presents in his hands. "You haven't changed a bit, you old scoundrel!"

"At least he's housebroken these days," said Vera, smiling at Gail. "Now if I could just get him to take a flea bath."

"Yeah, yeah, laugh it up, V." Bryan stepped back out of the embrace. "Laugh it up." He smiled at Gail. "Seriously, it's good to see you."

"I hope you make a habit of it." Gail slapped him on the shoulder. "Don't be a stranger, you hear me? You're not a Christmas card!"

"Yeah, yeah." Bryan smirked. He handed one box to Gail before he glanced back at Abby and Marlon. He pointed above them. "Hey, is that mistletoe?"

"What?!?" Marlon craned his neck to look, backed up and slid on a patch of ice. Losing his balance, he fell straight into a snowbank. "Grampa, sheesh! Don't do that!"

Abby felt her face heat up in the cold. She glanced up at the empty arch before offering her hand to help Marlon back to his feet.

"Were you *hoping* for mistletoe?" asked Dominic innocently.

Hush, you! Abby's face just got hotter. *It's none of your business.*

"Is that any way to speak to your grandfather?"

"Now, boy don't lie, you're dyin' to try... you wanna kiss the girl," Bryan sang then snickered at his grandson's protest.

I see why you two got along so well, Abby thought. *You're just as bad as he is.*

"Bumbler, I swear." Vera rubbed her temples. "Will you act your age for three seconds?"

"All of three?"

"Get inside, you fool," said Gail. "No sense standing out here freezing." She hugged Abby when she walked in. "It's good to see you, sweetheart."

"You too, Grandma." Abby reached into her pocket and pulled out a small wrapped package. "Merry Christmas." She ducked her head. "It's not much..."

"It's fine, dear, I'm sure it's perfect." Gail squeezed Marlon's shoulder. "Don't let that fool get to you. He's got a gutter mouth, but a heart of gold."

"I know, ma'am." Marlon grinned. "The first is gonna end up paying for me and my siblings' college."

Bryan joined them and held the second box out to Abby. "Merry Christmas, Dragonfly."

She took the box and smiled. "Thank you."

"He's not the only one with presents." Marlon reached into his pants pocket and pulled out a wrapped box. He laid it on top of the one in her hands. "Merry Christmas, Abs."

"Thanks, Mars-Bars." Abby sat both beside her then opened the smaller first. Inside lay a simple silver cross – at first glance – but when she looked closer, she saw the dragon engraved in the metal. It was clearly an eastern dragon; its serpentine body filled the cross's descending bar. The dragon's head rested in the center of the crossbar. She lifted it up by the chain and stared. "It's beautiful."

Marlon reached out and took the chain. He undid the clasp and placed the gift around her neck. He smiled and brushed his hand against the gold cross he still wore next to his family crest pendant. "Figured since I took yours I should replace it."

Abby whispered a soft thank you. Never would she have expected this a year, or even a month before. She then opened the box Bryan had handed her. She pushed aside the paper to find a black denim jacket. Why a jacket? She lifted it up then turned it over and her jaw dropped. Embroidered on the back was a black dragon outlined in gold. It curled around a white cross. Gold letters above announced, "I ain't into hiding," and below lay the words, "Jesus Freak."

Abby looked from the patch to a frame on the end table. Gail had brought out the photo around the third time she and Marlon visited. A larger version of the one Bryan carried in his wallet of him and Nick Whelan. The dragon on the jacket wasn't exactly the same as her grandfather's, but it was close.

Abby finally asked, "You... where did you find this?"

"Didn't. Made it," said Bryan smiling at her reaction. "I can sew after all." He lightly slapped Marlon's shoulder. "A little birdie told me your favorite song. Try it on."

Abby slid the jacket on. It fit perfectly. She spun around and froze at her grandmother's gasp. Gail crossed the room and spun Abby back around to look at the patch.

"I'll be darned!" She chuckled. "Guess we have a new Dragon in the family."

"Dragon*fly* maybe," said Abby stepping back. She glanced at Dominic out of the corner of her eye, then looked up at her grandmother. "What do you think?"

Gail had tears in her eyes but she quickly brushed them away. "I think Nick would be so proud right now." She smiled. "Jesse and Nicole, too."

Dominic came over and pressed against her leg. "I know so."

Abby smiled and looked at Bryan. She wiped her eyes, too. "Thank you."

"Anytime, Dragonfly. Anytime."

THAT'S ALL FOR NOW, BUT HERE'S
A SNEAK PEAK AT THE SEQUEL

Abby reread, for the third time, the official-looking letter she had found beside her breakfast plate. Finally, she met Gladys' smug gaze. "Is this some kind of joke?"

"I've afraid not, Abigail. As you pointed out, you are eighteen years old and can make your own choices." The older woman sipped her tea. "And I refuse to have a heretic in my home. I cannot support you returning to that house of sin." She tisked. "I so hoped I had raised you better."

"Heretic my ass!" shouted Dominic. "Guess it was stupid to expect understanding and tolerance from the old bat, but still she waited *this long* to pull this stunt?"

Abby started shaking, torn between fury and fear. *Why am I surprised?* She had announced her intentions to return to the Catholic faith on her birthday a month prior, hoping her great-aunt would respect her decision. At the time, Gladys had only asked if she had thought it through. Abby had assured her that she had, and as a legal adult the choice was her own. Gladys had simply nodded. Nothing more had been said on the subject, even when she and Marlon had started attending mass rather than Preacher Davidson's services. And now this. *What am I going to do?*

"You best be getting along, dear." Gladys looked at the clock on the wall. "You'll be late for school. I hope *that* still matters to you."

Abby pushed out of her chair, pocketing the letter and swinging on her backpack. She locked eye contact with Gladys before pulling her crucifix out from under her top to rest in plain sight. "Good day, Aunt Gladys." She turned on her heel and stormed out the door before her temper could get the better of her.

ABOUT THE AUTHOR

Ashleigh Daniellé Jaelyn Cutler is the daughter of two avid readers. She had a book in her hand before she could walk. One of her favorite phrases, when she began to talk, quickly became "Daddy book read". Her parents, Jay Cutler and Pam Stepp, offered constant encouragement and praise as she made her way towards becoming the artist and author she always wanted to be.

Her stories, supported by the various courses she took during her school years, explore a range of social topics despite their often non-human protagonists. Her artwork does focus more on wolves at times as well as the stars of these tales. Also known online as Ash Of Wolves until 2004, she adopted the handle AshWolf Forever in 2009 and still uses it today. She can be found on Facebook, Twitter, deviantART.com, GoodReads.com. Fanfiction.net and FictionPress.com.

She is currently working on her next book.

OTHER TITLES BY ASHLEIGH D.J. CUTLER
A Childhood Fantasy
Few Know You're Crying
and many more to come, including *Path of the Dragon*.